ILLUSIONARIUM

ILLUSIONARIUM

HEATHER DIXON

GREENWILLOW BOOKS
An Imprint of HarperCollinsPublishers

Illusionarium
Copyright © 2015 by Heather Dixon

The text of this book is set in Sabon.
Book design by Sylvie Le Floc'h

Library of Congress Cataloging-in-Publication Data

Dixon, Heather, (date)
Illusionarium / by Heather Dixon.
pages cm
"Greenwillow Books."
Summary: As apprentice to his father, the second-best medical scientist in the empire, Jonathan leads a quiet life in a remote aerial city until the king arrives, calling on them to find the cure to a plague that has struck the capital city and put the queen's life at risk, but the newly discovered chemical, fantillium, that may help will also put at risk all that Jonathan holds dear.
ISBN 978-0-06-200105-4 (hardback)
[1. Plague—Fiction. 2. Medicine—Research—Fiction. 3. Fathers and sons—Fiction. 4. Apprentices—Fiction. 5. Kings, queens, rulers, etc.—Fiction. 6. Hallucinations and illusions—Fiction. 7. Fantasy.] I. Title.
PZ7.D64433Ill 2015 [Fic]—dc23 2014041136

15 16 17 18 19 LP/RRDH 10 9 8 7 6 5 4 3 2 1
First Edition

 Greenwillow Books

To my grandpa Dixon,
the nuclear physicist & physics professor.
A man with an unfailing compass.

He's probably rolling in his grave with
the equations I've put in this book.

CHAPTER 1

Fata Morgana (Class. A Aerial City)
December 16, 1882

When storms like this hit Fata Morgana, the snow blew horizontal, glaciers formed over the buildings and walkways, and nothing—not airships, not light signals—could get through.

I sat at the top of Fata Morgana's semaphore tower, a tall, spindly telegraph structure in the center of our aerial city, looking out over the ice-encased rowhouses that receded into the howling blizzard. The sky glowed a bright polar blue.

Once more, I braced the levers on either side of the light signaler and twisted them forward, clicking and flashing a red-coded message out the shutters and into the bitter cold:

ATTN: LADY FLOREL KNIGHT -- VENEN INFO REQ. -- SYMPTOMS, TEST RESULTS, CHEMICAL BREAKDOWNS, ETC -- DR. H. GOUDEN -- ASAYAW

The message was dead important. It was a light signal to Lady Florel, the empire's head medical scientist, calling for more information. A highly infectious disease, the Venen, had sprung up in the center of the empire's capital city, Arthurise. Since we were residents of the northernmost mining city, we'd only just received the news by light signal two days ago. My father, the second-best medical scientist in the empire, had read the transcript with furrowed brow and had me, his medical apprentice, send out for more information.

And then the storm had hit, making it impossible for light sigs to pass through.

But that didn't stop me from trying. I stolidly braved the storm several times a day to send the sig out again. To no avail; the storm choked the light like a snuffed candle.

The movement of something below, traversing a nearby walkway, caught my eye. A figure struggled against the storm, seemingly headed nowhere, wrapped up in a thick coat, a scarf, and an academy skirt.

"You're *joking*," I said. I only knew one person

stupid enough to come out in a storm like this.[1]

Slamming the sig shutter closed, I broke the ice from the door behind me and ran/slid down the twisted staircase and into the icy inferno outside.

The storm assaulted me in sheets of slivered glass, stinging my face. I could only just see the figure up ahead, clinging to a railing. Taking a breath, I plunged forward into the storm, ignoring the burn of the cold.

When I reached her, I gripped her around the waist, looked around frantically to get my bearings, and made for the nearest building: the observatory.

The observatory was the large, cavernous building, with massive wooden doors and marble pillars, where my father worked. We stumbled up the stairs and through the doors with difficulty. I pulled her down the entrance hall and into the empty library, where a large heat lamp hummed in the center of the room. The warmth seared my skin. Annoyed, I turned on the figure.

"Hannah, you idiot!" I said.

The figure had thawed enough to throw back her hood and scarf, revealing the beaming face of my fourteen-year-old sister, Hannah.

"Jonathan!" she crowed, her blue eyes bright.

"You nearly killed yourself out there, you know that?"

---

[1] Besides me, of course.

"Jonathan, there's a ship!"

"You were lucky I was there!"

"At dock seven! And not just any ship! It's the *Westminster*!"

That gave me pause.

"The *Westminster*?" I said, confused. "Not . . . the king's airship?"

Hannah nodded, so excited she couldn't stand still. "I was hurrying home from classes and I saw something through the snow at the top of dock seven and so of course I *had* to take a look and it *was*! It was the *Westminster*, Jonathan! And it's the most beautiful airship I've ever seen. It looks like a giant cake dipped in gold!"

"Oh, come on, Hannah," I said. "The *king's* airship? What the devil would the king be doing this far north? In a raging storm, no less? Anyway, I've been in the sig tower all day and didn't see a thing. *You* were having a polarage."[2]

"No, Jonathan, I swear!" Hannah protested. "I hardly saw it, as well! Only because dock seven's near the academy. I'm not lying! Not this time, anyway."

I warmed my hands in the aura of the heat lamp, and

---

[2] polarage *pol-a-raj*\\ n: A mirage found in polar regions, when the cold air warps and forms floating icebergs and billowing shapes that could be mistaken for airships*

*but only by drunken airmen

examined her. With her drenched coat and dark, dripping hair, she looked like something the storm had chewed up and spat out.

It didn't diminish her a bit. Hannah was an *absolute* sort of person. She could stand there, leaving a trail of water on the dusty library rug, and yet command attention from just the delight in her eyes and the whip of her voice.

Unlike me, of course. I could only be described as *sort of*. Sort of tall. Sort of thin. Sort of brownish hair that was sort of curly and sort of not. I wore the same thing every day—a vest and cap and trousers that were all sort of beige. I was sort of smart, but not as smart as Hannah, who was two years younger than me but outdistanced me in every subject save anatomy, biology, and mathematics.

"I have a hypothesis," Hannah said excitedly. "For why His Majesty's here. Would you like to hear it?"

"Not really, no," I said.

"All right then, here it is: remember the sig that came a few days ago, before the storm hit? About that horrible disease in Arthurise?"

The Venen, I thought, remembering the light sig. A blood infection. Two weeks ago, it had reared its head in the Old London sector of Arthurise and had already claimed several dozen lives.

But the truly odd thing about the disease was this: it only infected women. And those it infected, it killed.

Hannah continued eagerly:

"I bet the research is going *really* poorly," she said with delight, "and Lady Florel is having difficulty, and she needs another scientist's help, and that scientist would *have* to be Papa!"

I considered her.

"Polarage," I said.

"Jonathan, it really is there!" Hannah cried. "I even took the lift to the dock!"

"Polarage."

"I even saw the *queen* through the aft windows! She was in her nightgown and she really *does* wear all those long strands of pearls!"

"Right, now I *know* you were having a polarage," I said.

"Jonathan!" Hannah wailed.

The library doors banged open, sending echoes fleeing to the ceiling. A gust of bitterly cold air blew over us, and we froze, seeing the man who filled the doorway. He wore a thick, perfectly fitted blue coat, had a graying beard that formed to a point under his round face, buggy eyes, and hands that could snap necks. He stomped into the library with such utter confidence that each stomping bootfall said CLAIMED.

I immediately recognized his sovereign visage. It adorned paintings and newspapers and Arthurisian coins. His Royal Highness King Edward VII had come to Fata Morgana. Hannah had been right!

Six men followed into the library after him in crisp blue uniforms and tall boots, sword clasps at their necks. Northern airguardsmen. The soldiers that patrolled the Arctic sector of our empire. Their ships often came to Fata to refuel or trade, and the men would even attend shows at our tiny theater. But now they stood guard, militaristic and grim.

"Where is Dr. Gouden?" the king boomed at me.

Hannah and I exchanged glances.

"In the laboratory," I said, keeping my voice steady. "We could take you to him?"

"Good idea!" the king snapped.

My father, the only scientist who remained on Fata through the long polar winters, worked on the second floor of the observatory. I hurried through the dark, cavernous halls with ice growing up the sides, the king and the airguardsmen marching after me, feeling a bit stunned. Hannah, jittery with excitement, ran on ahead.

I was familiar with my father's laboratory. I'd been his apprentice for nearly a year now. It was stuffed with cupboards and counters and microscopes and tables, laden with koch dishes and books and every shape and size of furniture crowded into whatever space was left.[3] It smelled of chemicals and old wood.

My father looked up from his work, with Hannah already hovering beside him, when I arrived at the doorway. The king and the soldiers brushed past me. My father smiled, carefully removed his reading glasses, carefully folded them, and carefully tucked them into his apron pocket. He was a careful man.

"*Goed sneeuwmiddag*," said my father, who was from the Amsterdam sector of the empire and often spoke HoLander in greeting. "Your Majesty."

He did not seem surprised at all to see the king here at Fata. Perhaps he wasn't. He wore his collar upturned in the old-fashioned way, and a heavy apron with his cravat tucked in, and the rest of him looked like me, thin, with his curly brown hair and yellow-brown eyes. He had a solidness to him that I didn't have, and wished I did.

"Are you Dr. Gouden?" the king said.

"I am."

"You are the scientist who found the cure to the London Fever?"

"The antitoxin, yes. I did."

---

[3] My father enjoyed bartering with passing trade ships for their most unusual pieces of furniture, collected from all around the world. As a result, our row house and observatory were both filled with strange, mismatched furniture. It drove my mother to distraction.

"Three days ago you received a light signal. About the Venen. Since then, it has become much, much worse. We need your help."

My father's brows furrowed.

"Will you have something warm to drink?" he said to the airguardsmen, noting their frozen state. "You're all quite ice."

Within minutes, the king had seated himself among the eccentric furniture, the airguardsmen standing guard around him, their hands clasped behind their backs, and Hannah and I hurrying to make tea for them at the orthogonagen stove in the corner of the laboratory. I pulled a lone mug from the empty cupboard, and it looked like it hadn't been washed in a week. Hannah made a disgusted noise in her throat and swept from the laboratory to find more mugs in the other observatory rooms. I set a kettle of water to boil, listening to the conversation between the king and my father.

"Less than a hundred had caught the fever, two weeks ago," said the king. "Now there are eighteen thousand. Everyone is under quarantine. Lady Florel is helpless."

My father frowned, touching his clasped hands to his mouth as the king explained the Venen. I listened keenly, washing the mug over and over in the laboratory sink.

The highly contagious disease turned women's veins black. It robbed them of their strength and snuffed the life from them in exactly six days. No one knew where it had come from, and no one—not even Lady Florel Knight, the empire's top medical scientist—knew how to cure it. The empire needed my father.

My father worried the pages of his research notebook.

"I am no Lady Florel," he said.

"You don't have to be," said the king. "I've brought her here with me. You will research with her."

My father brightened and straightened up in his chair. He had apprenticed with Lady Florel when he was my age, and even now, years later, admiration shone in his face.

"That is wonderful!" he said. "Allow me to gather my things—"

"A moment," said the king, cutting my father short. From the inside of his coat, he produced a tiny vial. It caught the light and danced and shimmered between the king's fingers. The black liquid inside glittered. I couldn't pry my eyes away from it.

"Lady Florel has found a new method of research," he said. "A rather incredible method of research. And she insists you study it—now—before you see her."

My father paced unhappily as the airguardsmen pushed the furniture to the sides of the room, opening an area of space around the orthogonagen stove. I could tell he did not like his laboratory changed about, and he did not like being told how to do his research. He crossed his arms as the king instructed me to remove the lid from the boiling teapot. It sent steam billowing into the air.

"This is fantillium," said the king, shaking the little vial. "It was discovered with orthogonagen, nearly a hundred years ago. We thought it useless—until several days ago, when Lady Florel discovered it to be a valuable research tool. And very unusual, too."

My father and I drew back as the king uncapped the vial and held it over the kettle. Three drops fell like black pearls into the boiling water. The steam around the stove grew opaque and glistened.

"Breathe it in," said the king.

"You are *certain* Lady Florel wishes us to use it?" said my father. "We ought to be spending this time collecting blood samples and speaking to Lady Florel, not playing with some unknown chemical—"

"She will not see you unless you do," said the king.

And that was that.

My father inhaled the steam first, and cringed. Then it enveloped me, several feet behind him, and a strange sensation filled my lungs as I breathed it in. It was like swallowing frosted spurs, or a scoop of diamond sand. The air prickled, freezing my throat and coating my lungs with frost. The steam that had been hot in our faces turned burning cold. Frigid.

The light above brightened painfully. I winced. Every highlight on the jars and glasses around us seared my vision.

"Turn down the lights," the king commanded. The airguardsmen, outside of the steam's reach, obliged.

The room fell dark, but I could see every piece of furniture perfectly. The clock in the corner ticked the seconds unbearably loud. I glanced at my father. His yellow-brown eyes had become black. He stared back at me, frowning, and removed my glasses to peer intently at my eyes.

"They're dilated," he said.

"So are yours." I smiled, and wasn't sure why. The pulse of blood through my veins gave my fingertips a fizz. My heart pounded. And yet, I was entirely calm. I felt asleep and awake at the same time.

"Lady Florel discovered," said the king, "that diluted with steam and inhaled, fantillium can give *shared hallucinations.*"

Stunned silence. I put my glasses on and looked about, half expecting hallucinations to jump out at me among the rows of jars. Nothing moved.

"I see nothing," said my father.

"There is one more element needed: an illusionist," said the king. "The illusionist envisions something in his head, you see, and the illusion appears before him and everyone else breathing the chemical. Lady Florel believes that illusionists are quite rare. They must know science—and have the talent to envision little bits of chemicals that everything is made of. I have tried to illusion and cannot. But Lady Florel can, and she believes that you, Dr. Gouden, will be able to, as well."

My father tugged his ear. He seemed uncomfortable with the whole situation.

"You know what water is made of, don't you?" the king continued. "The very basic structure?"

"Yes," said my father. "One part oxygen and hydrogen twice. It is so."

"Very well. Now, imagine those bits in your head. Exactly what they are made of."

My father bit the side of his lip and grimaced. Sweat beaded on his forehead. He held out a trembling hand. In the center of his palm, a glistening droplet of water formed.

"You did it!" I said, stunned. I dared reach out to touch it. It felt absolutely real and left a sheen on my finger, as actual water would.

The king looked relieved and considerably happier than he had the entire afternoon.

"Well done!" he said. "Try more! A lot of them! Make a rainstorm!"

My father closed his eyes, shaking.

Ping. A drop of rain pelted the tile by my foot.

Ping. Another drop fell on my shoulder. And another—*ping*—and another—*ping ping ping.* Rain sprinkled and then poured, pattering against the large oak table and checkered floor, the counters, the shelves and sink, and over the three of us. I shivered as rivulets ran down my neck, and peered up at the ceiling. The beams had disappeared into mist.

My father gaped upward, looking slightly frightened.

"If it's true," I broke in, excited, "that a person can illusion small things, like water . . . temperatures would be even easier, wouldn't they? All you would need to do is imagine the molecules spreading apart—"

The moment I thought it, the weight of the idea whorled in my head and warped my vision like a fever. An actual physical sensation. It pulsed with my heartbeat, down my neck and chest to my fingers. It emanated from my skin like vapors.

Whoosh. A void in my head made the laboratory spin. White.

When the world righted itself, I stood in the midst of spinning snowflakes. They fell cold on my head and glasses and hands, white crystals melting into drops. Snow began to frost the jars on the counters. I laughed aloud.

"Your apprentice!" the king said, delight in his booming voice. "He can illusion, as well!"

Grinning, I glanced through the swirling flakes to see the airguardsmen standing at attention against the walls of the room, regarding us warily. Far out of reach of the kettle's steam, they surely couldn't see the illusion. Behind them, in the doorway, Hannah clutched an armful of dusty mugs and stared at us with wide, frightened eyes. What did we look like to them? Laughing at invisible snow?

"Try something more difficult," said the king to me. "Try—say—a pocket watch."

In spite of the cold, sweat pricked my scalp. I thought of the mechanics of a watch. Metal gears. Springs. Glass. The sweat dripped as I tried to create iron, forming gears and screws in my mind.

The weighted thoughts expanded in my head and suffocated me. I gasped for breath as blotches filled my vision. Falling to my knees, I swallowed until my head cleared. It was like breathing water. No illusion appeared before me.

"It must only work for small things," said the king, disappointed.

"This is a toy," said my father, spinning the temperature wheel on the stove. The boiling halted, and the frigid air that had coated our lungs dissolved into nothing. It took my pounding senses and utter peace with it. The snow faded. The room darkened. Reality eased back in.

"What use could Lady Florel possibly see in this?" my father continued. "It isn't scientific. It is trickery."

"She has explained *something* of it to me," said the king, picking a koch dish—a round glass bowl about an inch deep—from the counter. "You grow the Venen disease in these dishes, correct? Lady Florel has said that she can *illusion time to go faster*. So, the disease grows more quickly, and you can test it immediately."

My father shook his head unhappily.

"I'm afraid you have no choice," said the king, his voice growing hard. "We don't have *time* to waste time. We only have four days."

"Four days—?"

"The queen has fallen ill!" the king snarled.

A *crash* sounded at the doorway. Hannah had dropped the mugs she held, her hands to her mouth, her face pale, shards at her feet. I grabbed the broom, suddenly feeling sick. So the queen was ill. No wonder the *Westminster* had braved the storm and the king's face had such desperation in it. Everyone loved the queen.

"Gather the things you need," said the king, face red from either anger or shame. He nodded with stiff politeness and made to leave. "Captain Crewe will see us to Lady Florel as soon as you are ready."

CHAPTER 2

"The queen is ill?" my mother whispered, arriving at the laboratory not long after the king had left, her face pale as a snowstorm. Hannah had run to fetch her from our row house, because our family was close and this was News.

My father answered her by pulling her into his arms and kissing her in front of the airguardsmen who remained in the laboratory. Hannah nearly fainted.

"Well, if anyone can cure her, our father can," I said, smiling reassuringly at my mother as I prepared my father's satchel. My mum was someone you never wanted to upset, as she was so quiet and sweet. Quite the opposite of Hannah, really.

"In four days?" said Hannah. "It took nearly four years for Papa to find the cure to the London Fever."

"Working with Lady Florel will speed things up," I said, shrugging.

"But *four days?*" said Hannah. "Even with that awful chemical—"

"Hold off, it wasn't *awful,*" I said, remembering how calm I had felt, and my focused, bright vision. "It was different, but—"

"It was awful," said Hannah, whipping around to face me with flashing eyes. "All three of you, staring up at the ceiling like demons had taken up residence in your head—"

"Hush," said my father, and we both fell silent. I could tell he agreed with Hannah. "We will speak to Lady Florel and see what can be done. Jonathan and I shall probably be sleeping here, in the observatory," he added to my mother, apologetically. My mother embraced him and promised to send Hannah with hot meals, and the four of us stood there in the laboratory, gathering strength from one another.

I embraced my mother as well, gently, because I'd outgrown her at age twelve and if I squeezed her too tight, she might snap. You didn't crush flowers, you didn't squeeze birds, and you didn't break your mum.

"Jonathan, please don't let your father bring the king in the laboratory again," Mum whispered, looking sideways at the mismatched furniture. "Perhaps the library, where the chairs aren't—so—"

"I heard that," said my father, with the hint of a smile.

"Mum, is that all you can think about?" said Hannah. "The furniture?"

"It is horrible furniture," said my mother.

"It is . . . *unique*," said my father. He nodded to the clock in the corner with so many carvings and pendulums that it couldn't possibly just be a grandfather clock. A grandfather clock had decency.[4] "That clock, for example. I doubt a person could find another clock like it."

"I doubt they could," my mother agreed.

I grinned. This was an age-old conversation in my family.

When Hannah and Mum left—Hannah sulking—the warmth they always had with them ebbed from the room, leaving my father with the cold and barren work.

Captain Crewe, a man younger than my father but with that same raw, honest look, introduced himself as the head of the Northern Airguard, promising us that he would do whatever he could to speed us in our work. And he went straight to it. In moments, we were out in the storm and following Captain Crewe to the largest airguardsman ship looming above the city: the *Chivalry*.

It didn't take long. Though Fata Morgana was the largest aerial city in the empire, it was only half a mile in diameter. I could walk across it in eight minutes. I'd

[4] A great-great-great grandfather clock, possibly.

grown up here, used to the brutal cold and the twirl of sun or stars overhead. Used to the white buildings, walkways, and cloud canals. Used to the rumble of the city's generator, its vibration like a heartbeat, keeping the city afloat above the Arctic Ocean. The inhabitants consisted mostly of orthogonagen miners and their families, but some, like my parents, lived here for the peace. Everyone knew one another. I'd be leaving Fata in just three months to attend the Arthurisian University, and I already missed the old thing.

The *Chivalry* bobbed at the top platform of dock three, a sleek metal beast the size of a building, double rows of cannon along the hull. The entire ship hummed with power. It must have fusioned through a maddening amount of orthogonagen fuel. The massive balloon provided an umbrella against the gale as we entered the ship into the command deck, full of more airguardsmen, and found the king waiting impatiently for us. More composed now, he led us through the dim, narrow halls to see Lady Florel.

Lady Florel was a legend. . . .

They said Lady Florel might have been royalty. Her family was one of the empire's wealthiest. They say she chose instead to become a surgeon and medical scientist.

They say she was a warrior, braving the Crimean

battlefield when she was only twenty-four, binding wounds and sewing bayonet gashes.

They say she was an angel, curing diseases throughout her lifetime, like the North Pox and the Paraphi, and establishing hospitals all throughout the empire.

They say that even now, at sixty-two years old, her spine was made of steel and her heart made of the sun, and when she spoke, no one disobeyed.

My father assured me the rumors were true, even the steel-and-sun one, if you were thinking figuratively. Steel, particularly. She had whipped him once, during his apprenticeship, for not washing his hands.

"Whipped?" I said, when he had told me the story.

"They did things properly back then," my father had said with pride.

Foreboding grew in me as we descended another flight of stairs into the belly of the ship, with lines of weak lights stretching down the hall, tang of metal and clang of engine pistons. Why was someone like Lady Florel being kept down here? Surely she would have a civilian's room?

We reached the narrowest and dimmest hall yet, which I recognized as a brig hall, a sweltering corridor with pipes along the walls hissing steam. The king called out, "Lieutenant?"

A uniformed boy, who had been polishing his pistol at the end of the hall, stood, holstered the pistol with sharp authority, and saluted smartly. His gun was so large the holster buckled to both his waist and his leg.

"Highness," said the boy.

"This is Dr. Heinrich Gouden, the medical scientist. He will be working with Lady Florel."

The boy saluted again, so sharply it sliced the air. He looked to be my age, sixteen, and everything about him was sharp. Crisp. Starched uniform, piercing blue eye, and so confident it was off-putting. An *absolute* person, like Hannah. But with one irregularity—he was missing his left eye. He wore an eye patch over it.

The name badge on his chest read *Lockwood*.

"Why is Lady Florel in a guarded prison cell?" said my father, frowning as the lieutenant unlocked the cell door.

"Because she tried to murder the king."

The lieutenant smiled at our shocked faces.

"I—beg your pardon!" said my father.

"I saw it myself," the lieutenant said lightly. "She had an entire officer's room for a laboratory, but she wouldn't even pick up one of those wossnames you look through—"

"Microscope," I offered helpfully, and the lieutenant glared at me with his lone eye.

"King went to speak to her," he continued, ignoring me, "to tell her to hurry things up a bit, she daggered him in the chest. Or tried to, anyway. I was there, so . . . she didn't." He crossed his arms and peered at me with smug finality.

"I do not believe it," said my father.

"Lady Florel is simply not herself," said the king, waving the entire subject away with monarchal grace. "None of us have been, of late."

"Some of us have been even . . . *better*."

The voice echoed sweetly from beyond the unlocked door. Lady Florel's voice. Attention now turned to the cell, we entered the tiny dim room under the lieutenant's watchful eye. Stuffed with a table, stacked with empty koch dishes, and books lying about. In the glow of a single light, an older woman in a heavy coat turned and smiled at us.

Lady Florel.

She was smaller than me, with a severe face, noble nose, and tiny lips. Her eyebrows arched over her eyes, giving her smile an edge. If she recognized my father, it did not show in her face.

"Have you brought me my illusionist?" she said.

The king spoke as though he were peeling the words from the back of his throat.

"Lady Florel," he said to us, with pauses, "has agreed to find the cure . . . if . . . I could find her an illusionist . . . to help her in her research."

I glanced at my father to see what he would say. He said nothing, but instead had taken a step back toward the cell door.

"That is not Lady Florel," he whispered.

"What? How do you know?" I asked in a low voice.

"Lady Florel never smiled."

I turned and examined Lady Florel again, standing behind the table. She looked like every picture I'd seen of her in every medical journal I'd ever read. Older, perhaps—and certainly a lot more pleasant, wearing a smile. She never smiled in any of the pictures. Now she almost looked like a grandmother. I paused as my eyes caught something new on her face. A divot lay between her eyes. A dimple.

I gnawed on my cheek. A person couldn't have something like that on their forehead unless they were missing bone. . . .

Warily, I picked up Lady Florel's research journal, which had been tossed to the side of the table. I flipped through the pages and found them all blank. No notes. Nothing.

"He could illusion water," the king was saying, having introduced my father to Lady Florel, who looked pleased beyond measure. She still had not shown any sign of recognition.

"Excellent!" she was saying. "That is a *start*. All

I need is a vial of fantillium, and we shall get the cure straightaway!"

"Capital," said the king, looking relieved. "I'll have Captain Crewe bring the vials—Dr. Gouden, you and your son—"

"We will not."

My father's voice hushed both of them.

"Dr. Gouden—" the king began.

"I once apprenticed with Lady Florel," my father said, drawing himself up and clutching his satchel. His hands shook and his eyes blazed. "And I knew her well. You, Madam, are not her, and I will not use the unsound methods of an unsound mind! Jonathan, come, we have no time to waste!"

I halfway tipped my cap to them, avoiding looking at the king's face, red with the affront. My father was just half out the cell door when a hoarse scream tore the air. Lady Florel lunged at my father in a blur of coat. In her hand flashed a bladelike shard of broken koch dish.

She plunged it into my father's neck—

BANG.

—*Almost* plunged it into my father's neck—

The glass in her hand exploded into dust with the steam pistol's bullet. Lady Florel retreated halfway bent, gloved hands held up in surrender. Standing casually at the door, Lieutenant Lockwood kept his pistol pointed at her. It steamed.

"Don't let's do that again," he said smoothly.

"I—I—I don't know what came over me. I'm so terribly sorry," she said, pressing herself against the back wall and truly looking apologetic and frightened.

Lockwood's pistol remained at the ready.

My father, stunned, touched his hand to his neck, where the glass had only just punctured his skin. His fingers brought back blood. The lieutenant had shot the broken glass from Lady Florel's hand at just the right moment.

"Right," I said, clapping my hands on my bewildered father's shoulders and steering him out of the cell. He looked as though he might collapse onto the brig floor. "No time to waste. Back to the laboratory, work to do!"

I'd never seen my father distraught. Not like this. Back in the laboratory he paced and spoke in HoLander to himself, saying, "It *is* her . . . but it is *not* her." He cleaned his glasses on his apron over and over. I was the one who reminded him that we needed blood samples of the Venen, if we were to do any kind of research at all.

The task at hand focused his attention, and Captain Crewe was once again at our side, escorting us to dock seven, where the *Westminster* bobbed. We had clearance to see the queen. The king, Captain Crewe told us, was taking a cold walk around the perimeter of the city to keep from bashing the walls in.

The storm had waned now, and a group of Fata Morganians gathered at the bottom of the dock's lift, bundled in thick coats and scarves and peering up at the ship, talking excitedly among themselves. Professor Stromberg, my academy physics professor, stopped me as we entered the lift.

"Jonathan?" he said.

"Nothing to worry about," I said jovially. "A hiccup, really. My father's going to save the empire from a pernicious disease, you know, that old thing, nothing to worry about."

Everyone looked pleased beyond words. They admired my father as much as I.

The *Westminster* was as royal and ornate as the *Chivalry* was austere. Captain Crewe escorted my father and me quickly and quietly through the airship, down long halls with crimson rugs so thick I sank into them with each step, and chandeliers that jingled with the ship's engine rumblings. We entered the lush captain's quarter's moments later, and here I witnessed the Venen for the first time.

Queen Alexandria lay on a bed by the fireplace, still among the mountain of pillows. She was familiar to me in the same way the king was—through newspaper prints and paintings—a slender and beautiful woman, always wearing pearls and her hair braided into a bun on the top of her head. Now she lay motionless, her eyes closed, her hair in tendrils around her, just as I'd imagined the Lady of the Lake. Even in her nightgown, she wore long necklaces of pearls.

And the Venen. It mottled her fingers black. The blackness had seeped up her milk-white arms, splitting into spindly strands and tapering like vines. It was as though someone had penned ink over her veins. Her neck, too, had the Venen's mark, threads of black reaching her ears.

She spoke softly when we entered, not opening her eyes.

"More doctors?" she said. She smiled, but a tear fell down her face. "I feel I have no blood left."

"Your Highness," said my father gently. "It is our life's work to keep people from pain. My son will be gentle."

Ah, but no pressure, I thought.

I *was* good at drawing blood, though. Remarkably good. Dr. Palmer, the physician here on Fata Morgana, often had me help in the infirmary. I had great plans to become a surgeon. Even so, my hands shook as I cleaned the queen's arm and injected the needle. I almost expected ink to flow into it and was grateful for the deep purple-red instead. I drew three vials and then softly wrapped her arm. I don't believe she felt a thing.

My father asked questions of her condition and the fevers, which she quietly answered and I wrote down. He begged permission to see her hand, which she couldn't move. It did tremble, however, as a gust of cold air blew over us. I turned and discovered that the mullioned windows along the walls were all partially open.

"Hello there," I said, stopping one of the servant boys who'd come into the room with fresh flowers. "Why are the windows open?"

"The king says she's to have fresh air," said the boy.

"Were they open earlier today? This afternoon?"

"Yes, sir. They've been open the whole journey, on account of the good air."

I tugged on my ear, uncomfortable, as the boy scampered out of the room. I drew my father aside, out of earshot.

"Hannah was by the ship this afternoon," I said in a low voice.

He glanced at the open windows, and his brow creased.

"I am sure she had enough sense to not draw near," he said.

Near enough to see the queen's pearls, I thought.

The visit to the *Westminster* had shaken me. I hadn't expected the Venen to be so . . . vivid. Every time I closed my eyes, I saw the spindly black threads coursing up her arms. And it was raging through Arthurise.

My father and I worked through the night and into the next day, labeling koch dishes with the Venen growing inside them and drawing diagrams of what it looked like under the microscope—spindly black creatures with diamond-shaped heads. The storm had cleared by now, and I jogged to the semaphore tower in the center of the city, signaling Arthurise for more information.

Captain Crewe arrived at the laboratory in the middle of our work, a metal box with fantillium in his hands, again informing us that the king wished us to work with Lady Florel.

"I will not," said my father, without looking up from his work.

"The king is insistent, I'm afraid."

"The king can illusion, himself, then."

Captain Crewe saluted, and left with the box.

"What do you think happened to her?" I asked him after the door had closed. "Lady Florel, I mean?"

"I cannot say," said my father. The color in his face, which had fled in Lady Florel's cell on the *Chivalry*, had returned to some degree. He continued to copy my semaphore notes from Arthurise into his medical journal, and spoke without looking up. "But Lady Florel—the true Lady Florel—would never work with something like fantillium. It causes acedia."

"Aced—what?"

"It means," said my father, "it dulls the conscience."

I paused. I hadn't noticed that. I'd felt more alive with the chemical in my blood—lights were brighter, sounds were clearer. The lab even smelled sharper. I hadn't really paid attention to much else.

"Well," I conceded, "it is strange. But we may have to use it. The king seems a bit on edge. . . . Can't say I blame him, either."

"It is better to disobey a king," said my father, "than to disobey my own conscience."

He touched a finger to the center of his chest, and that was that.

My father had this . . . belief.

It was that everyone had a sort of compass inside of him. One that you could feel. And if you were doing everything good and right, it pointed to a northernmost light, and if you did ill, it turned and twisted and caused a sort of southerly darkness inside your soul.

I myself had never felt a compass in me, figuratively or otherwise, and supposed it was just One of Those Things Fathers Say to get you to learn your sums or not hit your sister. But even now that I was sixteen, my father still believed it so ardently, he touched his chest whenever he felt the need to be Pointed.

I adjusted the microscope lens, frustrated. A person's conscience couldn't cure a disease like the Venen. And—a darker voice in me added—it couldn't throw you into a cell like Lady Florel's.

By evening, because I hadn't slept in two days, my father made me retire to the library, where the airguard had set up cots for us to rest on. I'd nearly fallen asleep between the freezing sheets when a banging on the window roused me. I had to break the ice on the pane to shove the window up, but when I did, I was face-to-face with Hannah and her friend Alice, bundled up in shawls and wearing their best dresses and beaming at me.

"Oh, ah, hello," I said, transforming my shivering into a laugh. Growing up I'd mostly ignored Hannah's friends, until one morning a year ago I woke up and they'd suddenly become funny and pretty and all shades of clever. I couldn't string a sentence together around Alice. It was maddening. She had a mass of red curly hair that fell to her waist and her face and arms had freckles all over them, which was utterly charming. At times I'd catch her looking at me after I'd said something funny, and she'd smile at her feet and hug her books to her chest, and insofar as I could see, it was the beginning of a very promising relationship.

Beneath all the shawls, I could see she wore a long homespun yellow dress with a bit of lace, which was dead nice, and she held a covered tray of what smelled like sweet rolls, which was even deader nice.

"We wanted to come through the door, but there were soldiers there and we were afraid they'd turn us away," said Hannah. "Can you come out?"

Without hesitation, I climbed through the window onto the metal walkway. We retreated into the warmth of the nearest heat lamp, a length away in the courtyard. It loomed over our heads and could turn snowflakes to steam so quickly they snapped. We huddled in the lamp's orange light, warming up and laughing in the shelter of the observatory walls. A lone light shone from a window on the second floor. My father's shadow paced across it.

"Sorry about the soldiers," I said, warming my hands on the lamp's metal rim. "The empire's a bit tense right now."

"How's everything coming?" said Hannah, her eyes alight.

"Great, great. Um, what are you wearing?" I said, because I'd caught a second look at her, and beneath the layers of shawl she wore a violet dress with masses of silk puffs. Her hair had been pulled up into ringlets and ribbons. Hannah was only fourteen but had a figure that made my academy classmates snap their slate chalks in half.

"Do you like it?" she said, twirling around, the ruffly bits poofing up around her. "There's twelve yards of fabric altogether! I can hardly lift my feet. We ordered it last summer, but now I can wear it *because there's a dance tonight*! At the Rosewine Theater, we're just on our way. Can you come?"

"A dance?" I said, laughing. "What, with who? All three boys who live here?"

"No, stupid." Hannah grinned. "The airguard is here, aren't they?"

That wiped the smile off my face. My head played mutiny with my soul as I imagined all the airguardsmen lining up to ask Alice for a dance. It double mutinied with the thought of that cocky one-eyed lieutenant snaking his arm around Hannah's waist.

"Oh, don't be like that; Mum will be there to chaperone," said Hannah. "Anyway, don't you think you could use a bit of a rest? Maybe you could slip away for just one dance?"

I glanced at Alice, who blushed at her platter, and I ran a hand through my mussed sort-of brown hair. Glancing up at the lit laboratory window, I shook my head.

"Sorry," I said, nodding to the second floor. "I can't just run off like that. Not when the old fellow's at work."

Hannah looked disappointed. Alice looked even more disappointed, which made me the most disappointed of all.

"At least have a sweet roll," Alice said, uncovering the platter. I eagerly took one, because fresh food was hard to come by on Fata, where most things were made with food from cans and bottles. Not to mention, I'd had Alice's sweet rolls before.[5] "Take one for your father, too," Alice added. "And another one, if you want."[6]

"Don't encourage him, Alice, or he'll eat the entire—"

Hannah stopped abruptly and leaned against the rim of the lamp. I hadn't noticed until now how sickly pale she looked.

"Careful," I said, drawing her away from the red-hot grid. "You'll get burned."

"She hasn't been herself all day," Alice said.

"Stop it, I'm fine." Hannah weakly pulled out of my grip. "Stop acting like such a—a *surgeon*—"

She halted once again and closed her eyes. Then in one fluid movement, she folded up into a giant silk poof ball on the walkway.

I dropped to her side and propped her up amidst the purple. Her eyelids flickered.

"Hannah!" I said.

"I'm fine—fine—" she said, feebly trying to get back up.

---

[5] More icing than roll. The proper kind of sweet roll.

[6] See what I mean? Charming.

I took her hand and pulled off her silk glove.

Her fingertips were mottled black. Little crisscrossing rivulets of black capillaries. Alice gasped.

I delicately slipped her glove back on with shaking fingers.

"You know, let's take a quick toddle to the infirmary, hey?" I said, pulling her to her feet. She hung limply on my arm.

"I'll be late," she moaned.

"Fashionably late," I said, half carrying her down the walkway. "You'll be back in time for biscuits and punch, you can bet on it."

CHAPTER 3

She wasn't back in time for biscuits and punch.

The infirmary, a long brick building with rows of tall windows and white rooms that smelled of laundry and disinfectant, admitted Hannah so quickly in a blur of nurses and purple dress that I'd been abandoned in the hallway with empty arms, a bit dazed. I was still there when Mum came, dressed in a proper coat and gloves—Alice had run to fetch her from the Rosewine. She stood on her toes and kissed my forehead.

"Hannah is in the wing?" she said quietly.

I nodded.

"Your father ought to know," she said, but when she stepped forward, she collapsed. I caught her before her knees touched ground. She hardly weighed a thing. I guided her to one of the lobby chairs.

"I'm sorry," she stammered. "I—I've felt so oddly today—"

I was already taking off her glove. Her fingertips were scored with black.

"Oh," she said, looking at her hand with great interest. "Is this what your father has been working on?"

"Oh, ah, I don't know," I said, backing out of the hall. "Um. Why don't I just go—and go—and go—and go and fetch him?"

I fled.

Minutes later I returned, this time with my father on my heels, his long coat flapping and his face ashen. He hadn't even bothered to remove his apron. My mother, at Hannah's bedside by the main wing, began to speak, but was stopped short by my father pulling her into a tight embrace and cradling her head against his shoulder. They remained still for a long time.

I removed myself from the room, and ran.

And ran.

And ran.

Into the freezing polar night, over the walkways and around the promenade that jutted around the perimeter of the city. The problem with Fata Morgana was that there was nowhere to *run to*. You either ricocheted back into the city, or leapt over the railing and fell into the ocean below. I ran until I felt my throat would turn itself inside out and collapsed onto the platform that led to dock three, on the south side of the city.

Here, in the warmth and hum of the heat lamps, I leaned against the railing. This dock had benches and a plaque that marked the establishment of Fata thirty-one years ago (1851). Three telescopes stood along the platform, which would play a jaunty tune for a coin and allow you to look out over the ocean for ninety seconds. On a clear day you could see the Scandinavian coast.

I drew a hand through my hair, shivering. The generator rumbled beneath my feat, chorusing with the jingle of piano and polite laughter that wafted out from the city's center. And far below, the ocean. A great black expanse of unending nothing. I could sympathize with it.

Six days.

It began with weakness and fainting, and the fingertips and toes would begin to color. That was day one.

Day two: Fever sets in. Discoloration spreads up the legs and arms and neck.

Day three: Fever gives way to periods of unconsciousness.

Day four: Loss of movement, loss of voice. The black spreads. The veins color over the face.

Day five: The discoloration reaches the center of the body, the heart.

Day six: Death.

I smacked the telescope. It spun unevenly and slowed to a stop, pointing northeast. Six days was nothing. A blink. You'd inhale and it'd be gone.

At the far end of dock three, the *Chivalry* loomed, all cannon and steel. Like Lady Florel, I thought. An idea took hold of me, and did not release. In a moment I was riding up the lift and recklessly hurrying over the platform to the ship.

Captain Crewe stood at the top of the dock, just exiting the massive airship with several other airguardsmen. He seemed genuinely glad to see me.

"Master Gouden," he said. "I only just heard. I am so sorry."

"I need to speak to Lady Florel," I said.

To my surprise he said, "Of course."

He led me down the main corridors that smelled of burning orthogonagen, past rows of sleek lights and endless doors and spiral stairs. None of the airguardsmen questioned us, but rather saluted when we passed. We arrived at the brig, pipes hissing along the walls, to Lieutenant Lockwood. He stood and saluted smartly to Captain Crewe. His lone blue eye narrowed at me.

"Lieutenant," said Captain Crewe. "This is Jonathan Gouden, Dr. Gouden's apprentice. He's come to speak to Lady Florel. You *will* allow him entrance and do everything you can to speed him in his work, is that clear?"

Lockwood clicked the heels of his boots together and saluted smartly again.

"Very well. Master Gouden, I will see you back in the observatory."

Captain Crewe left me alone in the brig's corridor with Lockwood. Lockwood's cold blue eye hadn't left my face.

"If you could open her door?" I said when he did not move.

"Why?" he said with a sneer.

"Um. Because half the empire is dying? That enough for you?"

With extreme bone-bending reluctance, Lockwood unlocked Lady Florel's cell door and bowed me in with exaggerated politeness. I ignored him.

In the darkness of the cell—koch dishes notably absent—Lady Florel stood behind the table, bundled in the coat, her graying hair pulled into a tight bun, facing away from me. She did not turn around as I removed my cap, but said, "Dr. Gouden. I knew you would come."

I coughed.

"His son, actually," I said. "But I can illusion, too. I think."

Lady Florel turned around with raised eyebrows and took me in. Something flickered in her eyes, and they glittered.

"Of course you can," she whispered.

I twisted my cap, wary.

"Lady Florel," I said, and the words dried in my throat. My thoughts scattered. People dying in droves. The Venen spreading. My mother touching my cheek with her black fingertips. Hannah's weight on my arm. You couldn't condense it into something as clumsy as words. Instead I said, "Lady Florel, you said you needed an illusionist to find the cure. I can illusion. Tell me what I need to do. My mother and my sister—"

I couldn't speak anymore.

Lady Florel smiled. Her brows wrinkled around the dimple on her forehead.

"Did you bring a vial of fantillium?" she said.

"Er—no," I said.

"Ah. Well, we cannot continue until then."

"What? Why not? Couldn't you just tell me what to do?" I said, thinking of all the trouble this would get me into. "It would be better if it was just me, illusioning in my father's laborator—"

"No," she said sweetly, cutting me off. "Bring a vial of fantillium to me. Then we move forward."

"Right," I said, kneading my cap like a loaf of bread and thinking of Captain Crewe's box. "Only—I mean, I'd probably have to take the fantillium from behind my father's back, you see, and that's—" I coughed. "That's, ah, that's stealing, you see. Textbook definition."

Lady Florel kept her cold brown eyes fixed on me.

"I don't care," she said. "Bring the fantillium, or the Venen's antitoxin shall never be found in time."

I placed my cap back on my head and turned to go, frustrated. This wasn't the Lady Florel I'd read about. She'd do anything she could to find the cure. Perhaps my father was right—she wasn't the same person.

Six days.

I turned sharply around, the scientist in me rearing his head.

"I need *proof*," I said. "Proof that you're not mad. Proof that you can get the cure in time. I need proof right now, Lady Florel."

Lady Florel, her smile unceasing, tore a page from her blank research book and wrote upon it. I frowned as she penned an equation:

$$\Omega = x \left(\frac{(2\pi r)\left(\mu \sqrt{\left(\frac{2}{\lambda} - \frac{1}{\theta} \right)} \right)}{\varphi} \right)$$

And then:

x = 288, then 1 Day = 5 minutes
x = 1440, then 1 Day = 1 minute
x = 86,400, then 1 Day = 1 second
φ = 1 Day in real time
Ω = Illusioned Time

"What?" I said, frowning at the paper.

"This is the Quickening Formula," Lady Florel said, handing the paper to me. "It's a modified orbital equation."

Real time? *Illusioned* time? I recognized the equation for circumference, then parts of the equation of orbital gravity; the Earth's distance from the sun; a semi-major axis.

Illusioned time . . .

The king's words rang in my head: *You can illusion time to go faster. . . .*

Realization dawned on me like an early spring sun: This mangle of an equation, with its odd symbols, harnessed the rotation and orbit of the Earth.

I could illusion time to go faster by illusioning the world to turn more quickly.

"This is mad!" I said, nearly dropping the note. "Illusioning the entire Earth! That's impossible! A person can't even illusion a pocket watch!"

"*You* asked for proof," said Lady Florel, steel in her tone. "And here it is. If you are a good illusionist—and I *know* you are—try it, and it will work. That's how you'll know I'm not lying."

Disturbed, I folded the note and put it in my coat pocket and left the cell without bidding her a good-bye. Lockwood slammed the cell door behind me with a *clang*. Just .005 seconds later, his hand grabbed me by the neck and shoved me against the steaming pipes. I gasped for air as he pressed his arm into my neck and I was nose to nose and eye to eye patch with the lieutenant's face.

"You were trying to help her!" he spat.

"What?" I said. "No, I wasn't!"

"You were going to help her *escape*!" he snarled. "I can sense these things, *Johnny*, the way I can spot an assassin's light sig in a sea of Arthurisian lights and the way I can tell you, *Johnny*, have about as much moral fiber as a dead fish, and the way I can tell there's something very wrong with her, *Johnny*, and that there must be something very wrong with *you* if you want to help someone who tried to kill your own father and let me tell you something, *Johnny*: I haven't been put guard over her to let her escape! Is that clear? Johnny?"

I shoved Lockwood away, which took a bit of doing.

"I don't even let my mother call me *Johnny*," I snapped. "And I *like* my mother."

"Let me introduce you to someone, *John-ny*," Lockwood continued, bringing his steam pistol up to my face. It was larger than my head. The pistons steamed and whirred in my ear. "This is a Benguela steel-forged new-model center-fire steam-powered three-piston revolver. So alive it nearly shoots itself."

"What is your *problem*?" I ducked away and retreated for the door. "Is that how you lost your eye? Playing with guns?"

"I lost my eye," he said, "scaling the Royal Palace of Madrid amid a hailstorm of bullets to save Robert the First, duke of Bourbon-Parma, and his wife, the Duchess Maria Pia of the Two Sicilies, from their impending assassinations."

The ship hummed.

"Oh, that old story," I said.

I turned to go.

CRACK.

Hissssshhhh . . .

I jerked away from the jet of superheated air that streamed past my head. The pipe by my ear had a bullet hole shot through it. My ear stung. I lifted my hand to it and brought back blood from a graze wound.

I turned around sharply to meet Lockwood's smug smile. The barrel of his revolver steamed in his hand. Airguardsmen appeared at the doorway, looking annoyed and twisting the wheel on the boiler at the end of the hall, and the steam sputtered and tapered off.

Lockwood holstered the revolver with finality.

"I didn't want you to think my depth perception was off," he said.

Oh please, I thought, and left the *Chivalry* with my ear still ringing.

CHAPTER 4

I couldn't keep my mind off the paper in my coat pocket. I worked with my father the next morning, impatient at how slowly the Venen cultures grew. If I had fantillium, I thought, I could at least try the quickening equation on them. I didn't dare bring it up with my father, however. Without a word, he soldiered on, his face rough and unshaven, his eyes sunken. Lunch was the same food the airguardsmen had—a soupy curried rice. Having no appetite for it, I allowed myself the distraction of quickly visiting Hannah in the infirmary.

I arrived in the warmth of the infirmary's main wing with Hannah's academy textbooks tucked under my arm. I'd stopped by the school to fetch her homework. Hannah hated missing class.

More beds were filled today. They lined each side of the infirmary's long corridor, white curtains separating each patient. The infirmary nurses had fallen ill. And—my heart sank—so had Alice, her fiery red hair a tangle over her pillow. Dr. Palmer stood in a room off to the side of the wing, holding a clipboard and speaking in a low voice to Alice's father, who wrung his miner's cap in his large craggy hands.

I walked down the long aisle until I reached Alice, lying asleep in her bed; I touched her freckled cheek, gently. She sighed and slept on.

"If she didn't know you liked her before," Hannah's voice broke in, "she really will now."

I quickly removed my hand.

"Checking for fever," I said.

"Oh, just."

I smiled and walked to the aisle between Hannah's and Mum's beds. Mum lay unmoving in a deep slumber. Hannah lay on her pillow, her eyelids half-closed, but brightening when she saw I'd brought her books, and with effort she pushed herself upright. I dumped the books on the table by her bed. She used all the same books I did. One, in fact, was even a year ahead of me. It didn't bother me, of course. Not in the least. Not at all.[7]

[7] Really*

*No, really.

"Does Professor Arnoth know I'm here?" she said, referring to our dusty old history professor. "If he knows I have the Venen, he's going to be so *cross*!"[8]

She struggled to lift a pen to her workbook, but her fingers, turning black, couldn't bend.

"I can't even hold a pen," she said with a wavery voice.

"'Course you can." I plucked the ribbon out of her hair and tied the pen to her hand. "There, see? Also, very fashionable."

She sniffed.

"I don't want Mum to die," she said, and burst into tears.

And that summed up the remainder of the visit. I left with my shoulder soaked and my knees weak. Hannah's last words rang in my head: "I'll fight it, Jonathan. I'm a fighter. I'll fight it, and Papa will find the cure."

"I think he's close to something."

"I *knew* it," Hannah whispered, falling asleep with the pen still tied to her hand. "I knew it."

"Arsenic," said my father, that night when the king arrived at the observatory unannounced with Captain Crewe to see how our work was coming along. My father presented the koch dish to the king, a round shallow dish he had swabbed with an arsenic compound, the

---

[8] He had actually started to cry.

black receding and leaving a ring around it.

"Arsenic?" said the king. He sat on one of the sofas crammed into the room, eating a large bowl of curried rice. He ate like he spoke, with gusto and little regard. Grains of rice were scattered by his feet and stuck to the sofa's embroidery. He wiped his hands on his napkin and sniffed. "That will kill the Venen?"

My father smiled.

"Arsenic kills everything," he said. "But it does seem to kill the Venen faster than the other tissues."

"Wonderful!" said the king, leaping to his feet and thumping him so hard on the back, his glasses slid down his nose. "We give the queen a dose and she'll be well straightway, will she?"

"Yes, it doesn't *quite* work like that," said my father, who tried to explain to the king about wrong dosages and imperfect compounds and refining the formula and how the research would take *time*; otherwise we would inadvertently paralyze or kill the patients—

The king chewed impatiently, face growing red as my father spoke.

"I should think I have been *very* patient with you, Gouden," he said in a slow and patronizing tone. "But we don't have time for this any longer. We hardly have two days!"

"I am aware—"

"We *must* consider more options, Gouden!"

"I will not work with Lady Florel or that chemical!"

"You will work however I jolly well tell you to work—"

"Is this a bad time?" a quiet voice broke in.

My father, the king, Captain Crewe, and I all turned and discovered Hannah, her hair tangled and leaning against the doorframe of the laboratory. She wore an overlarge coat, which her bare feet peeked out under. Her toes were black.

"I did it," she whispered. "I came the entire way myself. Huzzah."

My father and I caught her before she collapsed to the ground. She came to as we brought her to an orange chair with claws for legs.

"Come now, *meisje*," said my father, drawing her baggy coat tightly around her shoulders. It looked as though she'd stolen it from the infirmary supply closet. "We will visit you soon. But your place now is in the infirmary. We can have the captain take you back, hey?"

"Papa, I'm not five years old," said Hannah, pushing him away and struggling to her feet, which caused her to knock against the laboratory table. The koch dishes clinked. "I've come all this way, and I'm going to help! Jonathan said you've almost found the cure. So, I thought . . . you'll need someone to try it on. And that someone should be me."

My father blanched.

"Well!" the king bellowed, making everyone jump. He strode to Hannah's side and took her hand, which made her beam. "What a fine idea! You are a credit to the empire, young lady!"

"Does the queen really have eighty-two strands of rare pearls?" said Hannah.

"She does."

"I've always liked pearls."

"Then you shall have some!"

"I beg your pardon!" said my father, stepping between them, his ears flaring pink and his spectacles flashing. "My daughter will be no medical experiment!"

The king stepped back, stunned at my father's tone, then rebounded. An argument progressed. Louder, then louder, my father parrying with sharp words and Hannah declaring that she wanted to help, pleading over the king's booming voice.

I watched quietly from a distance. Gears whirred in my head.

She wouldn't be harmed, I thought. Not if the time, and the arsenic, were an illusion . . .

"What if we illusioned it?" I said aloud.

Hannah, my father, Captain Crewe, and the king stopped arguing. They stared at me.

There was a pregnant pause. The pause gave birth to a lot of little pauses. Foolishly, I spoon-fed them.

"Why not?" I barreled on. "We know the chemical structure of arsenic. So—we breathe fantillium and have Hannah drink an illusioned dose. If we illusion sped-up time, we could see if it will work. And Hannah wouldn't be in any real danger. Not if it were an illusion."

"Why, that's brilliant!" the king boomed, and immediately commenced into adulation about what *clever* children Dr. Gouden had. My father grabbed me by the arm and drew me to the far side of the room, just out of hearing.

"I should think I have taught you better than this," he said.

"Better than what?" I said, bristling. "I'm trying to help!"

"*If* fantillium truly creates an ersatz reality," said my father, "then Hannah will feel the pain as though it were real! Do you not remember the snow? We felt the cold of it upon our faces! We could deeply *hurt* her, even if it does not last! You would do that to your sister?"

I winced. "Well, no. Of course not. I just—"

"I *want* him to!" said Hannah.

"Dr. Gouden?" said the king. "A word, if you please."

My father and the king left the room. Ten minutes later they reentered, the king clapping his hands jovially and calling for us all to begin. My father's face was ashen. He kept his eyes firmly *away* from me as the king announced broadly that our father would very much like

53

to have me illusion the arsenic for Hannah. I wondered what the king had said to him.

I did know one thing: If anything went wrong with the illusion, I was going to be in deep, deep trouble. . . .

My father didn't stop us as we helped Hannah to the orange chair and pushed it to the orthogonagen stove. But he didn't help us, either. He remained by Hannah, arms crossed. I rooted through my father's notes myself and found the chemical breakdown of arsenic. Captain Crewe brought the teakettle to boiling and produced the small metal box with the vials of fantillium. Taking one, he set the box down, uncorked the vial, and emptied the black contents into the kettle.

We crowded around the stove. I clutched an empty mug in one hand and pages with the quickening formula and the arsenic compound in the other. My nervousness subsided the moment I inhaled my first breath of fantillium steam. Liquid ice. The world grew bright and sharp. The clock in the corner thudded the seconds . . . *clonk, clonk, clonk*. Captain Crewe turned down the lights.

Hannah gasped when she saw my eyes. Her eyes, too, had dilated to pure black.

We were ready.

I filled the cup halfway with water and studied the arsenic formula on the paper, a tangle of elements and chemical bonds. I'd illusion the arsenic into the cup, and Hannah would drink it. Easy enough.

The paper shook in my hand as I visualized the chemical in my head. I imagined threads of arsenic forming and bonding. It grew heavy in my thoughts, seeping to the front of my head, an actual physical sensation. I exhaled, pushing it to the mug.

I almost saw the thought glistening in the air, a long string from my face to the cup. The water sucked it in, and it became metallic.

"Right," I said, sweat beading my forehead. I'd produced the Quickening Formula from my coat pocket and smoothed it out on the counter. "Hannah will drink the illusioned arsenic, and then I'll illusion the days to go faster. Maybe—make the days last thirty seconds. That means it will only take about two or three minutes to see if it all works." I handed the mug of illusioned arsenic drink to Hannah. "That would be about right, wouldn't it?" I added, to my father.

He didn't answer. He remained with his arms crossed looking as though he very much wanted to hit me.

"Well, I guess we'll see," I said, rankling.

I stared at the page with the Quickening Formula, letting the numbers and symbols etch themselves into my head, redrawing it with mental pencil to paper. As soft as a sigh, the algorithm solidified in my head. Warmth like a fever evaporated from my skin. The formula swirled heavily around my brain. I closed my eyes and exhaled.

$x = 2880$.

Nothing happened. The grandfather clock *clonked* unbearably loud. *Clonk*.

And then . . .

And then . . .

The dust in the dim light began to swirl in patterns. *Clonk clonk.*

Shadows flickered with the lights. A buzzing filled my head.

Clonkclonkclonk . . .

Clonkclonkclonkclonkclonkclonkclonkclonkclonkclonk clonkclonkclonkclonkclonk

The hands on the clock spun and blurred and it groaned as though in pain, chiming a mangle of broken bells. Light grew through the frosted laboratory window. The polar sun, lifting above the horizon. The light faded as it plunged back into the sea. Thirty-second days! It was working!

On the sofa, Hannah began to tremble. The black on her fingers grew up her arms like vines.

"Hannah, drink the arsenic!" I said as the light grew and waned faster.

Hands quavering, Hannah lifted the mug to her lips, gulped, and gagged. She coughed and with sputtering defiance downed the entire mugful.

She began to shake.

Black spread rapidly around her ears and up her neck. Hannah gasped for air, and began to shudder and cry.

Quickly my father took her into his arms and held her tightly. The windless air whistled around us. The light strobed.

"Stop the illusion!" my father shouted at me. "You're killing her!"

"We see it through!" the king yelled.

I mentally flailed. I didn't know how to *stop* time! Thoughts in my head scattered. My focus blurred. Hannah's lips and eyelids turned black.

"Jonathan!" my father cried.

And as fast as time flew, it could have frozen at that one moment when my father held Hannah tightly in his arms, the luster of her skin dimming and her body falling limp like a rag doll.

I lunged at the stove and shoved the kettle off. It sloshed and hissed, burning my hands. I didn't care.

The laboratory darkened. The clock *clonked* its regular seconds. Sick, I ran to Hannah, my father holding her limp frame in his trembling arms, drenched in sweat. My knees gave way and I collapsed by them.

The king towered over us.

"She can't be dead," he said, alarm in his voice. "It— it was an illusion. Wasn't it?"

Captain Crewe turned up the lights, and as he did so,

the black that had scored Hannah's neck, hands, and feet slowly faded and receded back to her fingertips.

Luster returned to her face. She drew a shuddering gasp.

"Papa?" she whispered.

My father broke into a stream of HoLander and held Hannah's head to his chest. She wrapped her arms around his neck. I drew a shaking hand across my forehead, wiping away the dripping sweat. It had just been an illusion.

"Well, excellent," said the king in a relieved voice. "The—that dose of arsenic—didn't quite work, so—let's have another go." The king set the kettle I had shoved away back on the burner, and the water inside immediately rolled into a boil. Glistening steam rose out the spout.

"Another go?" said my father as the cold air stung our lungs. I winced as the room brightened.

"I expect this time, we shall require more arsenic."

"No."

My father stood with Hannah in his arms.

"A stronger dose of arsenic, then?" said the king. "I am not a scientist—"

"I will not illusion again."

The king slowly drew himself up, the buttons on his coat flashing.

"We will illusion," he said quietly, "until we find the cure, Dr. Gouden."

"I will *not*."

The fantillium air in the laboratory burned our faces and the king's face became red. My father remained solid beneath his glare.

With controlled delicacy, the king said, "I can see your daughter does not have the strength. You told me earlier your wife had the Venen, did you not? Perhaps she would volun—"

"I have a better idea," said my father, striding to the door. "Why don't we experiment upon *your* wife?"

The king's voice grew dangerously low.

"Because my wife is the *queen*, and your wife is a little *nobody.*"

My father whipped around, his coat snapping behind him, and threw his hand out.

Wind shrieked through the laboratory. A razor-sharp jet of air howled past my ear. It sliced through microscopes and glass bottles on the table, sending the pieces skittering across the tabletop and onto the checkered floor—

—the razor wind of air slashed the king across the face like an invisible sword. Blood splattered. The crimson droplets remained suspended in the air as the blast of wind threw our sovereign over the mismatched furniture. He toppled into lamps and chairs and globes, slamming into the wall with a thunderous *thumpf.*

He crumpled to the tile floor among the wreckage of furniture.

Blood speckled his heavy coat and the sofas around him.

The king did not move.

No one moved.

Captain Crewe drew away, looking horrified. My father gaped from the king's mountainous form, to his own hand, then back to the king.

I was the only one with enough sense to end the illusion. I threw the kettle into the sink and once again, the laboratory darkened. The broken furniture about the king faded back into their original whole forms, though askew from the king stumbling back against them. The gash across the king's face disappeared. An illusion.

"Jonathan," said my father quietly, Hannah still in his arms.

I hastened after him, out of the laboratory, with one last glance at the king as Captain Crewe helped him unsteadily to his feet. He touched his face where my father's wind-blade had struck him. His bulging eyes caught mine in a seething glare.

We're going to pay for that, I thought.

CHAPTER 5

Hannah curled up in a ball, shaking with silent sobs, when my father gently set her back in her infirmary bed.

I paced up and down the aisle of the infirmary, distracted, drawing a hand through my tangled hair. The infirmary was so crowded I had to step over the wheels of all the extra cots and carts and chairs they'd brought in, to accommodate all those infected with the Venen. Mum. Hannah. Alice. Nurses. The miners' wives.

And yet, everything was eerily silent. None of the figures on the beds moved. Entering day two of the Venen: fever, discoloration, and continued weakness.

My father seated himself next to my mother's bed and took her hand in his. He held it tightly, squeezing her blackened fingers as though they would slip away.

"They can't do anything to you," I was saying, my voice filling the sickening silence. "The king wasn't actually hurt. It was an illusion. Not even a bad one—just a cut. Even if it had been real, stitches, at most. He'll be banged up from throwing himself back against the furniture, but that's his own fault, right? And anyway they need you. You're the best scientist they have. They won't—"

"Enough, Jonathan," said my father. "Please, go away."

His tone drew me short.

"You're—not angry with *me*?" I said.

"I am angry with *myself*," he said, clenching Mum's fingers like a drowning man. "I have been a failure if my own son cannot even tell right from wrong."

I tripped over a chair leg.

"I'm—I'm sorry, what?" I said.

"You went to Lady Florel," he said. "That is how you knew how to speed time. You sought her help even though you *knew* something was wrong with her and that fantillium causes acedia and that—that it all points wrong!"

"Enough with the compass metaphors!" I snapped. "I'm not *two*!"

"And yet you act like it!" My father removed his glasses. "You are a child. I cannot believe you even *think* you are fit for the university when you seek solutions through *questionable* means—"

"What choice do we *have*?" I yelled. Patients stirred in their beds. "I had to go to Lady Florel! How else can we find a cure in *five days*? Hannah would agree with me!"

Hannah pulled the coat she still wore closer and curled up tighter against the pillow.

"Oh, right, you're such a *fighter*," I snarled. "That's fighting, Hannah. You might as well just die now and get it over with—"

I regretted the words the instant they escaped my mouth. The rest of the sentence died in my throat, choking me.

"I—I didn't mean it," I stammered. "Hannah—"

Hannah cried underneath her coat.

"Get out." My father stood. "Get out! I cannot even bear to look at you!"

"Right, right, I—I will," I said, my face burning with shame. I hurried from the main wing, hating myself, pushing past Dr. Palmer and retreating into the blistering cold lobby of the infirmary, a room with chairs and a reception desk, all abandoned in the wake of the Venen.

The front doors blew open, and a freezing gust of air brought with it ten airguardsmen, Captain Crewe bringing up the rear. The soldiers marched through the lobby with cold precision, but Captain Crewe stopped when he saw me.

"Your father?" he said.

I glanced at the main wing door before I could stop myself. Captain Crewe nodded.

"You are needed in the laboratory," he said. "Go, please."

I didn't leave, but waited until the soldiers were inside the main wing, and listened at the doors. Captain Crewe's voice said, "I am sorry, Dr. Gouden, but I'm afraid the king requests you work in a room on the *Chivalry*. Please accompany us."

A room just like Lady Florel's, I thought.

I pulled back into the shadows as the airguardsmen marched past in a series of blue uniforms, my father in the midst of them, his head bowed and graying hair mussed, his shoulders sagging. His hands had been cuffed behind him.

I followed after them at a distance, hardly breathing, my chest was so tight. I kept behind each heat lamp, running to the next one they passed, and halted as they took my father into the lift that led to the dock three platform. His long coat flapped in the wind.

The lift slammed shut.

If I did have a compass inside me, it would have broken the moment he disappeared behind those iron doors. It would have shattered. It would have smashed, leaving shards in my chest and running through my bloodstream.

Since I did not have one, I stood there, hollow. Two days ago, my largest worry had been asking Alice to write me when I left for the university. Now it was how to piece the world back together.

Somehow my feet led me to the abandoned observatory, its dome shadowing over me as I climbed the stairs, walked the hall, and climbed again to the second floor. Three airguardsmen worked in the laboratory, packing my father's things into boxes. I numbly helped them bundle his books and notes and wrap his microscopes to send to the *Chivalry*.

When the room had almost emptied, I packed up the kettle—now dry—cleaned a mug, and stopped at the papers I'd left on the counter. One was the arsenic breakdown. The other—the Quickening Formula.

I need proof. . . .

Lady Florel had been right. The equation had actually worked. The clock in the corner had agonized over days only seconds long, and the dust had jittered around us. It had actually *worked*.

My proof.

The small box of fantillium still lay in the corner where Captain Crewe had left it. I removed one vial of glistening black, extracted myself from the warmth of the observatory, and ran.

I arrived at the brig hall of the *Chivalry* ten minutes later. The airguardsmen had saluted me at the entrance of the ship, remembering me from before, and ushered me through each checkpoint. Now, after the long halls of flickering lights and metal staircases, I halted at Lockwood's checkpoint, the brig hall. The pipes hissed and sent steam into the corridor. Sweat dripped down my back. Lockwood had a presence that sucked air from the room.

He didn't stand and salute when I arrived. Instead he remained sprawled on the metal bench at the end of the hall, lazily touching his pistol to his lips and staring up at the ceiling.

"I thought," he said, not bothering to even look at me with his one eye, "I had made it particularly *clear* you were not welcome back in the brig?"

"Not as such, no," I said, standing my ground. "I'm looking for my father."

"Really. You know, you are a terrifically bad liar. If you were after your father, you would have asked the airguardsmen at the command deck. *They* would have told you he's in the civilian's quarters in sector one. This is sector five. Shove off, please."

"You know, I don't think I *will*," I said. I'd had enough with being ousted from the observatory, expelled from the infirmary, and now banished from the brig. My mother and sister were dying. I would not retreat any longer.

Lockwood stood in an oiled-gear movement of perfect control and strode to me.

"Out," he said, clamping his hands on my shoulder and directing me to the door.

Anger seared through me. I elbowed him sharply, whipped around, and punched him as hard as I could.

He dodged it. And laughed.

"Oh, Johnny, that's adorable," he said.

I threw myself at him. We banged against the burning pipes before he had a chance to reach his gun. I landed a solid punch to his neck. He threw me off by kicking me in the chest. I hit metal ground, and the fantillium vial flew out of my hand and across the grated floor.

Lockwood drew his pistol in a blur and pointed the barrel between my eyes.

"Pick up your little science toy," he said coolly, "and please exit to your left. Thank you."

My eyes not leaving the barrel, I slowly retrieved the fantillium vial. My cheek stung where it had scraped a bolt. I straightened, and my eyes caught the small, shoulder-height boiler by the doorway. It kept the brig warm, the steam pouring through the pipes, filling the air with hot mist, not unlike the teakettle in the laboratory. . . .

My hands thought before my head. In a flash, I'd spun the waterwheel, threw open the tank door, and smashed the vial of fantillium like an egg on the edge of the tank.

Broken glass cut my hand. Liquid and shards fell through my fingers and into the boiling water.

I banged the plate lid shut just as Lockwood grabbed my collar and drove me into the ground.

His gun pressed itself to my head. The grated floor glowed white in my vision. I writhed under his knee, which dug into my back.

"All right," said Lockwood in his lazy drawl. "I don't know what you just did, but on the *very probable* assumption you have just poisoned us all, you murderous piece of *filth*, I dare*say* we ought to speak to Captain Crewe, *hmmm*?"

He allowed me to shakily rise to my feet, the gun still at my head.

As we reached the door, the steam in the hall grew thick.

And glistened.

I inhaled. Frigid air coated my lungs. The rumble of the engine roared. The smell of burning orthogonagen grew so strong I could taste it, and my dilated eyes watered as the hall lights burned.

Peace filled my soul and pulsed with my heartbeat.

"What the—" Lockwood gagged. His eye had dilated full black.

I jerked around, pulling every wind current and aether stream of my knowledge together, and blasted them at

Lockwood. Wind sucked itself out of my brain and lungs. Lockwood had a fraction of wide-eyed surprise before the gust picked him up in a howling gale and threw him across the hall. He smacked the floor and skidded, hitting Lady Florel's cell door, the pistol spinning out of his hand.

I laughed.

"What was that you were saying, Lockwood?" I said. "Something about me being adorable? Would you like to say it again? Like, right now?"

He was on his feet so fast his brass buttons blurred. He dove for his pistol. I threw my arm out and wind-blasted it beyond his reach, sending it skipping in my direction.

"Oh *look*, I found a *gun*!" I said, picking it up. Lockwood halted, wary, his all-pupil eye glaring as I haphazardly brandished the pistol at him. I judged him to be about two centimeters away from murdering me.

"What is this madness?" he seethed.

"This, Lieutenant, is fantillium." I motioned to the steam issuing from the pipes around us. "Ah! If only you'd paid attention in chemistry class, instead of playing with your guns. Open Lady Florel's door. Now, if you please."

"Over your dead body, Johnny," he spat, and lunged.

The *Johnny* did it. The temperature plunged in my mind, and then plunged in the corridor around us. The pipes frosted. The hall turned white. Icicles grew from the ceiling and molded in glacial drifts around us. Ice froze Lockwood's boots to the floor and he fell to his knees mid-lunge.

"Very well." I sighed. "I shall do it myself." I reached for the brig keys at his belt.

In a blur, Lockwood removed a dagger from his boot and slashed at me with lightning dexterity.

The tip of the blade caught my arm and sliced neatly through my sleeve. I angrily knocked the dagger from his hand with a sharp gust of air, sending it flashing across the floor. Lockwood snatched at his other boot, extracting *another* blade.

"What? Another one?" I said. "Do you have any feet in your boots, or just knives?" I illusioned another gust of wind, disarming him as he hacked the ice that fused him to the floor. The dagger hit the wall behind him.

Lockwood clawed again at his boot and withdrew a third blade.

"You're *joking*—"

In a flash, Lockwood had grabbed me and was choking me in the crook of his arm, pressing the knife against my throat.

"You ruddy assassin!" I snarled. I hadn't gone this far to get my throat slit!

The temperature plummeted so fast the air snapped.

It stung my ears. It froze my sweat and frosted my skin. Ice grew up the walls in thick white sheets and florets. The blade against my throat seared, and ice formed over Lockwood's hand.

The knife dropped from his fingers. It hit the ground, blade shattering. I twisted out of his grip and unleashed.

Bullets of ice screamed past me. Sheets of ice. The ice at Lockwood's feet broke and he fell to the ground under the assault. The world around me spun in glimmering white, blocking everything from sight.

Frigid silence. The air glittered.

I collapsed to my knees as the last flecks of ice floated to the ground. Shaking. Dizzy. The air cleared, revealing a hallway that had transformed into an Arctic cave. Icicles stretched from the ceiling to the floor, giant stalagmites of blistering cold.

I swallowed, trembling, and got to my feet. Blotches grew in my vision and cleared. Lockwood lay against his bench, curled in a glacial nest of ice.

Unconscious.

I gulped. My throat stung. With a trembling hand, I unhooked the ring of keys from Lockwood's belt, breaking ice as I pulled it free.

"S—sorry," I stammered to his unconscious form. Cold sweat dripped from my forehead. I wiped it away with a shaking arm. It was just an illusion. An illusion. I would never do something like this in real life.

I stumbled to the cell door at the end of the hall, unlocked it, and pushed it open with my remaining strength. A gust of hot air swept over me, and I inhaled. The cell darkened even more as I breathed in the unaffected air. I glanced behind me. Without fantillium in my veins, the hall was back to normal. No ice. Only steam that glistened and hissed from the pipes. Lockwood lay on the corridor floor, breathing gently in the mist, eyes closed as though he'd fallen asleep.

Inside the cell, Lady Florel had not moved save to turn around, slowly, and smile at me.

"The quickening formula worked," she said.

"Yes—yes, quite," I said, removing my cap and twisting it like mad. "You—you were right, Lady Florel."

"Of course I was."

She walked around the table and past me, her heavy coat brushing me, and stepped out into the hall. I followed out after, and the fantillium air frosted my lungs again. Cold air hit like a hammer.

And the illusion returned. Ice blossomed up the walls as I felt my veins turn cold, the corridor growing white around us. Lady Florel stared aghast at the sheer winter beauty before us.

"Look, Lady Florel," I said, kneading my cap like bread. "I—I had a vial of fantillium and I—ah—I used it on the boiler to, ah, get to your cell. But I expect we can go to my father's laboratory and get another one. Er—if we can get past the guards. Actually, perhaps you ought to stay here and I'll be right back—"

"You illusioned all this?" she breathed. Her eyes glittered.

"Right, um, we don't have much time. . . ." I stepped quickly over Lockwood's unconscious form and grimaced. I was going to be in so much trouble. . . .

"No need," said Lady Florel, stopping me as I made for the door.

And she began to illusion.

She illusioned like it was an art, her gloved hands turning around themselves, glistening streams emanating from them in whorls. The air warped around her fingers and extended across the hall, growing in layers of white.

Awestruck, I stepped back as the illusion solidified and grew on the corridor's wall. First the white outlines of an arched doorway, which darkened into decayed colors of white and gray, and rotting textures of wood and brick. Rusty iron hinges and a latch formed. It looked like it could be a door from Old London and smelled thickly of must and rot.

My head swam, thinking of how many elements and metals she had to know to form something so complex. Wood . . . iron . . . stone . . . how was this possible? I stared at the illusioned door, stunned.

A voice from beyond the brig hall echoed distantly into the corridor.

"Lieutenant?" It was Captain Crewe's. My heart began to bang against my rib cage.

"Lady Florel—" I began, panicking.

Lady Florel swept up Lockwood's steam pistol, which had lain by her feet, and held it with experienced authority. She swept to the illusioned door, grasped the latch, and opened it.

Warm air blew into the corridor from the doorway. Watery sunshine and the smell of orthogonagen offal washed over us. I winced against the light, and when my vision caught up with me, stared at what stretched before us through the illusioned door.

It was a city.

An expanse of building and towers and bridges, black and gray stone in ruinous grandeur. I stepped forward, pinpricks of memory stinging; I recognized some of them! I'd seen pictures of Arthurise before. There stood the Elizabeth Tower before us. And there, like a golden sliver, the same river that ran through Arthurise.

And yet, it was not our capital city. It lacked the spires, the tall railway bridges, the semaphore towers. In the distance, an unfamiliar glowing white building with pillars and domes rose from the tangle. And above the expanse of the illusioned city, hundreds of airships bobbed, darkening the skies with their hulls. Beyond even that, high above everything, stood crisscrossed steel beams and glass. The entire city was encased inside a giant glass building.

"Lady Florel!" I choked, twisting the life out of my cap.

Lady Florel smiled at my reaction.

"This is Nod'ol," she said simply, motioning to the door. "The cure to the Venen is found here. Come along, no time to sit here gaping."

"*What?*" I said. I backed away sharply. "What is this, Lady Florel? How—how did you illusion all of this?"

"Lieutenant, have you seen the Gouden boy?" Captain Crewe's voice called into the brig hall. I whipped around as Captain Crewe stepped into the corridor.

Lady Florel raised her pistol and fired.

The crack shattered the air.

The bullet hit Captain Crewe.

His face registered surprise, then pain. He fell back, hitting the wall and then the ground. It vibrated under my feet.

"Captain Crewe!" I ran to help him.

An arm grabbed my throat and yanked me backward to the brig floor. My vision filled entirely of Lockwood, entirely conscious and seething in my face. His blue eye flared. Shouts filled the air from beyond the brig hall.

I writhed out of his grip. The ice around us had begun to fade. The boiler was running out of fantillium. With a futile effort I made for Captain Crewe; Lockwood pounced again and thwacked my head against the nearest pipe.

In a sweep of coat, Lady Florel fled through the illusioned arched doorway, into the city of airships and glass sky. She slammed the rotting door behind her, and—

Disappeared.

I gulped hot air. The brig darkened as the pipes sputtered and the steam grew transparent white again. The fantillium had run out.

Lockwood knocked my head against the pipes again, giving me one last glimpse of the corridor. The ice had gone. The illusioned door was gone.

And Lady Florel was gone.

My consciousness gave up, and I surrendered myself to darkness.

CHAPTER 6

"**G**et up! *Get up!*"

A large, thick boot attached to a large, thick leg attached to King Edward VII kicked me awake. I groggily peered up at the towering king, who glared down at me over his stomach and pointy beard.

I lay in the exact spot I'd passed out, flat on my back and surrounded by angry airguardsmen, a wall of blue uniforms, belts, and brass buttons. My father stood among them, a pillar of brown beside the king, looking pale and worried.

I leapt to my feet. A dozen gloved hands grabbed me and shoved me back to the floor.

"Captain Crewe!" I said. "He's been shot!"

"Not that you care," Lockwood spat, standing with the airguardsmen.

"What gives you the right to steal my fantillium and

attack my airguardsmen and release my prisoners?" the king yelled, dragging me back up by my collar. "Where is Lady Florel?"

I writhed and twisted out of his grip and straight into the airguardsmen's clutches, as the events before crashed over me. The illusion! The *doorway*! *She had disappeared into an illusion!*

"Your Highness." An officer saluted at the brig hall's entrance. "The ship has been searched. She's not here. All the dinghies are accounted for, as well."

"Keep searching," the king said. "Search the city."

"She's not in Fata!" I choked. "Lady Florel illusioned a door! She went through it and disappeared!"

The king's buggy eyes narrowed at me.

"I *know* it sounds mad," I pled. "But that is what happened, I swear it! The—the lieutenant saw it, too! Just before the illusion ended! He'll tell you!"

All eyes turned on Lockwood, who stood with a bruise across his hollow face and his yellow hair mussed. He turned his eye to the floor.

"I don't know what I saw," he muttered.

The king wrenched me up by my collar again, and with fists the size of boxing gloves, throttled me. My glasses shook off.

"Enough, please!" said my father.

The king gave me one last shake and shoved me away.

I fell to my knees by my glasses, hand at my throat and gasping for air. The blood returned to my head.

My father knelt in front of me, peering intently at me with his yellow-brown eyes. The past three days had drained years from his face.

"I *swear* it's the truth," I said fervently to him. "She said she could find the cure. All she needed was fantillium! I—I had to do *something*!" I pled.

My father brought a hand through his mess of graying brown hair and shook his head.

"If my son says she disappeared into an illusion," he finally said, standing, "then that is what happened. My son would not lie."

"And I suppose your son does not steal, either?" said the king. "Or help criminals escape?"

My father mouthed words, but no sound came.

"Two—two days ago, I would have emphatically said no." His shoulders began to shake. "But now, I am not sure of anything."

My heart sank in my chest. The airguardsmen seized my arms and wrenched me to my feet. They twisted my hands behind my back and clamped iron shackles around my wrists. I struggled.

"I had to do *something*!" I cried to my father. "I couldn't just let Mum and Hannah die!"

"Take him out!" the king yelled.

The airguardsmen dragged me into the hall. I caught one last glimpse of my father, his long coat unbuckled and his tie askew, and I could see him crying.

The airguardsmen forcibly escorted me to dock five on the other side of the city, up the lift, and into the old, small military airship, the *Valor*. I was locked in a brig cell. I lay there on the metal floor, exhausted, bruised, and sick inside.

My own father hadn't stood up for me.

I pulled myself up and paced—discontent, angry—and the feeling only intensified when the airship's engines rumbled to life and the brig guard informed me that I was being taken to Arthurise to await a trial there.

"What?" I said, grasping the crisscrossed bars on the cell door. "To Arthurise? But—no! I'm Dr. Gouden's apprentice, surely—surely they need me here to help!"

"King's express orders, I'm afraid," he said. "Can't go against those, eh?"

I nearly strangled him through the bars. Instead I returned to pacing, pitching across the tiny cell when the ship jolted forward. I peered out the tiny port window in my cell, watching Fata Morgana growing smaller and smaller in the pitch-black sky. It stung my vision. The dome of the observatory, the chimneys and roofs and row houses, the prickly mining towers, all suspended in the air like a sliver of the moon. The city grew small and disappeared into the distance.

It felt like my heart had waned and disappeared with it.

I'd never been to Arthurise, but I knew it was a full day-and-a-half flight away. All that time the illness would progress in Mum and Hannah. For hours on end, I banged around the cell, refusing the gloppy food they tried to give me, kicking the door and walls until I could see the bars and rusty bolts of the door when I closed my eyes, every inch of it copied in my mind.

When the *Valor* lurched out of the southerly aether streams, all I could think was: *Four days left. Only four days.*

Presently, a sturdy officer with his arm in a sling unlocked my cell door. I recognized his friendly face and straightforwardness immediately.

"Captain Crewe!" I said, relieved. "You're all right!"

The captain smiled. I noted Lady Florel's shot had hit him just below the shoulder. If he was in pain—and I knew he would be—he did not show it.

"Have you seen Arthurise before?" he asked.

"Only in books."

"Then come."

I followed him up a staircase and emerged onto the command deck, a large open floor with windows all around the sides, and officers and navigators at their posts. Weak winter sun shone over us. Afternoon. I walked to the side and peered, fascinated, at the expanse of city that stretched below the ship.

It was like the city Lady Florel had illusioned, but far grander. Steel and marble shone in the sun. Light semaphore of all colors made the city glitter over a tapestry of train tracks and commerce. Airships of all regulations and sizes docked to vertical ports and stretched as far as the eye could see. I could even smell it through the windows: burning orthogonagen and wet brick.

Arthurise. The City of Virtue. Years ago it had been called London. That was before the Assemblage of the Round Table. Now it stood before us, the largest and greatest city in the world.

"City is in mourning," said Captain Crewe as we waited for permission to dock in the Old London sector. "Quarantine, too—though it's doing little good. The Venen's already spreading to New England and India. I had hoped the king would let you stay and work with your father, but—" He stopped and shook his head.

I stared miserably at the towers and architecture that surrounded us as the *Valor* descended into the scrubbed brick of Old London. We docked; Captain Crewe and several airguardsmen led me out, handcuffed, into the docking lift. I couldn't believe how warm it was here. At least thirty degrees! And the sounds! Airships. Distant trains. The lift opened into a courtyard and I stepped onto grass—*grass!*—strange and spongy beneath my feet. Leafless trees lined the stone wall around the courtyard, their spindly branches like veins. It smelled so thickly of a hundred muddled scents that I gagged when I inhaled.

The Tower of London. I knew this place only from books. I stared up in awe at the water-worn towers attached to massive stone walls. Slotted windows and ancient doors punctuated the fortress. Queens and dukes had been held prisoner here hundreds of years ago. I hadn't realized it was still used as a prison. [9]

A large building stood in the middle of the courtyard made of brick, domed towers at each corner and arched windows in between. An Arthurisian flag flew from a pole at the roof, a blue-and-gold ensign. We climbed a wooden set of stairs to reach the entrance. I read a plaque next to the door that designated it as the White Tower, then my eyes caught the door.

It was wooden and arched, with iron hinges and latch, and I immediately recognized it.

It was the door Lady Florel had illusioned.

---

[9] Hannah would have known this. Also, she could probably list off all the queens and dukes who had lost their heads there, in consecutive order, or, quite possibly, alphabetically by either a) surname or b) title. Our long winters on Fata were, indeed, joyous.

And it *wasn't*.

This door had been tended to, polished and cleaned over the years, and the hinges weren't rusting. But it *was* that door!

I shifted impatiently, nearly bursting with the revelation, as the head yeoman—the main guard of the tower—reviewed my papers in his office, and exhaled loudly at me.

"Why is it," he said to no one in general, "that when the king is in a foul temper, *we* are always full?"

Passed over to the tower's stewardship, I managed one last word with Captain Crewe before we parted.

"This door," I said as we were led out the entrance again. "This is the door Lady Florel illusioned!"

Captain Crewe's brow creased and he looked at me, confused.

"It was older—rotting," I said. "But it was this *same door*. I'm sure of it."

"What can it mean?" he said.

"I don't know. "But—Captain—will you tell my father? He might be able to sort it out—"

"I am not returning to Fata Morgana, Jonathan. I have been given leave. My wife and daughter are dying."

I was struck speechless.

We parted without another word. Cold rain drenched me as my new guard escorted me across the courtyard, up slick stone stairs, to a jutting tower in the wall. Here they unlocked a groaning door, and a musty-smelling dank rolled over us.

"You'll have to share this cell," the head yeoman said wearily. "I *really* don't want to hear of any trouble, is that clear?"

I cautiously entered. My eyes adjusted, taking in stone, wood beams, an old empty fireplace, names carved into walls. A figure in the corner separated from the darkness. I noted the blue uniform, the glint of medals and buttons, a handsome figure with light hair and an eye patch—

Lockwood recognized me the exact moment I recognized him. A feral cat couldn't have pounced on me faster. My head hit stone and his hands gripped my throat.

"You little maggot!" he snarled. "You disgusting flap of cut-off flesh, you murky chunk of *filth*! Thanks to you I've been stripped of my rank!"

I kicked him off and dove, raining all my frustration and anger of the past four days upon him. He threw fists into my stomach and face. A *crunch* sounded in my head. I sputtered as blood poured down my lips.

I didn't care what I hit, so long as it was made of Lockwood. My glasses knocked off my face and skittered at our feet as he soundly thrashed me.

Yeomen's hands dragged us away from each other. Blood dripped down my chin as they held us apart, three yeomen keeping Lockwood from dismembering me. The head yeoman stood at the door, looking duly unimpressed.

"Gentlemen, *please*," he said. "Quite enough, what! I assure you, outside my office there is a *lovely* museum of torture instruments *heartily* used hundreds of years ago and I *have* always wondered what *exactly* they do. So unfortunate to have to use them on fellows so lithe and young, what! Shake your barking hands. Right now."

Lockwood and I glared at each other with concentrated loathing. His one eye had swollen up, giving me great satisfaction. With unexpected friendliness, he suddenly straightened and offered his hand. I grasped it to squeeze the life out of it, and was confused when he shook it firmly and fairly.

"There. See? Aren't we all so happy now?" said the yeoman.

Grinding glass sounded against the stone. Looking down, I saw Lockwood's boot driving my glasses into the floor with his heel.

I dove at him.

Five minutes later, Lockwood and I stood at opposite ends of the tower room, nursing our wounds as the head yeoman, still threatening us with all shapes and sizes of torture, locked us in. I fumed, face pulsing, as I examined the crack on my broken lens and slid them back on. I could hardly see without my glasses, so it appeared I'd spend my time in prison with the world half-broken.

Through the slit of the window in our cell, I watched the *Valor* discharge from the long line of airships above us and sail away. Back to Fata. I couldn't sit still after that; I paced the cell, and eventually settled on scratching the Venen's chemical makeup on the floor with a piece of broken stone.

"What are you doing?" Lockwood's voice broke the silence from the other side of the room, the first words he'd spoken in hours.

"Mapping out the Venen," I said, and added, "not that you care." I doubted he had any family that would die from it. Most of the airguardsmen—especially Northern airguardsmen—joined because they were orphans and could be on duty for months at a time with no one to miss them. That explained, anyway, why he was so miserable.[10]

Church bells an hour later startled me from my work. They rang from the White Tower in the center of the courtyard. On top of those, bells began to chorus all over the city in symphonic discord. The dissonance filled our cell.

"Why are the bells chiming?" I said, alarmed. "It can't be Sunday already! It's only just Monday, right? Wait—how long was our journey to Arthurise?"

I scrambled to the window, and called out to the

---

[10] Or, at least, I really hoped he was.

yeomen in the courtyard below. They patrolled the area, lamps held aloft.

"Ho there!" I yelled. "Yeomen! Why the bells? What day is it?"

The yeoman nearest called back to me, and his voice broke.

"The queen is dead," he said. "God rest her soul."

The bells were drowned out by my heartbeat thudding in my ears. I sank onto the stone under the window and buried my face in my hands, despair seeping into my soul. The queen. Our symbol of Avalon. My father had not been able to save her.

She had looked so much like my mother. . . .

I bit my tongue to keep from showing emotion in front of Lockwood, though I fear my shoulders shook. He silently watched me from the other side of the cell.

I must have somehow fallen asleep in the following hours, because abruptly I was shaken awake by Lockwood, his face so intense you could have sparked fires with it.

"Get up," he said shortly. "Something's going on."

I groggily pulled myself to my feet and squinted out the window, Lockwood poised beside it as tight as a wound spring. He nodded his head at the courtyard below, where the four dim pinpricks of the patrolling yeomen's lanterns swung.

"Two of them aren't patrolling anymore," he said in a low voice.

I saw he was right, even through my broken glasses. The two lanterns farthest had fallen to the ground, still lit but unmoving. As I watched, a third lantern tumbled, and the yeoman made not a sound when he fell. The winter air held its breath.

My heart began to thud.

The fourth lantern fell.

"Hello!" I cried out. "Hello, ther—"

Lockwood grabbed me by the vest and flung me away from the window.

"Idiot!" he seethed. "You don't make a move until you know what's going on!"

Silence encased us. It wasn't normal silence. It was the silence of a thick fog. The sort of silence you'd find in Fata's cloud canals. Suffocating silence.

"They're after us," said Lockwood.

"What? After us? How do you know?" I whispered back.

"We're the only tower in this direction. Don't you notice *anything*?"

"Of course I do," I snapped. "Just because it's all under a microscope—"

The hairs on the back of my neck rose. The silence had become thicker. Lockwood pressed himself against the wall next to the door, ready to pounce on whatever tried to come through. I copied him on the other side of the door. The silence was so strangling now a dropped pin would be a cannon.

A pin did not drop, but a voice beyond the door whispered, "*Jonathan.*"

And the door exploded.

The force threw me back against stone. Splinters rained over me; twisted iron and broken wood staccatoed over the wall. Smoke choked me. My ears rang and I couldn't inhale, the wind knocked out of me. Dust stung my eyes.

It settled like a snowfall. I coughed, my swollen nose throbbing, and in the thinning haze, a grandmotherly figure faded into view. She was surrounded by an odd assortment: a dozen men in facemasks and long red uniforms. They settled themselves about her in military formation.

"Well, Jonathan," said Lady Florel, beaming. "Shall we fetch that cure?"

CHAPTER 7

I stared. The scene could only be taken in by pieces, as everything all at once was too much whole.

Piece 1: Lady Florel. She wore a small red mask that covered the upper half of her face, and a costume that covered almost every inch of her in striped rags and gathers. She looked like a seabird that had got caught in an airship engine.

Piece 2: The guards that stood around her. Like Lady Florel, they wore masks, but these covered their entire faces. Their clothes looked as though they had been stitched together from pieces of various costumes from the past hundred years, and all of it—even the masks—had been dyed and painted a crimson red. Even the boots. They stood in broad-shouldered, perfectly symmetrical formation, silent and still as de—

Lockwood snarled and launched himself at the

crimson guard, a full-fledged assassin.

"Lockwood!" I yelled.

The following seconds blurred with blue uniform among the long crimson coats. Lockwood's assault created a flurry of torn fabric and sprawling men. I dove into the brawl to pull Lockwood away.

For a moment, I was suspended in a silent snarl of limbs and crimson.

The tangle of fight spat me out. I hit wall.

Lockwood fought on, and I didn't need to be an experienced fighter to see that with our fights before, Lockwood had *tolerated* me. With these trained guards, he slipped out of their grasp and twisted arms behind backs and used their own weight to throw them on their heads.

One pulled a pistol from a holster at his waist; Lockwood kicked it out of the guard's hand, sending it flying into the empty fireplace.

A blurred moment, and the fighting refocused and paused. The masked guardsmen untangled and stepped apart.

Lockwood had gone. Crisp footfalls faded in the distance, beyond the tower door.

"He'll be off to fetch the guard," said Lady Florel, motioning me out the door after her.

"Yes—yes, very keen, Lockwood." I ran down the

stone stairs after her, the broad subject of Hope speeding my feet. The crimson guards hurried us on in perfect step. "I'm—dead glad you're back, Lady Florel! Did—did you say *cure*?"

"*Quite* right," she said, flashing me a smile as we entered the grassy courtyard. "Follow me."

"That's grand!" I exulted, practically bounding after. "Let's get it to my fath—"

I tripped over something and knee-planted into the spongy grass. Twisting around, I saw it was a fallen yeoman, his lantern glowing on the ground a length away. The light reflected in his open eyes. Automatically I was at his side, checking his pulse. But his skin was already cold.

"He's—dead!" I said.

"Yes, my masked guard can be *very* enthusiastic," said Lady Florel. "Put this on, please."

Her guard promptly strapped a mask over my face. It covered my nose and mask, the tubing at the chin hissing. I gagged on a breath of ice-encrusted air as the Tower of London courtyard glowed on its own accord. Fantillium. Suddenly the world was sharp and clear, and my horror at the dead yeoman faded into a dull footnote. My lungs froze with liquid ice.

"It's a traveling illusionarium," Lady Florel explained, buckling a similar gas mask around her head. The guard surrounded us in a perfect crimson circle, each wearing his own gas mask over his facemask.

In the fantillium light of blues and grays that glowed almost white, in the center of the courtyard by the White Tower, Lady Florel illusioned. She illusioned with the brick wall of the tower as her canvas, her hands twisting in and out and thoughts pulling away from her fingers in thin wisps.

An arched doorway formed before her. I recognized it as the door Lady Florel had illusioned on the *Chivalry*—and the same door that stood on the other side of the building. The White Tower's door.

Except it was different. The wood was decayed and splintered, and moss grew in the cracks. Rotting. The brick around it crumbled at the corners with Lady Florel's illusion.

Her hands trembled as she finished, and the illusion on the wall before stood complete. An ancient door of old wood and iron pocked with age. Lady Florel twisted the rusting latch and opened the door.

It didn't lead into the inside of the White Tower.

I half recognized where it led now. Before us stood a mirror image of the Tower of London courtyard. The fortress walls lay before us, but crumbling and ruinous, and the scrubby grass of the rolling courtyard hills was an overgrown mess of weeds. An abandoned-for-years version of the Tower of London: a mess of broken buildings below a sea of airships.

Shouting filled the courtyard. Yells echoed across the stone walls. I whipped around to the sight of Lockwood charging from the far wall, leading the head yeoman—dressed in a nightshirt—and a flock of soldiers at his heels.

"Our Arthurisian friends!" Lady Florel cried with delight. "Why don't we give them a very *warm* Nod'olian farewell!"

On cue, a masked guardsman streaked past me in a crimson blur. Silent as a prayer and smooth as a zephyr. Several yeomen broke away from the group and chased after him, the head yeoman barking orders. I regarded this all with mild, fantillium-tinged interest, watching the guardsman dart to the vertical tower in the middle of the courtyard and then up to the airship dock, a structure of X-beamed steel. He leapt, grabbing the beams, and began climbing it, hand over hand with utter ease and speed, ignoring the lift entirely.

The dock platform loomed high above, old regimental airships docked along it in a neat row. The crimson guard leapt onto the platform in a graceful arch and leapt again onto the first airship, scaling it with dexterity until he reached the balloon's envelope. A blade flashed in his hand.

He plunged it into the balloon, making a long slit.

The inner workings of my soul, like an old clock, groggily awakened and groaned. Orthogonagen was dead flammable, and a lungful could kill a man, besides. The fumes of the gas warped the guard, who clung still to the ribbing of the envelope. With a twist of his hands, he produced something within his many-pocketed jacket. I instinctively knew what it was before I even saw the flicker of an orthogonagen match.

"Lady Florel," I said, alarm growing. "He's—"

Spark.

Boom.

I felt the impact before I saw it. The explosion threw me back and smacked me against the brick of the White Tower. The airship's balloon billowed into masses of yellow-orange florets. My eyes burned with the light. And slowly, slowly the ship pitched, a mass of fire, and began to sink over us, encasing the courtyard. Lockwood and the yeomen, who'd been racing to us, quickly raced to the lift to rescue those still in the airship.

Boom. The airship docked by the one aflame caught fire, the burning explosion throwing the yeomen back.

"Now is the time to make our exit!" Lady Florel grasped my arm and yanked me through the illusioned doorway, into the ersatz Tower of London courtyard.

The moment my foot crossed the decaying threshold, a change occurred.

Every cell and microbe that made up my entire self went . . . *blip* . . .

. . . and shifted one millimeter to the side. My vision flashed black. I tumbled onto the dew-drenched weeds, gasping for breath. Cool air kissed the skin around my mask.

I scrambled to face the doorway behind me. The courtyard beyond glowed brilliantly with fire. The burning airships had crashed into the courtyard, their flaming envelopes draped over the fortress walls, trapping everything in Death. The yeomen had disappeared.

One figure lay near the illusioned doorway, a dark silhouette against all the flames. Sprawled across the grass, unconscious. He wore an eye patch.

Lockwood, I thought, and my conscience roused.

"Lockwood!" I yelled as flames licked around him. I dove back through the illusioned doorway, back into the Arthurisian world.

"Jonathan!" Lady Florel yelled.

My organs reorganized, sending stars through my head. A barrier, a great wall of flame, surrounded us and seared my eyes and skin. I couldn't bear the light. I threw myself at the lieutenant, beating the flames out of his uniform. He roused and kicked me away.

"Stupid!" I yelled, lurching back onto my feet. "I'm trying to *help* you, idiot!"

The fire roared to an inferno, a vortex of blistering light. Lockwood struggled to his knees, coughing. Fire encased us. Our only exit was the illusioned doorway.

Which Lockwood could not see.

I inhaled deeply, held my breath, tore the fantillium mask off my face and pressed it against Lockwood's nose and mouth. He struggled against it.

"Breathe!" I seethed.

He cough-inhaled. I knew the fantillium was running through his veins when he threw his hand up and shielded his all-pupil eye, cringing. Blotches formed in my eyes, my lungs screaming for a breath of air. I grabbed Lockwood by the shoulders with one arm, dragged him to his feet, the mask still clamped over his mouth, and we dove together through the illusioned door.

Stomach, lungs, heart, and spleen all twisted themselves inside out. A hiccup of mortality—

—and cooler air swept over us. I gasped. The doorway behind me dissolved into the crumbling wall of the White Tower. I lost my grip on Lockwood and collapsed into the mess of weeds. The old brick fortress spun.

Around us, the masked guard stood like red chess pieces. The weeds parted with Lady Florel, who looked at us and shook her head.

"Oh, Jonathan," she said with a weary smile. "Welcome to Nod'ol."

CHAPTER 8

Lady Florel's masked guard spirited us away from the strange Tower of London ruins. I was so exhausted, everything passed before me like a dream. The sun rose, its light warped through the giant glass ceiling. A large, old-fashioned airship flew us across the city—a place of familiar and unfamiliar buildings, all in decay—to the center. Here stood an unfamiliar marble building of white pillars and domes. Unlike the rest of the city, it looked tended to.

The airship docked at a platform on the roof, and after disembarking and descending through a gabled rooftop, down stairs of thick rugs and corridors of large paintings, we were escorted to an atrium sitting room, a parlor of hanging plants and palm trees and spindly furniture. It smelled thickly of perfume.

Lockwood paced the far side of the room like a caged

tiger. I collapsed on the nearest sofa, smearing it with soot, fire still flaring in my vision.

Lady Florel arrived at the room just moments later, already washed and in new clothes of pieces and layers. I leapt to my feet and confronted her.

"What did you do that for?" I said angrily. "I—I—I hardly know what to think, Lady Florel! You didn't have to go and blow everything up! Isn't our life's work to save people's lives? I mean, didn't you used to save lives on the battlefield? What's happened to you, Lady Florel?"

Lady Florel ignored my words with a smile and turned to a long table at the side of the room, where a spread of food steamed in tureens. Unfamiliar food. Roasted orbs—probably potatoes—sugar-encrusted pears. Roasted chicken—*all* of the chicken, with wings and legs still attached. All our food on Fata had to be shipped from the south, which meant it came in pieces, and I didn't quite trust food that hadn't been cut up into God-fearing chunks. I fumed as she ladled food onto her plate.

"Lady Florel," I said slowly, putting the entire weight of it in my words, "I think you might have *killed* people."

"Oh, yes. I'm terribly disturbed by it, of course," she said. "Also, Jonathan, I'm *Queen Honoria* here in this world. I would appreciate it if you referred to me properly. Try the potatoes?"

"Excuse *me,*" said Lockwood, glaring at us both from the far side of the room. "But where, exactly, is *here*? Are we inside an illusion?"

"Lieutenant!" Lady Florel set down her plate of food. "What an—*unexpected* surprise to have you with us!"

Warily, Lockwood took a step back and eyed the windows behind him. Lady Florel strode to an ornate gold-trimmed chess set, sitting on a small side table, and turned her attention to its figures.

"In answer to your question, Lieutenant," she said, "no. We are not in an illusion. Tell me, have you ever played chess?"

"No," said Lockwood at the same time I said, "I have."

"Of course you have, Jonathan. How many different moves can you make? If you are the player to open?"

"Twenty," I said without thinking.

Lady Florel's hand hovered over the pieces of ivory and ebony. The craftsmanship was so fine, individual strands of hair had been carved into the horses' manes. She pressed the knight's head between her fingers and moved it over the pawns to a black square.

"The universe is . . . quite a bit like chess," she said. She smiled at my expression. "Let us say, in my first move, I choose to move my knight *here*. Then what happens? The game progresses in a very different manner than it would have if I, perhaps, moved it *here*." Lady Florel moved the knight two squares to the side. "It could be completely different, in fact."

"Perhaps," I admitted. "But probably not *entirely* different."

"Precisely. Let us say—" Lady Florel took the other knight, and mimed the pieces splitting apart onto the two legal squares. "Let us say that the *very moment* you decide to move the piece *here*, your same self decides to move the same piece *here*—and the game . . . *schisms*."

My brow furrowed.

"Sorry?" I said.

"So there are two games being played at once." Lady Florel set the knights back in place. "One, where you moved the knight here, and one, where you moved the knight *there*. Each on their own dimensional plane, invisible to the other. And let us suppose that each of *those* games schism at each move. How many different schisms and worlds where the same chess game is being played could there be?"

"Thousands," I said. "*Hundreds* of thousands." Comprehension dawned over me. "Lady Florel, are you—you're saying that—this world is a sort of—*other* version of ours? That we broke apart somehow?"

Lady Florel, beaming, tossed the knight at me. I caught it in one hand.

"Precisely!" she said.

"What an utter load of rubbish," said Lockwood.

"Fantillium is the key to the doorway between these worlds," Lady Florel explained. "If you can illusion something identical to another world—specifically, a door—down to the very speck, the mortar and brick— you can somehow *manipulate* the physics of the world into thinking it belongs to the other world. Do you see? *We can create gateways.*"

I sat down, head pounding in my ears. If this were true, it explained why this world had a Tower of London and other buildings like in Arthurise, yet different ones as well. When did it schism from ours? And—did this all mean there were *other* worlds? Hundreds? Or even thousands? My mind feverishly algorithmed. There could be *billions* of different worlds! I pressed my hands against my head.

"And you just discovered all this when you were curing diseases, did you?" said Lockwood coldly from the corner.

"Actually . . . yes," said Lady Florel, coldly smiling back. "Medical scientists work with a lot of chemicals. Several years ago, I began working with fantillium. I discovered it had *unusual* properties. And I became an illusionist."

"What, and you just *happened* to illusion the right door?" Lockwood spat.

Lady Florel didn't seem upset at all by his tone.

"Of course not," she said kindly. "It wasn't chance at all. There are other illusionists who have gone before me, years ago. I found their work, lost books in old libraries, hidden words. That's how I learned. Of course, it was easier to illusion a doorway that already existed. I have no doubt the Tower of London exists in hundreds of other worlds. Nod'ol is just one of them."

"Nod'ol, Nod'ol." I echoed the city's strange name. "But—Lady Florel—why would you even *want* to—to—go somewhere like this? What about Our Lady's Charity Hospital in Rochdale? Weren't you busy establishing that?"

The life in Lady Florel's face faded. She suddenly looked old, and sad.

"I came here, Jonathan, and I realized how much they needed me," she said. She walked to the wall of windows and looked out over the city. I got to my feet and followed her, taking in the expanse of city through the window. It really was an ugly tangle; buildings were missing their tops, and it looked as though holes had been eaten through their sides. The closer it got to our marble building, the more civilized it became, the more buildings appeared to be inhabited. And closer to us, rows and rows of brick walls and hedges surrounded the building. A maze.

"They don't need me in Arthurise," she said.

"Of course they—"

Lady Florel held up a hand.

"They don't," she said. "They did, once. But I'm old now. They see me as a relic, something to write books about and give medals to and dust off every few months."

I tried to speak up again, and she silenced me.

"But here—here in Nod'ol—they *need* me." She nodded to the landscape of dilapidated buildings. "Look at it. This city used to be the center of a vast empire. Look at the Archglass! Could Arthurise build anything so *massive*? But it's fallen, Jonathan. There's nothing outside the city—No Kowloon, no New Amsterdam . . . it's only us in the city now. And everyone here lives in airships. They don't even live in the buildings anymore. This empire, unlike your Arthurisian Empire, is almost fallen."

Lady Florel's brown eyes glittered with tears.

"When I came here, years ago," she said quietly, "I promised I would save it. I would bring it back to its glory. It's a marvelous feeling—like stitching up mortal wounds on the battlefield. *Nothing* matters more to me than this."

She was almost crying. I shifted, uncomfortable.

"Not even finding a cure to the Venen?" I said. "Arthurise is dying, too, Lady Florel. And Arthurise was your city first."

Lady Florel unexpectedly brightened and said, "That *reminds* me!"

From the inside of her many-pocketed jacket/dress, she produced a tiny brown bottle and offered it to me.

"The antitoxin," she said.

I snapped to life and snatched it out of her fingers, cradling it like a starved man. I examined it, reading the label, and though I didn't recognize the compound listed—*arsenic trioxide*—I *did* recognize the arsenic part. So my father had been right! Arsenic was a key piece in the cure. Administer by mouth, three doses in the bottle. So you *could* bottle Hope!

"The Venen has been in this world long before me," Lady Florel was explaining as I turned the bottle in my hands. "They found this cure years ago. No one even contracts it anymore."

I could have wept. Instead, still gripping the bottle in my hand, I swept Lady Florel into a bone-crushing embrace.

"Really, Jonathan!" she said as I released her. "That was very nearly inappropriate."

"May I keep this?" I said. "Are there more?"

"Yes to both. Though I suspect your father could formulate something from just that sample."

"He could," I agreed, and collapsed into a nearby chair. "Marvelous! Lady Florel, let's illusion that door and get back to Fata! Ha!"

"Of course, we ought to discuss how you will pay for it."

I slowly placed my feet on the ground.

"Pay?" I said.

"Naturally. Did you think you could just take it?"

"But—Lady Florel, people are dying," I stammered. "King Edward would pay you, I'm sure of it—"

"I want payment from *you*, Jonathan. I want you to illusion for me."

I shifted uncomfortably on the chair and glanced at Lockwood. His narrowed eyes darted from Lady Florel to me.

"Nothing difficult," she assured me. "Something like what you illusioned in the *Chivalry's* brig hall. There's an illusionarium that begins in only a few minutes, and I want you to illusion for it. It won't last longer than an hour, I swear it."

I frowned at the brown bottle, turning it from side to side. Payment? That didn't seem like Lady Florel.

"There are people dying, Lady Florel," I said. "Even waiting an hour could kill them. Surely we could bring this to my father, and then come back? I'll illusion for you then."

"There's no time," said Lady Florel. "If we go now, you'll miss the illusionarium. But if you participate and do well, I'll illusion the door and we'll leave straightaway after. I promise."

I pressed the bottle between my hands. The glass cooled my skin.

"You *swear* it won't last longer than an hour?" I said.

Lockwood made another feral noise. Lady Florel smiled.

"Not even that long," she assured us. "Last year, this same illusionarium lasted only ten minutes."

I stood.

"Fine," I said. "And if I make the illusion last a half minute long, we'll leave after a half minute, right?

Lady Florel beamed.

"Anything you want," she said.

A regiment of the strange red-uniformed masked guardsmen arrived at the door, rifles in their hands. I drew back slightly; Lady Florel adjusted her gloves and said, "Excuse me," and egressed with them, leaving me alone with L—

Lockwood attacked. The room spun. In a flash he'd slammed me against one of the glass windows, wiping it with my face, and had taken and twisted my arms behind me like a pretzel, sending pain coursing up and down my shoulders and spine and rendering me incapacitated.

A voice close to my ear snarled, "Do you know what this is, Johnny? It's a Knutsen hold position number one, a military fighting technique that twists the arm far enough you could scratch the back of your eyeballs with your thumbnail. Position number two—"

Lockwood adjusted his grip slightly, twisting my arm further and sending stars in my vision. Anger seared through my bones. Lady Florel was still talking to the guardsmen at the door, ignoring us both.

"—may very well snap the nerves in your joints and possibly cause paralysis and you *don't* want to know what position number three can do—"

"What is your *problem*?" I managed to gag.

"Hmmm, let's *see*," he drawled. "Maybe because you're helping a ruddy *murderer*? Possibly?"

"Oh, that's right!" I snapped back. "*You* want Arthurise to die of the Venen, I remember now!"

"I'm going to sort this out the *right* way, and I won't make deals with liars and demons to do it!" he snarled in my ear. "I'll find the way back home myself, Johnny, because if you think she'll *actually* curtsy us into Arthurise, that makes one of us incredibly stupid and the other one incredibly *dead*—"

"My dear lieutenant," Lady Florel's voice broke in. Lockwood's pressure eased one iota; I managed a glance back. Lady Florel was smiling as her masked guard streamed around her to us, bearing hissing steam rifles, their emotionless, masked faces fixed on Lockwood.

"I really think we've had enough of you," she said.

The meaning of her words hit me as the next two seconds . . .

. . . happened:

Lockwood released me, banging my head against the window. In a blur, he yanked a hanging plant off its chain and threw it at the glass. It smashed through the pane, shattering it as the masked guard seized upon him.

—a strange, silent brawl—

—that left three masked guards unconscious on the tile floor, the other guards tumbling back, their top hats strewn, and Lockwood had thrown himself out the broken window in a graceful arch. The brass buttons on his uniform glimmered in the sunlight.

He fell.

I raced to the window. The ledge below sported a pair of sooty footprints. Three stories below that, a wisp of blue uniform disappeared into a tangle of hedges. I peered through my broken glasses at the miles of broken hedges and buildings, massaging my arms as the blood returned to my fingers. Lockwood's figure disappeared completely into the tangle of labyrinth.

Lady Florel's masked guard rose to their feet and gathered around me, picking up shards of glass piece by piece like a flock of crimson pecking birds.

"Leave the glass," said Lady Florel sharply. "Find Lockwood. *Bring him back*."

The masked guard dropped their fistfuls of glass. A *pinging* shower of shards at our feet was the only sound they made as they swept from the room. A moment later, they streamed out of the building's entrance below, over the sweeping pavilion of marble and gardens, and into the maze. I bitterly rubbed my throbbing arms.

Good riddance, I thought.

CHAPTER 9

Still disheveled and streaked with soot, I followed Lady Florel through the theater. That was what this building was, Lady Florel explained, leading me down an ornate hall and an elaborate staircase. A theater where the monarch—who was also the best illusionist in Nod'ol—and the lesser illusionists lived.

And it did look like a palace. But a strange one. Everything had been decorated as though the builders had taken pieces of architecture from the past five hundred years, chewed them up, and vomited them into building materials. Carved cupids were everywhere.

Lady Florel was quickly explaining the nature of the illusionarium I'd be participating in in just a few minutes.

"It's part of an annual festival we have here in Nod'ol," she said. "A winter solstice festival. It's called *Masked Virtue*."

"Masked Virtue?" I repeated.

"Quite. This is the first illusionarium, and it's a small one. It's just for the miners. You'll illusion with the only other two illusionists in the world. *This* world, at least," she corrected. "They're young, too. Your age, as a matter of fact. Each of you will illusion your own bit. If you do well, and it's entertaining enough, the miners will decide to support your color in the festival, which begins tomorrow.

I frowned up at a massive chandelier. I had no idea what I'd illusion. Gross incompetence hit me like an ocean wave. So far I'd only illusioned things like snow and arsenic. And temperatures. I'd done the Quickening Formula—that was a complex equation, right? It had flowed right from my fingers. And I'd transformed the corridor on the *Chivalry*. But was it enough to put an early end to the illus—illusiona—Whatever it was called?

"Lady Florel—" I began.

"*Queen* Honoria. Please, Jonathan."

"Right—that. Illusionarium. What is that, exactly?"

"Ah. It's when you—the illusionist—illusion with an audience. Illusionists are rare, which means illusionariums are even rarer."

The hall opened up onto the main level, with vaulted ceilings, a mezzanine and a large staircase. The theater's lobby and reception hall. The wood floor gleamed below us. A ballroom, too. I'd never seen anything so grand. I tugged on my ear, thinking.

"Lady Florel," I began again.

"Queen—"

"Right. Queen Honoria," I said. "Look, are you really the queen here? Whatever happened to King Edward?"

Lady Florel smiled and descended down the staircase, which split into two and rounded to the floor. I hastily followed, wary of the time slipping away.

"I am," she confirmed. "Things are done differently, here in Nod'ol. The miners elect their monarch."

"They—elect? Really?" I said. "The miners?" Every miner I knew on Fata wasn't exactly nobility.

"Yes," said Lady Florel. "Here in Nod'ol, they control the airstreams, which means they control the orthogonagen fuel and the fantillium. Nod'olians are *very* fond of fantillium and illusions. I arrived here years ago, illusioned like a dream, enchanted the miners, and was elected."

"And since then, you've had one foot in Arthurise and one foot in Nod'ol?" I said, sorting it out.

"Something like that, yes." Lady Florel paused at the base of the stairs. Between her and the other staircase, almost in the center of the room, stood a display case. It was a round cabinet with glass around the sides, the display inside split like a pie into six sections, which were all locked and empty.

Except for two. The first one held an airship ticket on a green velvet pillow. It read:

PASSAGE TICKET
Airship #278, Theater Station
Destination: Sussex, dock 4

The section next to it had nothing but a slip of paper on an orange pillow, with one word:

ANNA

And the section next to that, swathed with gold velvet, lay empty. Lady Florel unlocked it and opened the little glass door.

"The antitoxin?" she said.

I'd been holding the brown bottle in my hand so tightly that it had imprinted itself into my palm. My fingers automatically and painfully unclenched. The moment the glass flashed in my hand, Lady Florel had swept it up, laid it on the velvet, shut the case, and locked it.

"Hold off!" I began.

"These are the prizes each illusionist earns." She cut me short. "You don't need to win to get it back.

You simply need to illusion *well*. There will be a large reception here after the show, and you can have it back then."

"What?" I said. "It doesn't need to be locked away!"

"Oh, Jonathan," said Lady Florel, sweet as icing on a cake. "Yes it does. I'm afraid you won't try hard enough if it's *not*. You see, if you do well, the miners grant me more orthogonagen and fantillium. The theater and the airships are powered, and the masked guard is paid in fantillium. It's the key to reclaiming this city."

"What about reclaiming Arthurise?" I protested.

"Arthurise can wait a few more minutes, Jonathan. I've been working on this city for years. I've already rescued this theater—it used to be overrun by . . . decay, and everyone lived up in airships. Slowly, we're spreading our tendrils of civilization. One day—*one day*—Nod'ol will regain its glory."

Lady Florel's lined face had turned rather glazed and thoughtful, and she stared off into the distance. I followed her eyes to the wall above one of the arched glass doors to the courtyard outside. A rough, craggy patch marred the marble, as though it had been scratched and chiseled away completely. It did not match the lobby's grandeur.

She stared at this marred patch of marble with glistening eyes.

Just as quickly, she snapped to.

"Well, Jonathan!" she said, adjusting her sleeves and mask. "Let us haste. I want you to meet the other two illusionists before the show begins."

And haste we did, back up into the many floors of the theater, the seconds feeling like they lasted hours. The sooner I met the illusionists, the sooner I could get the illusion over with and get back to Arthurise. To my chagrin, it took ten entire minutes to reach the other side of the theater, at a backstage room of the main theater. It had a wood floor and mirrors for walls, glistening lamps, and spindly white chairs. It was beautiful and sparse. A girl's voice rose from the inside of the room, delicate and chiming, and it made me pause a moment.

"Queen Honoria says he's good. *Very* good. She says he's already illusioned the Quickening Formula."

They were talking about me. My haste faded a milligram as I listened at the doorway. Another voice, muffled and guttural, rasped, "He's a scag."

The girl's voice, impatient: "You think *everyone* is a scag, Conny."

"That's because everyone *is* a scag, Divinity," the raspy voice said. "And you're the scaggiest of them all, you little piece of garbage."

I'd never heard anyone speak to a girl like that. Vexed, I followed Lady Florel into the room of mirrors. My reflection repeated in long rows of mussed, soot-streaked Jonathans.

A . . . thing . . . stood in the center of the room. I could only tell he was human by the general form. He wore layers upon layers of leather and linen, all in varying shades of orange and brown, thick nobbled gloves, a long coat with a hood, under which peeked a mess of blood-red hair. He also wore a mask shaped like something between a jaguar and a wolf. His eyes shone black through the mask's eyeholes, because over all this, he wore a fantillium mask. It buckled awkwardly over his mask's snout.

He seemed to be illusioning by himself. With quick, violent gestures, he was creating things I couldn't see. Turning, he swiped his hand at a girl about my age, who lay on a white settee, reading a book. She shook her head and laughed a sweet chiming laugh.

"Illusioned sticks and stones won't break my bones," she sang.

They both noticed us enter at the same time, and the boy quickly stopped his gestures. The girl stood, and they both bowed to Lady Florel. Lady Florel raised a hand, and they straightened.

I looked at the girl with the chiming laugh as she straightened, and couldn't stop looking.

Golden hair, with little diamonds in it, cascaded over

her shoulders. She wore a strange combination of long green skirts and black corset and jackets in a stitched sort of piecemeal that, unlike Lady Florel's, worked. She looked like a fallen queen. Her hair bounced as she straightened and smiled—at *me!*—with white teeth and deep red lips and long lashes and delicate features that put such a fizz in the air my knees nearly gave way. I'd never seen anyone so beautiful. I wanted to touch her, just to see if she was real.

"Divinity and Constantine," Lady Florel introduced us, "this is Jonathan. Our newest illusionist."

I held my hand out to the boy with two masks, Constantine, and smiled tightly.

He didn't shake it. Letting out a feral scream, he leapt and shoved his arms out in illusioned fervor, sending a blast of invisible, illusioned something at me.

It was almost amusing. I didn't move a hair. Constantine, breathing heavily, had landed in a crouch, his gloved hands outstretched. They had claws at the tips.

"Sticks and stones," I said coolly.

"He can't hear you," said the girl.

I glanced at her, then at Constantine, whose all-pupil eyes appeared to be staring straight through me, to the mirror on the wall behind.

"In the illusion, he's thrown you back against the wall," she explained. "At least, I think so. That's what he's staring at. He illusioned something at me, too. That's why he can't hear me. I'm probably in pieces across the floor."

The girl laughed a bright, chiming laugh. I smiled weakly.

"Watch," she said. She swept to Constantine's side in one smooth, graceful motion, dug her delicate fingers underneath his fantillium mask, and tore it from Constantine's face, revealing his mask's snout. It had rows of pointed teeth. We both jolted away sharply as he swiped, blindly, and the pupils in his eyes contracted. His eyes were bright orange.

He lurched to his feet and lunged for me. I dodged. He careened past.

"Constantine!" said Lady Florel quickly, hurrying to his side and halting his attack by weaving her arm through his. "Have I told you we found Anna? Tucked away in a corner of the maze, hiding from the Riven, poor thing. She won't run off this time, I'm sure of it. You'll see her tonight. . . ."

Anna. From the slip of paper in the round cabinet. So Constantine's prize was a person. Lady Florel led the hunched and growling Constantine out of the room, his long coat trailing after them. Whoever Anna was, I felt sorry for her.

The girl behind me, Divinity, was laughing. I smiled sheepishly and shoved my hands into my pockets.

"His eyes," I said, nodding at the door Constantine had just exited. "Are they really that color?"

"No," said Divinity, still laughing. "He has them injected with dye. It changes every day."

"Really!" I said, intrigued. "Is that medically possible?"

Divinity giggled, scrunching her nose. If I had a cap right now, I'd have twisted the life out of it. She paced around me, her dress sweeping the floor, sizing me up and down with her glimmering green eyes. They reminded me of gems. I made an attempt to comb through my matted curls with my fingers. I looked a wreck and smelled of smoke. I vainly wished I had taken the time to wash up.

"Queen Honoria says you're from the far north," she said, the gems glittering with delight at my disheveled clothes.

"Oh? Ah! Quite," I said.

"How far north?"

"Oh. Ah. Pretty far," I said.

Divinity wove her arm through mine, apparently not caring about my appearance. Her layers of silk brushed my skin, and her perfume made me dizzy.

"Let's sit down," she said, dimpling.

She led my completely unresisting self to a spindly sofa and nestled next to me, taking my hand and tracing her gloved finger over my palm as though it pleased her extraordinarily. It was like flying on an airship through a rainbow while the sun set during a hailstorm. . . .

"Oh. Ah. So. What were you reading?" I said, hoping for a good long conversation.

Divinity shrugged, released my hand,[11] and strode to where she'd discarded the book on the floor. She handed it to me.

"I can't make heads or tails of it," she said as I flipped through the pages of the tome, recognizing it as an old biology textbook. "I'm trying to study chemical structures," she continued. "Well, there's not a lot of books anymore that tell you how to illusion. They've disappeared over the years. So we're stuck reading these awful things. Do you want to practice?"

She nodded to Constantine's fantillium mask that had been left on the floor. I distastefully shook my head, rather not wanting to share something Constantine had been breathing in.

"Probably not much time for it, anyway," Divinity conceded as the doors opened and several masked guards issued forth. Their numerous reflections turned them into an endless regiment of crimson. "Come with me—we'll have you trussed up as well. You certainly look like you could use it."

[11] Blast!

Divinity had a suite nearby with mirrors and a pool. Everything in it—the furniture, the pictures, the curtains, the wallpaper—was in various shades of green. It was like I was trapped inside her glittering eyes. Flowers were everywhere. On the tables, by the emerald sofas, in large pots on the floor. I'd never seen live flowers before, and touched the petals and traced the veins on the leaves, and smelled them. They really did have a fragrance, just like the books all said.

Divinity sat at a vanity chair as the masked guards flitted around her like birds, puffing white powder over her face and rouging her lips and cheeks and adjusting each lock of her hair.

"What do you think you'll illusion tonight?" she said as I awkwardly and discreetly tried to brush the soot from my clothes.

"I—I don't know," I admitted, my face growing warm.

"You don't *know*?" she said, turning around to face me, her eyebrows knit. "I've been studying for this for *months*!"

My palms suddenly started sweating.

"Well—ah, what do you think I ought to illusion?" I said.

"Hmmm. Well. What's your specialty?"

"Um," I said. Illusionists had specialties? I scrambled.

"I'm—very good at . . . temperatures," I finally managed.

Divinity coughed. It sounded very much like she was stifling a laugh.

"Well, all right," I admitted. "I'm open to advice. I'm not terribly experienced, to tell the truth. It's my first real illusionarium. What do *you* think I ought to illusion?"

Divinity pursed her perfect lips together, thoughtful.

"Something sweet," she said at last. "Sweet, and beautiful, and innocent. Oh *do* put some powder on him; he's *so* . . . messy."

The masked guards attacked me with their brushes.

"*Puh,*" I said, spitting powder.

I let her advice sink in through my Divinity-induced stupor—which intensified as she wove her arm through mine yet again, and, smiling, tugged and led me out of her suite. Something sweet . . . well. I knew how to illusion ice. And arsenic. Neither of which were exactly beautiful.

Sweat was running down the back of my neck when, after our long walk, she'd taken me to the theater backstage. The entire theater was so large the red velvet chairs seemed endless, and theater boxes gaped at us. The curtains disappeared into the ceiling, and chandeliers lit everything. So different from the Rosewine Theater, which had only a platform and lamps that worked but half the time.

Only a few minutes, and the doors at the sides of the theater opened. The floor rumbled with the miners assembling, filing into their seats. There weren't many—maybe seventy or so—and they wore outfits like Queen Honoria and the illusionists, except . . . more. Buckles and jackets and wigs, green tresses with ships sewn to them, and hats that tied under the chin, and overall, a mess of clothes that completely hid their forms. And masks. They all wore masks. White masks trimmed with gold, masks with pearls and lace hanging from them, even masks rimmed with glittering gems. *These* were miners? I warily eyed the crimson guardsmen, who lined the aisles. Next to me, Divinity chattered on about every miner who took a seat.

"He's new. Her, too—oooh, lovely mask. A half mask—definitely hasn't been a miner long. Oh, look—there's Edward the Pathetic Miner. I can't believe he's not dead yet."

"Divinity," I said, for she still had her arm around mine. "Why does everyone here wear masks?"

Divinity's chattering halted. Her brow furrowed at me.

"You . . . don't *know*?" she said.

I quickly clamped my mouth shut. I was doing a wonderful job of proving how stupid I was.

I remained in silence as the illusionarium began.

Lady Florel—face rouged and powdered white—swept from the wing and onto the stage. The crowd hushed and no one applauded as she announced, "The Eighty-second Annual Masked Virtue Pre-ceremony" and the names of the illusionists taking part. Divinity. Constantine. The Young Promising Talent from the Far North, Jonathan Gouden. An honor. Please welcome.

And the raspy breaths of the audience indicated they were still alive.

Divinity slipped her arm from mine, leaving me bereft with a brush of her hair as she took Lady Florel's place onstage. I stayed back. Amidst her chatter, Divinity had let me know that I would be the last illusionist to have a turn, which gave me all the more time to worry.

A *hissssshing* filled the theater.

Gold-painted pipes along the perimeter of the seats in the audience, and the stage, hissed out thick billows of steam. A boiler somewhere backstage groaned. The steam around us grew in layers, billowing over the miners, who disappeared in the opaque white, then Divinity, on the stage, faded from view as well. I was alone in the dark, blistering steam.

I inhaled, slowly. My lungs froze and the lights brightened. The anxieties about Nod'ol, about illusioning and about the cure, all faded to nothing. The hissing roared and the steam thinned.

Divinity illusioned like her beauty. With grace, charm, and delicacy, sweeping her hands out and turning around, twisting the steam around her in long strands of white. She caught me in her spell.

A figure formed of steam, growing from it with long arms and legs, a rounded form of a man. It burned white hot, then cooled and solidified transparent. I couldn't tear my eyes away. Glass! That was a structure I hadn't learned. And the glass man moved! It turned to her and bowed! She curtsied back to it, and they began a flitting dance. As she danced, she created more and more glass figures of men, melting up around her in the mist, elongated pillars of ersatz gentlemen. Light danced in long glass strands and highlights.

Divinity touched the shoulders of the nearest glass figure and rested her head against its chest, then flitted away, dancing around it, her dress brushing its legs in layers of lace. I marveled at how she illusioned the glass to bend and mold, and managed to control all the figures at once. She leaned forward, lifted to her toes, and kissed one of the figures on the neck.

Lucky glass man, I thought.

Something formed from the steam in Divinity's hand, and when she raised it, I recognized a dagger made of glass. She reared back.

And plunged it into the glass man's chest.

"Gah!" I croaked. The chest cracked.

Red light poured from it and drenched Divinity and

the stage. The glass figure fell to its knees. Divinity thrust her hand into its glass wound and retrieved a *beating glass heart*.

She held it up to the audience, red light dripping down her hands. They cheered hoarsely and clapped.

Divinity threw the glass heart onto the stage floor, shattering it into a thousand pieces. A shard of it skidded backstage and hit my foot. I stumbled back sharply.

The rest of the glass men lined up in rows on the sides of the stage and held as still as soldiers. Divinity bowed as the audience applauded broadly, her hand still dripping red light. When the clapping died, she hurried offstage, looking faint.

Constantine, who had been standing in the wings on the other side, glowering at me with beastly hatred, took his eyes away and strode out. He was still dressed like an animal, with crimson hair and coats that encased him like a badly stuffed pillow. He didn't bother with the formality of bowing.

And when he began to illusion, I saw he didn't need to. His movements were so powerful and sharp he commanded the audience into rapt silence. The steam billowed up around him into eight columns, then formed a large ceiling over him, connecting the pillars.

In his gazebo of steam, Constantine leapt and threw himself to the stage floor with a yell. The ground vibrated.

The steam swept instantly from its formed columns, revealing not a building—

—but a giant eight-legged spider, made entirely of metal and gear works.

My brain turned, fascinated and feverish. Bronze! And *steel*! And piping and pistons, connecting each reticulated leg to the center. The spider clicked and groaned and rose up, curling its two front legs high above Constantine, moving with his harsh movements. The center of the spider had an engine that whirred with steam. Incredible! I grudgingly admitted: Constantine could make the pocket watch King Edward had asked me to illusion.

Constantine threw his arms forward, and the spider leapt over him, striking the ground just before the front row of the audience—making them cry aloud and jump back—and then the mechanical spider clicked and reticulated forward to the wall of the stage, testing it with its pointed feet before climbing to the ceiling with each leg sucking itself against the wall. Peering up, I could see smaller mechanical spiders piled on its back, crawling over one another in a mess of mechanical legs and *hisshes* and clicks. I wiped my arms, trying to brush away the shuddery feeling.

The audience stood and applauded. Constantine didn't bother bowing—he didn't need to—and left the stage in a brooding hunch.

The giant spider remained curled at the top of the ceiling. My ears rang.

"Go, Jonathan," Lady Florel whispered behind me, and two masked guardsmen pushed me out from the shielding curtains.

I stumbled onto the stage and couldn't even make it to the center. The miners, a cacophonic mix of all ages and clothes and masks, struck panic through me. I ran off the stage, to the safety of the wing where Lady Florel stood, unsmiling.

"I don't know what to illusion," I said, panicked.

She said, coldly, "You'd better figure it out if you want the antitoxin."

And with that, the masked guard shoved me back into the center of the stage.

I stood there, swallowing, as the steam misted around my feet, the mechanical spiders above me and the glass men behind me. A glance back at the stage's wing, filled with the crimson masked guardsmen, reminded me I was trapped.

The cure. The cure. Focus on the cure.

I closed my eyes, and all I could see was my family; Mum and Hannah ill in the hospital wing, their skin mottled black, and my father gripping my mother's hand as though if he'd let it go, he would drown. Interminable homesickness choked me.

The room hushed.

Sky came first, the thoughts pulling themselves from my head and fingers. I spattered stars over the theater with quiet movements, pinpricks of light, and willed them to sparkle over the room. You could reach up and flick them.

I envisioned ice, and it formed upon itself in the center of the stage. The energy radiated from my fingers and neck like a fever and I pushed it out, the wake forming into white tendrils and flakes and shimmering around the audience, in the aisles and up the gilded walls.

Towers grew. Rows of housetops, vertical docks, and the observatory dome. Bridges formed over the audience, making them gasp. Airships made of ice hung, connected to docking towers with delicate ice threads. The theater filled with ice of every transparency, forming the city I knew by heart. I'd even created canals of generator offal, the rivers of white rolling over the sides of the city and billowing into the feet of the audience.

I fell to my knees, gulping air. The theater and masked faces spun around me.

"Where is this, boy?" came a hoarse voice from the audience.

I swallowed.

"North," was all I could say.

"Fascinating," rasped another voice. "And how, exactly, will you fight with it?"

"Fight?" I said.

"And *begin*!" Lady Florel's voice rang out.

The world exploded around me.

Divinity's glass figures came to life, swarming around me and leaping onto my city of ice. They bashed the observatory dome in, smashing over cloud canals and destroying the walkways. The spider dropped down from the ceiling with a *clongggg* and the little spiders scattered from it. Stumbling away from them, I whipped sharply about to see Divinity and Constantine back on stage, bringing their illusions to life in violent, sweeping gestures.

"Just a ruddy minute!" I said, pulling together a gust of wind and shoving it at a trio of spiders skittering toward me. The wind picked them up and threw them into the audience, causing some of the miners to scream.

The glass men threw themselves at my illusion, bashing the towers and bridges, sending shards of ice raining over the audience. I cringed as they smashed my family's row house. With a sharp movement I illusioned a gale at the offending glass men, throwing them into the mass of spiders that skittered down the aisles.

The spiders crawled over them, puncturing the glass with their pointed legs. Divinity illusioned sharply; the glass men glowed molten hot and melted into the gears of the spiders attacking them, then solidified, causing the spiders to stiffen and tumble to the side, useless.

I shoved another gale at a glass man kicking the dome of the observatory, and he smacked against an empty chair. His head broke off and he flailed to death like a struggling corpse.

The remaining glass men pivoted and turned on me, running back to the stage in a mass. Divinity's giggle screeched through the air behind me.

The giant mechanical spider, puffing steam, rose in gargantuan monstrosity over me. It kicked one of the nearest attacking glass figures away. I turned quickly, seeing Constantine at the helm of the illusion.

"You stupid idiot," he rasped. "You let Divinity tell you what to illusion, didn't you."

He swiped his hand sharply. The giant spider's front leg swiped and knocked me across the head with the force of a speeding train.

I folded up, joint by joint, and smashed face-first into the floor.

CHAPTER 10

The masked guard had to remove me from the stage and escort me to a suite that was supposedly mine. It was like Divinity's, except gold. The furniture was gilded. The wallpaper was striped yellow. The chandeliers dripped amber diamonds. Even the flowers in the vases and growing at the top of the fountain were yellow roses. I was trapped inside a giant gold music box.

Fuming, I hurriedly washed in a steaming basin of water. The bruises I'd gotten from illusion-fighting had faded, but the humiliation remained. Divinity, that little viper.

As I dressed in new clothes however—all varying shades of gold and yellow, ridiculous with ruffles and carved buttons—hope began to replace anger. The illusionarium was over. I'd be back on Fata with the cure in just minutes! I quickly put on the mask left for me, a gold half mask with smiling eyes, then placed my glasses over it. They rested neatly on my long nose. I grinned, thinking of what my father would say when he saw me wearing it.

One last glimpse in the mirror—I looked like a gold nightmare from a traveling circus—and I rushed down the long halls and stairs, leaving the masked guard behind, until I found the theater lobby, alive with more masked guards. They swept about in silence, carrying glass bowls full of punch and tureens of food, setting a long table in the center of the lobby floor.

I ignored everything and ran to the cabinet between the two staircases. It was still locked. The little brown bottle inside seemed to be mocking me. I paced around the cabinet until Lady Florel appeared at the top of the stairs, wearing a mask, descending in a lacy gown that looked like it was made of lumpy spiderwebs. Her graying hair fell over her shoulders, making her severity strangely softened.

"Hulloa there, Lady Florel!" I said jovially when she'd reached the last step. "Unlock the cabinet, that's the ticket!"

"Jonathan, what *were* you thinking?" she said, crossing her arms.

"Not much time, don't you know," I said.

"That was the most useless illusion I have ever seen!"

"We've still got to illusion the door to—"

"I will not!"

I drew up short.

"Hold off," I said, the glee inside me ebbing to anger. "Lady Florel, you said—"

"I *said* if you illusioned *well*, you would get it back. Your illusion was terrible. You earn *nothing*."

"But—but—" I floundered. "You—you—you never ruddy told me I had to ruddy *fight*!"

"I'm sorry, Jonathan," she said. "But you'll have to do better than that if you want the antitoxin."

She smiled and turned away.

Anger building hot in my veins, I made after her.

Before I'd taken half a step, two masked guardsmen swept up, grabbed me in midair, escorted me forcefully to the end of the long table, and sat me in a chair. Hard.

Lady Florel was at my side as the pain cleared, arms still crossed.

"Illusion in the Masked Virtue illusionarium tomorrow," she said. "If you illusion well, it may only last a few minutes."

"But—I—I only have two days!" I said.

"If you illusion *well*, it may only last a few minutes," she repeated. She smiled. "Do eat some food. You look starved."

She strode away. The two masked guardsmen who

had shoved me into a seat took posts next to the cabinet and stared me down through their dark eyeholes as though daring me to come near them. I glowered at my plate.

Constantine, who sat the mirror-image distance across from me on the other side of the table, made a guttural noise through his lynx-shaped mask. It might have been laughter. It might have been a train running over its own engine. He sat with his feet kicked up on his plate, leaning back into his chair, arms crossed.

"Who's Anna?" I said, wanting a fight. "Your girlfriend?"

Constantine silenced, his orange eyes fixed stonily on my face.

"Only Lady Florel said she kept running away," I said. "Sounds like she *really* likes you."

It was Constantine's turn to be slammed back into his chair by additional masked guardsmen. Plates clattered across the floor.

Divinity's shrill laugh echoed down the stairs.

"Silly boys!" she said, descending like a waterfall to the table. Her eyes glittered when she saw me, and immediately she was at my side, lacing her fingers through mine and beaming.

"Your illusion was very good," she said. "I was impressed."

"You lied to me, Divinity."

Divinity had the nerve to laugh.

"Wasn't that so *funny*?" she said.

"No, Divinity," I said with an annoyed smile, unweaving my fingers from hers and pushing her hand away. "No, it wasn't."

Divinity took a seat at the middle of the table, still laughing brightly. The table, an odd gathering of lanterns and silver, progressed in color from Constantine's end—orange, set with brown whole roasted birds—to the blues of tarts, purple-brown soups and stuffed vegetables, green salads, where Divinity sat—to platters of golden potatoes and bright yellow curried rice where I sat. None of us took any food.

"Sometimes I imagine this is what a real family's like," Divinity said airily. "Getting in fights and all. And Queen Honoria is the mother, and Jonathan can be my brother and Constantine can be the family pet. . . ."

"Shut *up*," Constantine and I said at the same time.

Her delicate lips turned up, as though we highly amused her.

I processed the evening in a haze of anger. Miners poured into the lobby, descending the stairs and taking seats at the table in their bizarre parade of priceless masks, wigs, corsets, coats. They spoke in croaking voices, and the chandelier shook with their footfalls. They flocked to Constantine, already serving themselves the food as he sat among them, unmoving and cold. They doted on Divinity, who laughed like wind chimes and sat on the table and teased them and flicked ears. They bowed to Lady Florel as she directed the masked guard. And everyone completely ignored me, at the abandoned end of the table.[12]

Not quite ignored. A thin—bordering on starved— man, a little younger than my father, broke apart from the assemblage of the crowd. He was different than the miners. He wore shabby, plain clothes that hung on him like a clothesline, his hair was parted in the middle, and he didn't wear a mask. He almost looked like an Arthurisian clerk. A little tag pinned to his pocket said PRESS.

He approached me, timidly fiddling with his notebook.

"Jonathan . . . Gouden?" he said.

"What?" I said.

"May—may I interview you? The paper would like an article on the newest illusionist."

I didn't answer. He possibly took that as encouragement, and nervously sat on the chair next to me, pencil at the ready.

"Where are you from?" he said, keeping his eyes on his notebook.

---

[12] More food for me.

"North."

The reporter didn't press for more details on that score.

"It—ah. It has long been the duty of the press to come up with an illusionist's name for Masked Virtue. Do you feel there are any virtues that describe your nature?"

I paused.

"What?" I said.

"The Illusionists are . . . named somewhat after virtues," the reporter ventured. "Queen Honoria used to be . . . Florel Knight, and Divinity was . . . Jane Miller, and Constantine . . . was . . ."

He trailed off and looked away. I followed his eyes to the marble above the lobby's main archway. That marred bit of wall, the same Lady Florel had been staring at. He drank it in with a starved kind of hope. And he really did look starved.

"Hey," I said, a little concerned. "You look famished, what? Have something to eat?"

The reporter tore his eyes away from the wall.

"I'm not allowed to eat the food," he said.

"What? Why not? What a stupid rule." I took the plate in front of him and dumped a spoonful of yellow rice and a pasty on it. "Eat, already."

I couldn't believe I hadn't offered him food earlier. He positively engulfed his plate with his mouth, spraying crumbs everywhere, a pasty in one hand and two yellow pears in the other. It could do a person's heart good, if it didn't make them sick.

"May I take some for my wife?" he said, between mouthfuls.

"What? Oh. Yes. Do. Plenty here," I said.

He stuffed his pockets. Either he was a very bad reporter, I thought, or Lady Florel had been right about things being dim in the rest of the city.

"Get out of here, begone, you little pencil-pushing whelp," boomed a familiar voice.

The reporter grabbed one last pasty and fled, his frayed suit coat bulging.

The man who took the abandoned seat wore gloves the size of dinner plates and hulked over me in an array of ruffles and buttons. He wore a tiny mask over the upper half of his face, and a pointy gray beard clung to his cheeks and chin.

My silverware clattered to the table.

"*Booooy!*" he boomed, and thumped me on the back. My glasses fell onto my plate. "What a show. What a *show*! So different from the other years; you have potential, I say, *potential*. Some would say aligning with you is a poor choice, but I say *otherwise*! Your illusion may not have won you the battle but it had *heart*, I say! *Heart*!"

"King Edward," I said.

"Sorry I'm late, lad!" he thundered on. "Lost my way to the lobby, can you believe that? But now I am *here* and I am willing to offer you everything I have for the festival! It's not much, I grant you—I only have half an aether stream to my name—but you have my airship at your service and that's better than nothing! I have a good feeling in my *gut* about you. My *gut*!"

"King Edward!" I repeated.

And it was him. Right down to how he massacred the food on his plate and sniffed after each bite. I wanted to dive at him and give him a jolly good embrace. Instead, I leaned forward and spoke in a low voice.

"Right!" I said as he attacked the pears. "King Edward. You've found your way in. My father must have sorted out how to illusion the door! 'Course he did! Right. Your Highness—turn around slowly—don't attract attention—behind you, that cabinet being guarded? *The cure is in that cabinet.* If we can—"

I stopped. King Edward was staring at me with wide, buggy eyes, fruit dripping from his hands and mouth stuffed with food.

"Your . . . *Highness*?" he said.

I stood, slowly, put my glasses back on, slowly, and the world happened around me s-l-o-w-l-y.

This wasn't King Edward. Something about him . . . the hairs of his beard, or the grooves of his eyes, or something in his face, or just . . . *something* . . . was . . .

. . . off.

In the periphery of my vision, masked guardsmen flurried, undressing the table, clearing plates and taking chairs away. King Edward, his mouth still full, clapped his hands with delight as the masked guardsmen took his plate and music sounded. An orchestra on the mezzanine had begun to play, and as the table was carried away in pieces, the miners filled the floor. Before I knew it, I was surrounded in a snowstorm of a dance.

They danced like everything here in Nod'ol. A mess of stitched-together steps pieced from various dances of the past two hundred years. There seemed to be no particular rules or partners or order to the rhythmic chaos. They danced on the mezzanine and they danced on the stairs. Some buckled fantillium masks over their regular masks, and their movements grew fluid and drunken. I guessed the experience was rather uninteresting without an illusionist.

In the whorl of chaos, a regiment of crimson order pressed through the mismatched crowd to Constantine, who stood petulantly still in the middle of the dancers, arms crossed. He straightened as the masked guards pushed the crowd aside, bearing a girl within their ranks. An utterly beautiful girl. Prettier, even, than Divinity.[13]

---

[13] Divinity had become a lot less pretty since the illusion.

She wore a long ballgown with odd bits of lace and purple flowers pinned in her dark brown hair, pulled back in curls. Her lips and cheeks were rouged, but I knew her instantly.

"Hannah!" I yelled.

"Anna," Constantine rasped, hurrying to her, forcing his way through the crowd.

I plunged into the mass of dancers. *"Hannah!"*

Constantine reached her first and grabbed her wrist.

"If I may have this dan—"

Hannah reared back and slapped him across his orange lynx face. It did not appear to affect him in the least. Hannah retreated, nursing her gloved hand. She turned this way and that, trying to pull from Constantine's iron grip. I shoved my way through, knocking miners to the ground.

"I *said*," Constantine growled, "May I *have this dan*—"

"Nope, sorry, cutting in," I said, throwing myself between them, breaking their grip and grabbing Hannah's gloved hand.

And in the .5 seconds of confusion between Constantine, the dancers, and the masked guardsmen, I broke into a run, dragging Hannah after. She stumbled but caught my lope, and we fled through the dancers, banging one of the arched glass doorways open and plunging into the theater gardens before anyone could even react. We leapt into the garden hedges beyond, which gave way to a hedge maze. Hannah matched my stride, her dress billowing behind her.

"Find them!" Constantine hoarsely yelled. *"And don't hurt Anna!"*

The walls of leaves became thick and snarled as we turned corners and ran on, thoroughly lost.

We only slowed when the yelling grew distant, the miners and the ballroom orchestra became a hum, and the hedge maze opened up to a small sitting area with crumbling marble benches and a dried-out fountain.

"That—was close, right?" I said, panting.

Hannah retreated against the leafy wall, twigs snagging her dress, her eyes wide with fear. A small curved scar marked her left cheek, just below her eye. I frowned at it.

"Who are you?" she said, backing away further when I tried to get a better look at the scar.

"It's—oh—" I removed my glasses and pulled off my mask. Air cooled my face. "Hannah, it's me!"

Hannah gazed up at me with wide blue eyes—

—and *kicked me* so hard in the knees I buckled over. Pain shot up my legs. My eyes watered.

Hannah untangled herself from the overgrown twigs and fled.

"Hannah!" I yelled, limping to my feet. My knees felt like they'd been kicked concave.

I stumble-ran after her, catching glimpses of lace before losing her completely at wrong turns. I yelled her name, fervently, until my voice grew as hoarse as Constantine's, and the stone beneath my feet became thick with weeds, and the hedge walls were a bramble of feral, untrimmed branches.

"Hannah," I said, coughing. I'd lost her.

Or . . .

Had I?

My thoughts became as snarled as the maze. It didn't make sense. Hannah was in the Fata Morgana infirmary, ill with the Venen. Wasn't she? No—that girl was her, right down to the curve of her jaw and her rounded lips and devil of a temper. Hannah to the iota . . . except for that scar.

And slowly, like the monstrous grandfather clock, my mind went *clunk* and everything suddenly came together like a well-oiled mechanism.

That girl wasn't Hannah.

And she was.

Lady Florel had said this world had schismed from ours. If Nod'ol had some of the same buildings as Arthurise, why shouldn't it have some of the same *people*? That explained why Hannah was here! Or—no. Not Hannah. *Anna.*

It explained King Edward, too. He wasn't a king here in Nod'ol. Only an aether miner.

Was *I* here?

I laughed aloud, forging through the overgrown bushes, imagining myself running around in ugly Nod'olian clothes, then stopped when I realized I *was* running around in ugly Nod'olian clothes. I shook my head. If my Nod'olian self existed, Hannah—Anna— would have recognized me. Perhaps I hadn't even been born.

I'd stumbled into an overgrown topiary. The cats had grown into lions and the elephants loomed as woolly mammoths. In the distance, the theater, with its lit domes and pillars, glowed. Constantine's voice still hoarsely yelled.

Run, Anna, I thought.

"Jonathan!"

Lady Florel appeared at the arched entrance of the topiary, accompanied by two dozen masked guards. She gripped her dress, clumsily picking her way through the weeds. The crimson masked guard stood at attention around her, silent as always.

"Well, *that* certainly was an exit!" she said breathlessly, though she didn't sound impressed. "Jonathan, I would ask you not to leave the theater. It's not safe here in the lower city. And far too easy to get lost. It took us weeks to find Anna, and now you've lost her again."

The guard poured around her and past me into the hedges of the twisted maze beyond. To find Anna, I supposed.

"What, exactly, do you want with Anna?" I said, twisting a leaf around my fingers.

"She's a favorite of Constantine's," said Lady Florel.

The twig snapped off in my hand. I wished it had been Constantine's neck. I stormed through the hedge maze after Lady Florel with glowering anger, the remaining masked guard ushering me through the mess of leafy corners, bridges, and pathways, until the hedges behaved themselves into rows and opened upon the theater. The windows cast a glow over Lady Florel's smiling face.

Lady Florel never smiled. . . .

I halted in the middle of the path.

"You're not Lady Florel," I said.

And for the second time that night, the gears *clonked* together and formed a whole mechanical picture. She wasn't Lady Florel. And she *was*. I was speaking to the Nod'olian Lady Florel Knight.

"You lied," I said.

Lady Florel—*Queen Honoria*—paused at the top of the veranda that ascended to the theater, and her eyes glistened at me.

"No, Jonathan," she said, smooth as a dream. "Not

lied. It's still the truth, all of it. Nothing means more to me than rebuilding Nod'ol. *Nothing*. If I have to find ways to other worlds to do it, to find more illusionists and orthogonagen and fantillium, I will. All I need is for you to illusion in Masked Virtue tomorrow. All I need is for the miners to enjoy the illusionarium. Then you will have the cure and can go home. I *swear* it. I'm not the Arthurisian Lady Florel, Jonathan, but I still am Lady Florel. It was a five-percent lie, at *most*. A small impurity."

"Where is the *real* Lady Florel?" I said coldly. "There weren't two of you running around in Arthurise."

Queen Honoria smiled, then turned on her heels and hurried up the stairs back into the theater, the hollowness she left answering my question:

Queen Honoria had killed her.

CHAPTER 11

I fell out of bed the next morning in my golden room, aching everywhere after the worst sort-of sleep of my life. My nose throbbed, my kneecaps hurt where Anna had kicked them, and oddly, my fingers hurt, too. I examined them. They looked swollen.

I dressed haphazardly in a yellow arrangement of odd-ended clothes. Masked Virtue, their illusioning festival, began this morning, and the sooner I illusioned for it, the sooner I could get out of here. My door was locked—it had been locked and guarded all night—but on the floor next to it lay a steaming tureen of mush, toast, and eggs. Underneath the breakfast plate was a folded newspaper. I slipped it out and unfolded it, and found my picture staring back at me.

It had been taken in the theater last night, just before I'd started to illusion. In varying shades of gray it portrayed me staring widely ahead, looking lost and frightened. My hair was a snarl of curls, and my soot-smeared clothes hung on me like a drowned rat. Around it, headlines percolated: *Riven Restless. Sacrifical Speculations.* And the largest headline of all:

NEW ILLUSIONIST— A SAD DISAPPOINTMENT

I frowned and continued reading.

> After her two-week disappearance to find a new illusionist, Queen Honoria reappeared with a new player for the Masked Virtue: a sixteen-year-old Jonathan Gouden. While his illusioning history is unknown, his first presentation to the Miners was considered a universal disappointment, as the boy inexplicably chose to illusion a miniature city made of ice, which, two minutes later, was destroyed and—

I crumpled the paper and threw it across the room. You're welcome, Press, for giving you my food!

A gentle knock sounded; I pushed the plate of food

aside just as Divinity opened the door a crack, revealing milk-white skin and one glittering green eye.

"Queen Honoria sent me to fetch you for the opening ceremonies," she said. She opened the door a little wider and slipped in, wearing an emerald dress of corset and gathers and torn ribbons. She clutched the old biology book to her chest. "They start in about an hour. In the lobby."

Her eyes caught the crumpled newspaper I'd just thrown.

"I read the article," she said. "It was rather harsh, I thought. That reporter is *so* annoying; he always tells the truth. Are you all right? You look awful."

"I can't *wait* another hour," I said. "I only have a day and a half!"

"That's too bad," said Divinity. She unfolded the biology book from her very fine chest and offered it to me. "You might need the hour, though. I brought you the textbook. I remember how nervous I was, last year. It was my first Masked Virtue. I hardly knew what to illusion. So . . . I thought you might like to study a bit. Before it begins."

I eyed her warily, hesitated, and took the book from her hands.

"I—thank . . . you," I stammered. I'd paced all night in agony, wishing I'd had a chance to get my hands on this book. Guilt engulfed me, remembering how I'd hated her. "I—I really mean it, Divinity. You have no idea how much depends on this, and . . . I . . ."

I trailed off. Every page I flipped through had been drenched, blotted, splashed, and scribbled over with black ink, rendering the book entirely illegible. Divinity's chiming laugh escalated as my hopes sunk like an airship on fire.

I slammed the book shut, reared back, and threw it just left of her head. It ricocheted off the wall and thumped to the floor.

"You know, Divinity," I snarled, bearing down on her. She cowered against the wall, giggling like mad. "You are *really* lucky it's against my upbringing to knock a girl's head off!"

"Do you even *know* what we do for Masked Virtue?" she said, countering me with narrowed eyes. "It's a death pit! The entire Archglass fills with fantillium, and all the illusionists try to illusion-kill each other! And if you *think* I'm going to go through death again—"

"Wow!" I said brightly. "We *kill* each other! What an absolutely unsurprising discovery and completely in keeping with this wonderful city of Nod'ol!"

Divinity surprised me by touching my face. It surprised me so much, in fact, that every thought fled. She traced her fingertips delicately up the side of my cheek. My face had never been touched by a girl before.[14] It wasn't . . .

. . . unpleasant. . . .

"Jonathan," said Divinity with a voice like a dove's coo. "I—I know I can be a bit of a *naughty* child—"

"Yes—well—" I stammered. Divinity silenced me with a finger on my lips.

"It's just, I'm afraid of Constantine," she said, her green eyes grave. "He's won these past *five years*. Dying *hurts*. An awful lot, Jonathan." Her lips formed my name with pink softness. "I—I was wondering if . . . perhaps . . . you would like to team up with me? We could defeat Constantine together. Please, Jonathan. Help me."

Common sense broke through my Divinity-induced haze. She blotted out the ruddy pages of the ruddy book! She doesn't want you to win!

I pulled away.

"Really," I said. "And what happens after that? We'll just get along until the illusionarium's over?"

Divinity smiled softly, her half-moon eyes glistening. It was the same sort of glittering smile she'd given when she'd torn the glass heart away from her illusioned man.[15]

---

[14] Please. Your mother doesn't count.

[15] I suddenly realized what Divinity reminded me of. One of those female insects that, after they mated, would bite off the male's head and lay their eggs in his body so that when larvae hatched and burst through his headless body's abdomen, they would eat his entrails.

"Yeah, no thanks," I said.

"Not even—" Divinity lifted herself on her toes, her lips close to my face, "for a kiss?"

I stepped back. Divinity lost her balance and stumble-sat on one of the gold chairs.

"Not for a hundred kisses. Get out of my suite, Divinity."

"Oh, please," said Divinity. "Everyone knows *kissing* is all boys ever think about."

"Yes, that's right, Divinity. That's all boys ever think about. Every bit of me can be reduced into one word: *kissing*. Thank you, Divinity, good-bye."

I ushered her out of the room, and she stormed down the hall like a queen, chin up, golden hair swishing to her waist, her ears red. I had the feeling she wasn't told *no* very often.

I slammed the door.

So *that's* what Masked Virtue was. What kind of city was this? This was the sort of thing you read about in history books, stories of barbarous civilizations that would massacre their own people for entertainment. A Coliseum circus. I sat down on a gold-striped chair and rubbed my face with aching fingers. I couldn't kill anyone. Not even fantillium-kill.

You fantillium-killed Hannah.

That was an accident! I never would have hurt her on purpose!

And she came back to life. So will they. It's not real.
My fingers throbbed.

Still conflicted, I arrived just minutes later at the theater lobby, watching the scene before me from the mezzanine banister through my broken glasses. Hundreds of Nod'olians filtered in from the arched glass doors below, descending from their sea of airships. Rows of crimson masked guards ushered them into place. Like the miners and the guards and nearly everyone I'd met here, the Nod'olians wore masks. Some of them expressionlessly peered up at me, pointed, and whispered to one another. They wore clothes like ours, but worse—torn and dyed so much they were colorless shades. Their raspy voices wisped into the domed ceiling and the prisms on the chandelier jingled.

Pipes had been set up around the perimeter of the lobby below, with vents along them to release steam. Masked Virtue, apparently, began in this room, then extended into the city and airships beyond.

Constantine appeared at the mezzanine entrance behind me. We spotted each other at the same time. Taking a page from Lockwood's book, I dove at him like a released spring, knocking him into the wall with the full force of my shoulder, stirring up the audience below.

"You!" I snarled. I punched him again and again,

frustrated I couldn't make any impact with his layers of vests and buckles. "You stay away from Anna! You keep your ruddy claws off her, you piece of filth!"

Constantine kicked me so hard in the chest my lungs felt turned inside out, and I tumbled back.

"What's she to *you*?" he snarled.

"Enough. On your feet, please."

Lady Fl—*Queen Honoria*—entered the mezzanine, gracing the scene in an outfit as ridiculous as her others, with lumpy, torn pieces of red velvet, high-heeled boots, and a half mask. Her graying hair was pinned around her head in dozens of tiny loops, making her head look a bit like machinery.

I managed one last kick to Constantine's ribs before leaping to my feet and ducking out of his clawed hands. In a moment I was at Queen Honoria's side, descending the stairs.

"So we have to kill each other in this illusionarium?" I said, bristling. "Is that what happens in Masked Virtue?"

"Fantillium-kill, Jonathan. It's a very different thing." Queen Honoria nodded at the landing before us, which had chairs lined up across it and a polished wood platform in the center. "Take a seat, please. Masked Virtue begins with an opening ceremony, in which I illusion. Then, you go with your miners into their ships, and the Archglass fills with fantillium, and—well, what you do after *that* is up to your discretion."

"But we kill people," I said.

"Do you want that cure or not, Jonathan?"

I angrily sat myself down in one of the landing's chairs, next to Divinity and Constantine, thinking of the cabinet holding the antitoxin. I couldn't see it due to the masses of Nod'olians below. They all bowed as Queen Honoria stepped up to the banister, then hoarsely cheered as she raised her hand and introduced us one by one.

Constantine stood first and strode to the railing by Queen Honoria, his cloak billowing out behind him. By the rise of rasping and unintelligible words from the crowd, Constantine the Beast was the obvious favorite. He bowed sharply, and the crowd went mad.

Divinity took his place next, gracefully blowing a kiss to the slightly more subdued crowd. Her lacy collar slipped back, revealing something on the base of her neck, half-hidden by her golden curls. I adjusted my glasses. A curved rim of hair. Very much like . . . eyelashes.

A crescent glint of something white and green glistened just below them. Divinity lowered her arm, and her collar straightened over the odd growth once again.

"Your Riven is showing," Constantine muttered as she sat down.

Divinity gasped and hastily pulled her collar tight

around her throat, blushing furiously. I couldn't tear my eyes away from her neck and had to be shaken from out of my chair to face my own introduction.

The crowd silenced as I stood by the wooden platform, staring down at the emotionless sea of masks.

Someone coughed.

Only one large man, wearing a tiny gold mask, pumped his fist in the air from the middle of the crowd below.

"That's my boy!" he boomed.

I smiled wanly and waved to him. Edward the Pathetic Miner, my one supporter. I stormed back to my chair.

Queen Honoria then began a long speech about Masked Virtue and the Writing on the Wall and Traditions. A cough sounded next to me; I turned and found the emaciated reporter I'd met last night. He cowered, half-hunched, against the railing, as though afraid I'd bite him, and held his pen poised above his notepad, ready to spring at an interview.

"I suppose I owe that wonderful introduction to you," I said in a bitterly low voice. "Thanks for that really great piece in the paper. That's really going to help me in the competition. I really appreciate it."

"I always tell the truth," said the reporter, his pencil quivering against his notebook. "I will never lie. You can kill me and yet with my last dying breath, I still shall—"

"All right, all *right*," I said, annoyed. "I'm not going to kill you already. All right? You ruddy sound like my father."

"And who, exactly, is your father?" said the reporter, daring to pluck up courage. "Because, you see, *Jonathan Gouden*, I have spent the entire night looking up every parish and government record of every town and city up north and there are *no Jonathan Goudens*. Not one. Where are you *really* from, illusionist?"

I stared blankly at him.

The crowd burst into deafening cheers. Their cries were so loud I could *smell* them, perfumes with undertones of dankness. They screamed themselves hoarse. Movement stirred beyond the masked guard at the top of the stairs.

"What's going on?" I said, confused at the suddenly excited crowd.

"The ceremony is beginning," the reporter said. He'd suddenly gone white. "Oh . . . I hate this part. . . ."

"What? The ceremony's been going on for the past ten minutes!" I said.

"This is the part where they make an offering," he said. "A sacrificial offering. The queen kills a selected person."

"*What?*" I said.

"Oh, yes," he said mildly. "Only fantillium-kill, of course . . . which really, hardly makes a difference to the person offered."

The cheers increased in decibels as the pipes along the walls billowed thick steam, howling and rumbling with their voices. Clouds of hot, metallic white fogged over everything. The crowd became lost in the steam and so did we. The masked guard standing around us faded to crimson silhouettes.

With the steam came the stinging cold fantillium. I coughed and inhaled, and the chemical coated my lungs with liquid ice.

The change of fantillium swept over me. The world brightened. Each individual breath from the crowd rang in my ears. The overpowering smell of perfume. Divinity's green eyes had dilated full black, and the chandelier prickled my vision with blasts of highlights.

Calm settled over me like a blanket of snow. I couldn't remember what I had been so upset about.

Queen Honoria, standing by the raised platform, closed her eyes and exhaled. Glimmering strands formed from her fingers. They filled out and grew opaque, then melded together and formed steel. I watched, fascinated, as it molded and blazed white hot in her gloved fingers, then cooled to a spike of a dagger the length of my forearm.

The frenzy of the crowd multiplied as the masked guards on the staircase behind parted and carried a struggling person with them. The sacrifice: a girl dressed in the best clothes I'd seen a Nod'olian wear, only a few patches sewn to her white, simple dress. Her hair was an array of soft dark curls over her shoulders.

Anna.

I curiously watched as they wrestled her to the raised platform.

Someone probably ought to do something, I thought.

Constantine was on his feet and at Queen Honoria's side.

"I thought it was going to be the reporter!" he growled over the crowd.

"Anna," said Queen Honoria coldly, "needs to be taught a lesson, Constantine. We spent all night looking for her. If she's not punished for running away, she'll keep doing it."

Constantine's black eyes flashed. His hand twitched, as though he very much wanted to box Queen Honoria's head off.

He did not. Instead, he lowered his masked face, took a step back, and slowly sat down.

Queen Honoria raised the illusioned dagger. Anna gave a sob, pressed against the platform. Memories suddenly drowned me. Hannah gasping for air on the laboratory floor. Hannah trembling in the infirmary bed. *Might as well just die now and get it over with—*

Stronger than the pull of fantillium, something in my chest went *click*.

"Stop," I said in a strangled voice. It was like lifting an anvil from my soul.

Queen Honoria raised the dagger over Anna.

"I said *stop*!" I yelled, leaping to my feet. I reared back and illusioned a stream of air so powerful it whipped the knife from Queen Honoria's hands and set it spinning to the wall. It hit the base of the ceiling dome point first, vibrating with a *wuhwuhwuhwhuhhh*. A collective gasp sounded from the crowd below.

"I'll be hanged if I let you do this, Queen Honoria!" I said.

Queen Honoria's eyes narrowed at her empty hands, then at me.

"Hold him," she said quietly, and the masked guard herded around me and pinned my arms back. With sharp gestures, Queen Honoria illusioned a new dagger, this one poorly formed in haste, with a mottled blade.

I tried to illusion wind again, and found it difficult without my arms to gesture the illusion away from me.

Temperatures, I thought desperately. I was . . . good at temperatures.

I sensed the heat of the knife, still warm from being illusion-forged, and mentally brought it to a searing point. I multiplied that point in my head. Squared it. Cubed it time and time again, the equation swirling through me. I exhaled the thoughts to the knife.

It sizzled, then glowed in Queen Honoria's hands. Her gloves caught fire. She dropped the blade in a flash and batted the fire out in her skirts.

Just as fast, I imaged the heat of my hands and arms squared a dozen times over, multiplying into unbearable temperatures at the guards' hands that held me. Flames sprang from their gloves. They released me.

I hastened to Anna's side, focusing on the guards' hands that held her down and multiplying their heat by a thousand. They jolted back, burned. The crowd stirred with excitement.

The temperature plummeted, and not by my doing. It dropped so low that as I grabbed Anna's hand, ice froze our fingers to the platform. Queen Honoria loomed over us, smiling so coldly it matched the temperature.

"What you are trying to tell us," she said very calmly as I gathered my scattered thoughts of warmth together, "is that you don't really *want* to return to Arthurise. You wish to stay in Nod'ol forever. Is that what you're saying, Jonathan?"

In spite of the cold, I began to sweat. At the bottom of the stairs, the reporter scribbled in his notebook like mad.

"Step *aside*," said Queen Honoria.

I managed a rise in temperature—just enough to melt the ice at our fingers. I gripped Anna's wrist and pulled her into my arms.

Queen Honoria lunged. Arrows of light streaked from her hands, and past my cheek, striking Anna in a spray of white sparks. My grip broke. Anna cried and fell back. The light faded, revealing a gash in her arm.

The crowd burst into roaring cheers. A masked guardsman threw me back from Anna, and I hit the marble stairs. Queen Honoria threw another arrow of light, this one slicing Anna's leg, just below her skirt. The exultant cries of the crowd could have shattered windows and broken the chandelier.

I stumbled to my feet and ran to Anna again.

"What is *wrong* with you?" Divinity yelled above the crowd.

"What is wrong with *you*?" I countered. "What is wrong with *all of you*?"

Queen Honoria reared back to shoot another arrow at Anna, who lay on the platform, a bleeding mess.

I logarithmed the flame just as it left Queen Honoria's hand, and it exploded into a fireball, throwing her and the masked guard across the landing and stairways. It burst into tongues of flame and set the velvet carpet alight, streams of fire arcing into the audience and walls below. Everything caught fire. Flames licked the air.

"Jonathan!" Queen Honoria yelled.

Anger had taken over. It multiplied the heat in me, sucking the warmth from my skin. The fire consuming the lobby transformed into a firestorm. Hot wind whipped us in stinging strings. The painted cupids above bubbled and burned. Divinity's hair combs fell out and her hair tangled. Constantine's many layers of vests and jackets snapped in the wind, and hats blew from the crowd. They screamed.

Queen Honoria tried to feverishly illusion away the blaze, but the illusion had grown too strong.

"Make it stop, Jonathan!" she yelled. "End the fire or you can forget ever going back to your precious Arthurise!"

A burning wind swept over the staircases, cinders stinging our faces. It threw Queen Honoria to the ground and tumbled the masked guard down the stairs. I alone withstood, illusioning a cool, swift airstream in a maelstrom around me. I hurried to Anna's side, willing the cool air to gust over her as she lay on the platform. Blood streaked her clothes. She shook like a sig shutter caught in a storm.

"Han—*Anna*," I said, scooping her up into my arms. She hardly weighed a thing. Blood trailed from her leg as I ran down the left staircase and into the crowd. Above us, the masked guard fought the raging fire. Divinity and Queen Honoria illusioned water, which evaporated from their fingers in an instant.

"Constantine, illusion a pump!" Queen Honoria yelled above the inferno.

"Hang the pump!" Constantine roared, leaping up the stairs. "I'm shutting off the boiler!" He disappeared into the flame.

The crowd pressed us, shoving us to the staircase balustrade. My funnel of cool air put the licking flames out before we touched it.

"It's all right," I said in a quick stream of words to Anna, who trembled in my arms. I wove my way through the hundreds of masked Nod'olians pressing through the arched doorways in a rush to escape the fire. "We'll be out of this soon. One whiff of fresh air and the illusion goes away. Put your arms around my neck, there's a good *poppetje*."

I fell in line with the panicked crowd, burying us in the chaos of masks and rags. Sparks and ash rained over us.

The crowd pulled us through the bottlenecked doorway. I leapt over fallen Nod'olians, stumbled across the marble and, like the night before, made lopes across the terrace and plunged into the maze of gardens. My ears roared.

One gasp of air.

The fire and smoke and singed air faded. The soot on everyone's masks disappeared. I dared a glance back at the lobby. The panicked Nod'olians inside pushed one another out like mad and ran from an invisible nothing.

There was no fire. As soon as they inhaled a true breath of air, they slowed and looked back at the panic inside the lobby, and laughed raspily.

In my arms, Anna's wounds faded. So did the blood over her clothes. Her skirt lightened back to white. Mended in record time. I picked up my pace, escaping into the maze as the crowd behind us poured through the theater doors, red figures among them. The crimson guard was coming.

Anna writhed out of my arms but gripped my hand as we ran, once again, deep into the maze, a tangle of hedge that descended into the metal and grit of the city beyond. The figures in red fell farther and farther behind us as we escaped into the labyrinthine city.

CHAPTER 12

It wasn't until our lungs nearly burst that we stopped running. Our escape took us beyond the weeds of the theater and plunged us deep into the city, a mess of crumbling buildings and rusting pipes. Here, on grimy locomotive tracks, we paused for breath, gasping on stale, gritty air. I leaned against an abandoned railway car, in the middle of an abandoned train, in the middle of the abandoned rail yard, muscles aching and feeling . . . well, abandoned.

The immensity of what I'd just done poured over me. My one ticket back to Arthurise. I'd just torn it up. How could I be so *stupid*?

Still bent halfway with stitches, Anna leapt forward and grabbed a broken pipe from the piles of rubbish around us and backed away from me, sharp, brandishing it like a cricket bat, her blue eyes flashing. It looked as though she could barely lift the thing.

"All right, who are you?" she said. "Why did you help me escape?"

"Oh, ah," I gasped.

"You helped me last night, too. Why?"

"Well, I—"

"Do you know me? You act like you do. I have no idea who you are. I should bash your block in right now and run!"

"I say," I said, rather hurt.

She lowered the pipe a little and considered me. I considered her right back, taking in her mud-streaked skirt and tangles of hair. She was thinner than Hannah, with hollow cheeks, and her hair had overgrown like weeds, lending her prettiness an edge of feral. And then there was that scar. . . .

"Anyway, hello," she said, backing away warily. "Nice to meet you."

"Nice to meet you, too, I think," I said, still eyeing the pipe in her hands.

"We're lucky we ended up in this part of the city," she said. "I know this section. A little. I've been lost here before." She nodded to the misty railway around us, then, eyes still narrowed at me, slowly set the pipe down.

It *clanged* against the metal of railway track at our feet.

A snarl emanated from the railcar at my back. Claws

scrabbled on the metal inside. I jolted away from the railcar.

"Riven," Anna whispered, and she began to tremble all over.

"Riven?" I said, trying to decipher where I'd heard that word before. "What's—"

She clamped a thin hand over my mouth, cutting me off. We stood as still as death until the thumping in the railcar subsided. I exhaled, unsure what I was relieved about.

BANG.

In shrieks and howls, three figures smashed themselves through the railcar door between Anna and me, bending it off its sliding railing and sending iron plates across the tracks. Anna cried aloud. I grabbed her by the arm and shielded her from the . . . creatures.

That's the best word I could find for them. They were human only by default. Their torn clothes flapped wildly around them. Remnants of vests, dresses, coats. But it wasn't the clothes—it was their *faces*. It looked like someone had molded two faces from clay then squished the faces together. Where a human had one nose, the noses of these creatures had split off in the center of their faces, creating two noses. One of them even had three, the third growing on her cheek. Extra eyes, too, pocked their faces, blinking at us or swollen shut.

They gathered around Anna and me, hunched. Their legs had been wrapped in rags, and instead of tapering to the ankles, they grew *wider*, until they had actually split into two extra pairs of feet, stunted and purple. The creatures stumbled on both pairs.

"Lookee here," croaked one with five eyes, two of them swollen in the folds of his neck. "Fe upper crust come to visit us poor folk belo-w-ow."

"Lookette them fine clothess," said one, who probably was a girl, because she was shorter and thinner than the other two. She had two mouths. Complete with two sets of teeth and two tongues. They grew sideways down her neck, like a melting wax figurine. When she spoke, I could see the other mouth through her teeth, separated only with strings of sinew.

"All themsss flessh on themsss bones," drooled the third.[16] "'N' I bet thems is too high 'n' mightsy to share. . . ."

O-kay, I thought, turning as they hungrily circled. Anna had grabbed the pipe again. I carefully removed my golden coat.

"Han—*Anna*," I whispered, nodding to the rusted ladder attached to the car behind us. "Start climbing over the rai—"

---

[16] He really did drool it.

Anna dropped the pipe with a *clang* and threw herself up the rungs in a blur of white skirt.

The creatures lunged. I flung my vest into their faces and dove forward, shoving my fingers into their extra eyes, digging into soft tissue. I kicked and gouged again, until their many-fingered hands ceased clawing me for a fractioned moment. I leapt onto the ladder and pulled myself on top of the iron car—it clanged a giant echo—and rolled over, falling knee first onto the gravel on the other side of the train. I grabbed Anna's hand, and we fled.

The chorus of shrieks and bangs grew to a symphony of chaos. Every single railcar behind us burst open and more of them poured out and became an advancing army. Creatures with three legs. Extra arms and heads splitting faces. They hissed and howled and ran on all twos and threes and fours, blazing in the morning light.

"There's hundreds!" I yelled. "Anna, there's *hundreds*!"

"I *know*!" she yelled. *"Run!"*

Their stench of unwashed human grew closer, their craggy breaths at my heels. Anna and I halted short at the end of the pavement, the river slogging below.

Anna leapt first, throwing caution to the wind. I followed after, and as soon as I'd smacked into the sour black water, I realized: I grew up on an aerial city. *I didn't know how to swim*!

I flailed and sloshed, spitting mouthfuls of filthy water, and fell into a rhythm of not-drowning by swiping the water. I swiped after Anna through a stone archway.

I'd swallowed my body weight in foulness by the time I lunged my last water stroke to solid stone and inhaled precious air. Steps rose from the water, led up to a decaying door, and beyond, a very familiar courtyard. Anna and I staggered to our feet and broke into one last run through the old door. I found myself, once again, in the knee-high courtyard weeds of the Nod'olian Tower of London. And we did not stop running until we were up a crumbling set of stairs along the wall to a familiar tower. We dashed into a cell, and Anna shoved the door closed and threw her weight against a rusty deadbolt. It slid into place with a heavy *dooong*.

Outside, there wasn't a scritch of sound.

"We should be safe here," said Anna, between breaths and shivers. "I know there's a few Riven in that big building in the courtyard, and there's some on the other towers along the wall, but I've hidden here before, no trouble. I know a bit of the unRivened places left, here in the lower part of the city. There's not a lot. That's why most everyone here lives in airships or the theater. Are you all right? You look pretty sick."

I felt green with moat water, and wiped my head on my sleeve. I recognized the walls around us. This was my cell—the one I'd been prisoner in before. The Nod'olian version had most of the same names scratched into the stone. It lacked everything else, except a pile of old ragged blankets. It had Smell in spades, however. Foul Air of Moat.

"What," I said, letting my heart settle to individual beats, "were *those*?"

"Riven," said Anna, pulling a ragged blanket from a pile in the corner and wrapping it around her wet self. "You know. People who've had too much fantillium. You must be from pretty far north, to not know what the Riven are."

"People who've had too much fantillium?" I echoed.

"Mm. They're practically all that's left in Nod'ol. Are you hungry?" she added lightly.

I tugged my ear. "Well, yes, actually," I admitted.

"Me, too," she said sadly.

She stood there, drenched, the spitting image of Hannah the day I'd dragged her into the observatory library and she told me about the *Westminster*, her hair black and curly with water and her boots squishing with each step. Anna brought me back to the present by looking at me curiously.

"It's nothing," I said, quickly lowering my eyes. "You just—you look like my sister, that's all."

Anna hesitated, then grabbed a blanket from the pile

and threw it at me in a wad. It smelled rancid.

"I'm Anna," she said. "Anna Goodwin."

Goodwin, I thought. A schism from Gouden.

"Everyone knows who you are, of course," Anna continued, entirely as cheeky as Hannah was. "Jonathan Gouden, the newest illusionist. You're not bad at it, either. But don't let that go to your head. Anyway. Thank you for— for not letting me die." She turned away from me, digging through the pile of blankets for nothing in particular. "I—I fantillium-died last year," she stammered in barely discernable tones. "During last year's Masked Virtue. It's—horrible." And then, with the mental gymnastics of an acrobat, she flipped to a new subject with a glance back at me. "You look a lot like my father. And I'm from the north, too. Maybe we're distantly related!"

"Oh, I suppose it's possible," I said vaguely, pulling the blanket around my shoulders. "Is your father here in the city?"

"No," she said lightly, peering into an old rusty kettle, which she had dug up from the bottom of the pile of blankets. "I have some old tea leaves, fancy chewing on those? It's something, at least."

I remained silent, my eyes fixed on her, waiting for the rest of her answer.

She threw the kettle aside and began digging through the blankets again.

"He's on our ship," she finally said to the pile of rags. "Outside the city. The *Compass Rose*. That's why I'm trying to get beyond the Archglass. There's no way out of the city from down here; you have to get permission from the miners and Queen Honoria to even get on an airship. And it's not often they open the panels above to let ships in or out. But I'll get out, right? I've gotten out of the theater four times this past year. So how hard can it be to leave the Archglass? I'm pretty much halfway there."

She said it all carelessly, but her voice was taut. I dared to lean forward and put a hand on her shoulder.

And that's when I got a clear look at my fingers.

My fingers, which had been swollen this morning, had widened slightly. The thumb of my right hand had swollen so much it was beginning to split. My thumbnail had widened to two thumbnails, the skin smoothing over another thumb tip protruding from the side. It eased down into my knuckle.

I jerked my hand back sharply, examining it with horror. Anna quickly wiped her eyes and leaned in.

"Oh," she said, not sounding concerned at all. "You're Rivening."

"*What?*" I said.

"You've been breathing in too much fantillium. That's what happens. You'd better not breathe in any more until it heals."

I bit my lip and examined my other hand. The fingers on the left hand were wider, too, and a thumbnail had started to grow by my thumb's knuckle. I felt my face. The bridge of my nose was wider. I'm splitting in two, I thought. I'm schisming.

"I'm turning into one of them," I said hoarsely.

"Look," said Anna, kneeling in front of me, matter-of-fact, and tracing the thin purple scar below her eye. "Do you see this? That's when I started to split apart, during last year's Masked Virtue. It was an eye. It had eyelashes and everything. I saw things all broken, probably like what you see through those." She pointed at the broken lens on my glasses. "But," she continued, "I didn't breathe any more after that, and it healed up all right. And yours will, too. It's not too far along. It will take a few weeks, but all the extra bits will shrivel and scab over. Just don't breathe any more of the stuff, and you'll be fine."

"And what happens if I do?" I said warily, prodding my extra thumbnail.[17]

"You'll turn full Riven. Your face will split into two faces and your hands into lots of fingers and you'll have extra eyes and ears and toes and pretty soon your heart

[17]Absolutely *fascinating*, how everything split, sorting out how the veins and the nerves and the muscles grew apart—yes, it wasn't *quite* bone in the new fingertip but there was definitely cartilage. . . .

can't push blood to all of it. And then your *brain* starts to split, and that's when people *really* go mad, all those disconnected thoughts, and that's when you die," she finished.[18]

I fell back into the pile of blankets, my head throbbing. Perhaps my brain was splitting already.

"So that's why everyone here wears masks," I said. "To cover their extra faces."

And that's why Queen Honoria wore a mask over that divot on her face, I thought. By now, it must have developed into a full eye. And Divinity—well, now the eyelashes on the back of her neck made sense. She was growing a face down her back.

And *Constantine*. I didn't even want to imagine what Constantine's face was like. He wore a mask with a *snout*.

Anna sat next to me and pulled the blanket tight around her shoulders.

"I—had an older brother," she said. "Once. He died, when I was six. His name was Jonathan, too."

So I had existed in this world. I shifted uncomfortably. It was rather like attending my own funeral.

"How . . . did he die?" I said.

Anna shrugged.

"The masked guard," she said quietly. "My—mother

---

[18] With *far* too much relish.

was pretty. *Really* pretty. I mean, the sort of pretty that poets write sonnets about and men duel over. Anyway. Queen Honoria sent the masked guard to the countryside to find the prettiest and smartest people to take back to Nod'ol, and they found my mother, and it all went bad. At least, that's what we think happened."

Anna's eyes became distant. Rain pattered against the Archglass high above. The theater was a smudge in the distance.

"I'd taken ill, you see, and my father brought me to York to find a proper doctor. And while we were gone—"

The rain was a thunder of a thousand drops. When Anna spoke again, I could barely hear her whisper.

"And when we came back . . . there wasn't much left." She seemed to pluck up some amount of courage as she continued. "At any rate, it's my papa and I, now. We sail all over the empire in the *Compass Rose* and he barters at ports, when we can find one. At night he opens the stove and we roast bread and cheese and he tells me stories of Mum and all the places we would visit. We never can dock anywhere long. The masked guard is always after us."

"Why?"

"That's just what they do. They're children who were taken to Nod'ol when they were little, and Queen

Honoria trains them to be her guard. And when people in the city turn into Riven, she sends the masked guard out for more. She's dead set on keeping the city alive."

I remembered Queen Honoria's impassioned tears the night before. "Well, that makes sense, anyway," I said, and added, "They seem to take especial interest in you, though."

"No idea why," Anna said lightly. "I wish they would give up."

You do have an idea why, I thought. You're just too polite to say. She, like Hannah, had Mum's looks. She could make Renaissance painters drink their tubes of cadmium red.

"A year ago the masked guard found the *Compass Rose*," Anna said with difficulty. "They took me away from Papa and brought me to Nod'ol. That's when I first met Constantine."

My hands clenched involuntarily.

"It's been all right, though," Anna said quickly, noticing. "I manage to escape the theater before we even say *hello*. And—I hide in the city and find what food I can, and look for a way out of the Archglass. I'll be with my papa again soon."

She shook her curls back—they looked a bit like a rat's nest—and then changed the subject.

"I saw your prize in the lobby. During the ball. The

cure to the Venen. Did your sister catch it? The one who looks like me?"

I nodded miserably.

"I have a day and a half," I said. "Less than that."

Anna put a thin hand on my shoulder.

Her touch released a pour of words from me. I wasn't even quite sure what my mouth was saying. It simply spilled everything that had been bottled up into piles of words and heaps of sentences, all over the floor. And Anna listened, her hand still on my shoulder, her eyes wide.

I began with Fata Morgana. The Venen infecting my mother and my sister, and then all of our aerial city. I told her about Lockwood, and the Tower of London, and Queen Honoria bringing me to Nod'ol to illusion for Masked Virtue. When I told Anna about the illusioned door, she gasped.

I continued on about Lockwood's escape from the theater and my botched illusion the night before. I told her everything, straight up until the masked guard brought her to the wood platform.

When I finished, the words just sort of lay there. Anna blinked at me with wide blue eyes.

"Ah," I said uncomfortably. "Ha-ha. You probably think my brain is splitting now. . . ."

"Probably," said Anna slowly. "Of course, it *does* explain why you don't know anything."

"Thanks," I said.

Anna grinned.

"Well—it does," she said. "Queen Honoria's been looking for another illusionist for a while now. The last illusionist—Justinian—Rivened five months ago. The miners are desperate for new illusions, and she's desperate for orthogonagen. But illusionists are really rare. No one thought there were any left anywhere."

Anna lowered her voice.

"Only a few weeks ago," she said, leaning in, "Queen Honoria said she'd found old illusionists' secrets, and she disappeared."

I nodded, the pieces of numbers and symbols formulating a whole equation. That was when Queen Honoria had illusioned a doorway to our world.

"And when she came back," Anna continued, "she had *you*!"

She beamed, the Mystery Solved.

I picked at the threads on the edge of the blanket. Outside, airships stirred, maneuvering around one another beneath the Archglass. I hadn't seen movement like this in the Nod'olian sky before. Like a flock of sluggish ravens.

They were looking for me.

"I'm going to have to turn myself in," I said to the blanket. I shook my head. "I've got to get that cure."

"And you think Queen Honoria will illusion your door back to Arthurise?"

I scratched my head, distraught. My fingers tangled in the snarls of my curls. I knew she wouldn't.

"Jonathan, why can't *you* illusion a doorway back?"

I frowned at Anna.

"Of course I can't," I said. "A door—even a simple door—I mean, I'd have to know every chemical construct of wood and metal and—no, that's impossible in such a short amount of time; it's far too many elements—"

Anna laughed and stood.

"You're joking, right? Jonathan, have you even *seen* yourself illusion? That illusion today! You set the entire *theater* on fire! You made Queen Honoria's arrow into an—an—an inferno! *How?* Not even Constantine could illusion it away! And this is—what, your fourth illusion? Do you realize *how powerful you are?*"

I stammered, pride surfacing in my chest. I'd been so used to being *sort of*, that being *something* surprised me.

"Maybe I could," I said, hope stirring within. "I'd—I'd have to find the right chemical structures, of course. Divinity had an old biology textbook but—well, it's ruined now—"

"I know where to find books!" Anna crowed. "Old books! Books about how to illusion, even!"

"Really?"

"Sure as the sun rises. I know the city quite well—when I'm not lost. What else?"

"The cure. I'd need that, too, of course. It's still in the theater."

"Oh, I've broken out of the theater *loads* of times," Anna bragged. "Getting back in will be a morning breeze! What else?"

"Fantillium. We'd need that, too, to illusion the door."

"The miners usually have fantillium," Anna said. "I'm sure we could find our way onto one of their airships. This is exciting! What else?"

"Lockwood," I said, surprising myself. It felt so astoundingly right the moment I said it that I repeated it fervently. "We're going to need Lockwood."

CHAPTER 13

Back at home, Hannah had outdistanced me in light signal terminology. She had a better sense of rhythm, I supposed. She disliked it, however, which didn't seem quite fair. If you hated something, you shouldn't be good at it. Especially if you had a brother who was required to take all of Light Semaphore Basic, Intermediate, and Advanced because he was a boy.

Anna had scrounged through the moldy pile of blankets and produced an orthogonagen lamp with a mostly used cell, which would give us about thirty minutes. I sparked a light in it and filled the tower with brightness and shadow and set it at the window, hurriedly explaining the system of light signal semaphore and sending messages through the sky, what the flashes of shorts and longs meant, and how different colors were different channels. She nodded as though she understood—and if she was anything like Hannah, she probably did.

"If Lockwood is out there, he'll see this," I said, turning the dimming knob on the side up and down with a *clickety-click-click* rapidity, sending flashes of light in a sequence of bursts. It was daytime and the lamp was faint, so I assured Anna with: "Airguardsmen scout like mad for this kind of thing. And Lockwood's the maddest of them all. He'll see it."

"So will everyone else," said Anna forebodingly.

I glanced up at the airships, streams of bronze and black over us, and continued to signal with the lamp in coded flickers.

When my hand grew tired, Anna took over. She didn't know what the string of *clicks* meant ("ATTN: LOCKWOOD—TOWER OF LONDON ASAYAW,"[19] over and over) but she had memorized the rhythm, and the light flashed in perfect sequence. I took over again when she started to slow.

A quiet *clink* sounded behind us. Anna and I turned around sharply.

A masked guard, dressed in layers of crimson, stood at the open door. The deadbolt hung limp from its screws.

---

[19] ASAYAW = "As Soon As You Are Willing"*

*Which is the Arthurian way of saying, "We're Dying! DYING, I SAY!"

Anna lunged and was tearing at his uniform in an instant, yelling and throwing herself against him. I hurried after and grabbed her wrist, ready to flee with her out the door. Anna writhed from my grip and made a great effort to slam the masked guard against the wall, which was about as effective as attacking a brick.

The masked guard did nothing to stop her; he just stood there under her delicate assault, somehow managing to look amused through the mask.

"Hello," it said. A familiar voice. Only one piercingly blue eye shone from the eyehole of the mask.

"Lockwood!" I said.

Lockwood took Anna's hand as she lunged and spun her away as though in a dance. She stumbled, then rebounded and was at Lockwood's jugular once more—to no effect.

"This is a lot like fighting a butterfly," said Lockwood, spinning her away again.

"Anna, stop—"

"I'll fight! I'll fight!" Anna snarled, raining blows over Lockwood. "I'll fight until I die!"

"Hold off," said Lockwood, looking concerned. He quickly removed his mask, revealing his roguish face, mussed blond hair, and eye patch. Anna froze mid-blow. "No need for that," he said. "See? I'm nothing worth dying over."

"To be sure," I agreed.

Pink flooded Anna's cheeks, and she withdrew to my side, mortified.

"Oh," she said.

"Sorry," said Lockwood, and he actually did sound apologetic. "Didn't mean to frighten you. Couldn't guess what I'd find here. Certainly not Johnny with a *girl*."

"Thanks for coming, Lockwood," I said, and meant it. *Meant it*. I was glad to see him. Never would have thought.

"You're still alive," he said as he removed his numerous crimson coats and threw them aside, revealing the blue uniform underneath. He straightened himself crisply, re-pinning the crooked sword clasp at his neck. Like me, he was a scratched-up mess. Unlike me, it served to make him look rakish. I only looked pathetic. I tried to straighten my collar. My clothes had dried stiff with mud, and I reeked of moat.

Lockwood glanced at Anna again, and then Glanced at her. An odd expression crossed his face—the same expression a fellow gets when he watches airships crashing into each other and can't tear his eyes away from the brilliant, beautiful explosion.

Immediately, he smothered the expression into Slightly Bored.

"So," he said smoothly, producing a freshly printed newspaper page from his uniform pocket and unfolding it. "You're the girl from this article, then?"

Anna and I gathered around it. Above a large picture, the headline read:

QUEEN HONORIA COMMANDS: "FIND HIM"

The picture below was of the theater lobby. A blurred, panicked mass of people running for the doors. Masked guardsmen among them. Queen Honoria and Divinity flailing wildly, and Constantine running up to the mezzanine. In the very center of the staircases, I held Anna in my arms with the same dazed expression I'd worn in the picture before—but also, with a sort of . . . solidness.

There was no fire captured in the photograph. The masked Nod'olians all looked mad, running from nothing. Of course the camera wouldn't capture an illusion.

"Yes, that's me," said Anna, after a pause.

"Ha. So, Little Johnny does have a spine after all. Never would have guessed."

"Thanks, Lockwood," I said. "Good to see you're still a classification A twerp."

"I've actually been looking for you." Lockwood strode to the window and peered out into the sky of glass and airships, where the sun shone through the Archglass like a severed gem. He looked worn out. "The whole city's hunting you down. Can't let them kill you; you're my only way back."

"That's why we need you," said Anna.

Lockwood looked rather pleased by this.

"Well—let's have a merry chat about it on the way out," he said. He nodded upward. Several airships had broken away from the sea of balloons above and were steadily flying in our direction. Including one with crimson pennants, that looked similar to the *Westminster*. "I'm not the only one who saw your sig. Paper says they won't start Masked Virtue without you, and they're hunting you down like a three-legged fox."

We left the tower as the airships slowly converged, slipped out of the broken front gate as they docked, and descended into the dark grime of the city. Anna led the way, cautiously, and Lockwood and I followed after, navigating with care through abandoned, fallen buildings, broken statues, and pieces of giant, fallen skybridges. From the ruins, it looked like this city had been even grander than Arthurise. Now, it stank of decay.

Lockwood held a dagger that he had produced from the endless supply in his boot, watching warily for Riven and listening to Anna's hurried whispers with a tightened jaw. He gave a short nod after each point Anna laid out to him, and she tied it all up in a bow with, ". . . and I know where to find the sort of book he needs. There's a giant library not far from here. It's *really* old. It has to be there."

"And Jonathan's just letting you do this out of the kindness of your heart, is he?" said Lockwood.

" 'Course I'm not," I said, bristling. "I'm going to get her out of the city."

Anna halted, the grit scuffing at her feet, and slowly turned to look at me with wide eyes. I ignored her, locked in a Death Glare with Lockwood. His eyes could have pierced a boiler plate. I didn't back down—the words had come out unexpectedly, but felt exactly *right*.

"Will this be before or after you save Arthurise?" said Lockwood.

"Either. I'm not choosy."

Lockwood blinked first.

"You surprise me more and more, Johnny," he finally assented. "I might as well help with that, too, as you'll probably bungle it all up."

"Thanks, Lockwood."

He spun the dagger in his hands, and we continued on through a giant unused aqueduct. It was strange to walk through such large structures and be so alone. Beetles scurried beneath our feet. Lockwood went on ahead to scout for Riven, claiming he'd become very good at it in a day's time.[20]

---

[20] We'd also been curious as to how he'd gotten a masked guard uniform. He grimly answered that with a "Don't ask."

"You don't have to do that," Anna whispered to me, when he was out of earshot. "I know you don't have much time. Anyway, you saved my life! This is repayment. I *want* to help!"

I smiled at her and said nothing. Frustrated, she kicked a piece of broken pavement at me. It was just like being with Hannah back on Fata.

Somehow, amid the shadows of airships high above and Riven hiding behind every corner, we arrived an hour later to a more organized piece of the city. An open courtyard with a dried and weedy fountain stood among rows and rows of genteel abandonment. A townhouse loomed at the end in decaying grandeur. Water had stained the brick white, and mold grew black in the windows.

"Here it is," Anna whispered.

She led us up through the rusting gate, and quietly, without knocking or ringing, she opened the creaking door and slipped into the dark entrance. It smelled of rotting wood and polish.

"Lord Glamwell is a Riven," Anna whispered as we followed after.

Lockwood and I jolted.

"Sorry, should have told you that," she added.

My eyes adjusted, and across the walls and up the vaulted ceiling, mounted animal heads hung. Things I'd only seen in books: tigers, deer with fangs, a massive beast with tusks and trunk and ears the size of heat lamp wheels. An elephant! They had been stuffed, frozen with glassy-eyed ferocity.

"Hello?" a man's voice called out when I *clicked* the door shut behind us. It came from a closed, musty parlor just off of the hall. "Who's there? Someone's here! I know it! Come out!"

And then:

BLAM.

A hole blasted through the wall by my shoulder. It steamed, the wood splintering out. I grabbed Anna's hand and with Lockwood, we fled down the hall.

"Oh. He's a hunter," Anna panted. "Sorry, I should have said that, too."

"Great, thanks!" I said as another shot rang— *BLAM!*—and a puff of smoke shot through the wall, right where I'd been the moment before.

"I'll track you down!" the man's voice hoarsely yelled.

I caught a glimpse of a limping beast of a man, perhaps as young as an airguardsman, stumbling out of the parlor door, wearing a torn dressing gown and mussed necktie, his face a pasty white and his nose-and-a-half flaring. I counted three eyes, two of them swollen shut from sagging forehead skin, before I pitched around the corner. We followed Anna up a flight of stairs and across a mezzanine—the wood had rotted out in the center—

and careened through double doors into a library.

Anna had been right. The observatory library was nothing to this. Books covered every surface—from ceiling to floor, levels upon levels of mezzanines and leather-bound books, ringed with tall ladders. Books strewn across the floor, as though a hurricane had hit the library. It all smelled of rancid pages. The ceiling stretched high above us to a distant skylight.

"This is going to take hours!" I said, hurrying to the nearest wall of books. *Philosophy*, they read.

"Don't have hours," said Lockwood. "How fast can you two find it?"

BLAM.

"Twenty minutes?" I said.

BLAM! Closer now.

"Make it ten!" said Lockwood, bounding for the door.

"You're going to get your head blown off!" said Anna, pale and running after him.

"And I will savor every second of it!" he said with cavalier energy, taking her hand. He parried with an underarm turn and sent her twirling back into the room. He dove out the door and slammed it as another *BLAM!* sounded.

"Ha! *Missed* me!" Lockwood's voice rang. "You're a pathetic shot! Those animal heads can't be real!"

"Reckless idiot!" Anna said, pale as snow.

Lord Glamwell yelled something back. I threw a book of geography down and ran along the wall, the spines' titles blurring past in my broken-glasses vision. Biographies. Some names I knew. Some I didn't.

BLAM BLAM! More shots sounded. Lockwood's laughter rang in the distance.

Anna hurried up a ladder with wheels and shuffled through books. I ran across to the other side of the library, treading on books and torn pages. The books here: *Fiction.* Who read that stuff? I punched the spines in disgust.

"Botany," Anna called. "Sciences! I bet chemical books won't be far from here!"

Unless illusioning books are as rare as Divinity said, I thought. Then he'd keep them somewhere else, like a glass case or his desk—

—which would be the place an illusioning book *would* be kept, in which case, he'd hide it exactly where no one *would* look—

I hated my brain sometimes.

"He's going to get killed," Anna said through gritted teeth.

"Not Lockwood; he's like the undead," I said. "You couldn't just shoot him; you'd have to sever his head and bury it before he actually died." I bounded across the room, slipping on books and almost crashing into Anna. Books in this part of the library had fallen from the shelves to the floor, lying in tall neglected piles. I picked one up and found a how-to-build-a-cozy-hothouse diagram on its pages.

"Great," I said, throwing it down.

The library doors banged open.

"Lockw—" Anna said.

BLAM.

Wood splinters showered over us. The bullet had gone through the walnut shelves. Great job, Lockwood, I thought, and grabbed Anna's hand, my heartbeat roaring in my ears. Lord Glamwell's face appeared at the end of the aisle.

"Thieves!" he yelled. "I'm tired of you—breaking in and—stealing my furniture and—my food—" *BLAM!*

The rows of books flashed by, and Anna and I hit a wall displaying marble busts. We turned around and ran along them, their faces staring pupil-lessly ahead. Another *BLAM!* and the head of Bach behind us exploded into powder.

I threw myself to the ground, dragging Anna with me and smashing my face into a book—

—which read, ". . . *must know the very basics of the elements, to start with, the chemical makeup and bonding, iron, for example—*"

I slowly picked it up.

The Illusionist's Handbook, it read at the top of the page.

"Anna," I said, flipping through the pages. Diagram

after diagram of elements, chemicals, and equations fluttered in my vision. I laughed. "Anna, I found it!"

Anna answered me with a grip on my arm so tight it cut off the blood flow. I looked up quickly.

And met the barrel of a hunting rifle, pointed straight at my forehead.

Lord Glamwell was attached to the other end, every one of his eyes narrowed at us, breathing raggedly. The pistons of his weapon hissed and reeked of bad oil. I stared transfixed at his bared teeth, rows and rows of them. . . .

"Drop the book," he growled.

I gripped the volume so tightly I couldn't feel my fingers.

"Drop the *book*," he said again.

"Drop the *gun*," growled a different voice behind Lord Glamwell.

Lord Glamwell straightened slightly and slowly opened his many-fingered hands, and the rifle clattered to the wood floor.

Behind him, Lockwood stood with an ornate hunting rifle pressed to Lord Glamwell's back. Two more rifles were slung over Lockwood's shoulder, and he had a hunting knife tucked into his belt.

"Hello, Johnny, Anna," said Lockwood conversationally. "You can stand up now. Find what you needed?"

I nodded and stood slowly, keeping a wary eye on the penitent Glamwell. I held the book up for Lockwood to see.

"Well done, Johnny!"

"Please," Lord Glamwell wheezed, half-bent, his hands up in surrender, as we skirted around him. He looked pathetic. "Don't kill me. I—I'm not myself lately—"

Lockwood slung the rifle over his shoulders. It clattered against the others.

"I don't shoot people begging for their lives," he spat. "Even if they tried to blow a hole in my head."

Lord Glamwell closed his good eye and exhaled, and across his distorted face were distorted emotions—years, maybe, of regret and sadness and one fleeting iota of hope.

"Lord Glamwell?" I said, stepping forward and clearing my throat. "Could we borrow this book?" I held *The Illusionist's Handbook* up. "And—by borrow, I mean, probably, we won't be able to return it. Is that all right?"

Lockwood rolled his eye.

"Ahhh—I—ah—I suppose?" Lord Glamwell wheezed.

"Thanks!" I said heartily, and tucked it underneath my arm, Hope almost seeming to emanate from it.

CHAPTER 14

It was Lockwood who insisted we stay, undetected, in Lord Glamwell's manor until I had the chemical structures in my head; then we would head for the theater. "Don't you worry, Johnny," Lockwood had said as I paced. "You won't take long if you're as smart as Captain Crewe said you were."

It was the first compliment I'd heard coming from Lockwood. I couldn't tell if he was joking.

Lord Glamwell had slunk off, back to his parlor, like a cuckoo clock figure getting ready for the next hour, and Anna cautiously led us away from the library, through the halls of fallen grandeur. The portraits along the walls had numerous bullet holes through them.

"There's Riven in the basement and attics," she warned us quietly. "I've stayed here before."

"Stick to the devil we know," said Lockwood. "Better Riven than the masked guard."

She led us to the kitchen, an enormous room with three stoves and numerous cupboards and fireplaces, and locked the doors behind us. Like everything else in Nod'ol, it was abandoned. Pots lay strewn about the stone floor, flour containers lay on their sides, licked clean. A broken table. The rancid smell of some vegetable gone liquid.

"It'll do," said Lockwood, and he slung the rifles he'd brought from his shoulders and rested them against an overturned chair. His left arm sleeve had been torn and was soaked with blood. One of Lord Glamwell's bullets had grazed him. I inspected it, declaring it "not bad," but when Lockwood glanced at the wound himself, he grew sickly pale and averted his eyes.

"Lockwood?" I said, realization dawning. "You're not afraid of *blood*, are you?"

Lockwood gritted his teeth and refused to look at his arm.

"Poor ickle Lockwood!" I said.

"Shut up and bandage it, Johnny."

I grinned. So! Here was one area in which I outdistanced Lockwood exponentially. Blood didn't bother me in the slightest. I rummaged about the kitchen, shook the dust off a linen napkin, and had the wound bandaged in two seconds. The color returned to Lockwood's face, which made Anna grin.

"I have a healthy respect for mortality," he said, examining the bandage. A grudging amount of respect glinted in his eye as he nodded a thank-you to me.

To celebrate his Healthy Respect, we scrounged for food. Starved, all three of us. I regretted not eating breakfast that morning. Or dinner the night before. Or lunch before that.

We found some old potatoes in a neglected bin, molding bread at the back of a cupboard, and a jar of preserves. Lockwood discovered a ginger tea biscuit, which he promptly bestowed upon Anna. Anna promptly split the biscuit into three even pieces and gave one to each of us. Lockwood promptly made a face at his.

Meanwhile, I studied *The Illusionist's Handbook*. It began with simple things, like temperatures and light. Fire and ice weren't explained until halfway through. The breakdowns of wood and metals like steel were at the end. And it wasn't just the formulas I needed to memorize—I had to learn how to form them, so several compounds and illusions would be happening at once.

Anna quizzed me on the structures, which swirled in my head and solidified into bonds and letters. Lockwood quizzed me on the observatory entrance doors, which I had confessed were the doors I knew best.

"Two doors, are they? Made of what?" he said.

"Wood. Heavy walnut, with carved panels—three on each side. No—four. Four—I'm pretty sure there are four panels. Right. And there's lions' heads above the latches.

And the latches are iron and have little florettes around the top and bottom, where they meet the wood."

"And you're absolutely *sure* there are four carved panels in the door?"

"Lockwood, you're making it worse," I said, digging my fingers through my snarled hair.

Lockwood grinned.

Anna quizzed me again, then Lockwood, talking to each other between intervals until they ignored me altogether, lost in their own conversation. I frowned at my book, trying to study. They wouldn't shut up. Anna spoke of growing up on an airship, and how her father had so many books the ship was low-sailing, and he made a living for them by bartering at each port, though there wasn't much to barter for. The world outside Nod'ol was, apparently, quite bleak.

Lockwood, by contrast, talked about the places in the world he'd sailed to, places like Kowloon and Calcutta, their exotic foods and bustling ports and thousands of people and buildings. As they continued on, their conversation grew closer, and Anna asked him about his own family, drawing answers from him that I doubted he'd ever told anyone.

"Actually don't have a family," Lockwood admitted, cleaning one of the rifles. "Mum died when I was four or something. Wasn't much of a mother, anyway. So I grew up in the Arthurise gutters. Nearly starved to death before I was six. A boy found me and took me into his home with his family. Crewe, his name was. He joined the airguard and when I was old enough, I did, too. He's a captain now."

"Where was your father?"

"Don't have one."

"Oh," said Anna, coloring. "Right. Sorry."

"Why? I'm not. You know, I actually searched for him, before I joined the airguard. Thought maybe he'd want to see his long-lost son or something. Hunted him down through parish records and light sigs. Found him in Parii. Most pathetic man—*coward*, he's not a man— you'd ever meet. Has maybe a dozen other children, not the same mother with any of them. Never knew about 'em, never cared whether they went hungry or not, only cared about his jollies. Piece of filth. I decided then I'd never be like him. *Never*."

"You're not," Anna agreed fervently.

"Ha! Well, I'm not as noble as Crewe, anyway," said Lockwood, though he looked pleased. "Crewe's a straight bullet. Believes things, you know? *Really* believes them. Says the soul's an airship, and you've got to steer straight for your destination, or the winds'll blow you anywhere. So, I'll stay on course or die lashed to the wheel rudder."

"My father believes something like that," I spoke up, surprising them. I flipped thoughtfully through the handbook's pages. "Every soul has a compass, he says. And if you don't keep it pointed north all the time, you'll end up miles away and lost. Even just a degree off." I frowned and closed the book. "That's what happened to Nod'ol, isn't it?"

Lockwood and Anna looked at me, confused.

"It is," I said. I pushed aside the broken chairs, pots and pans, clearing a space on the floor. I drew a line in the dust. "Nod'ol is a schism from Arthurise, right? Once we were the same world. But something changed. Something in the past made them split apart." I drew a line breaking off from the other line, creating an angle.

"What was it?" said Anna.

"I don't know," I admitted to the floor. "Some of our buildings are the same. Like the Tower of London. So, after they were built. Fourteen-hundred, or something."

"And before Queen Honoria became queen," Anna said, getting on her knees next to me. "She's never been queen in your world."

"The airships here look stunted," said Lockwood, setting his gun down and kneeling next to us. "Right? Like they haven't progressed past the turn of the century. But they have airships, right? So, after they came 'round."

"—And we both discovered orthogonagen and

fantillium at the same time—over a hundred years ago—
seventeen seventy-nine—"

I drew dates and events in the dust, marking each line
and comparing historical events with each other. Venturing
through the wars, massacres, discoveries, events of each
world, we became more and more excited the closer to
the schism we came. By the time we finished, a network
of events and dates etched the dust all the way to the
kitchen wall. Anna had painted a grim picture of Nod'ol:
an empire that had risen to massive power, building an
undefeatable army of airships, then terrorizing the earth.
Nod'olian monarchs, who had once been the same as
ours, had been overthrown by those who mined the
aether streams, and illusionists reigned.

"Fantillium changed everything in our world," said
Anna, frowning at the timeline. "The rulers. Even the
name. So many people went to illusionariums that my
father said more people lived in dreams than real life, and
he said it turned everything backwards. That's when they
started to call London *Nod'ol*."

"London backwards?" I said. "Wouldn't that be
Nod*nol*?"

"Don't use logic; they hate that here," said Lockwood,
which made Anna laugh. Lockwood looked dead pleased
with himself.

"Arthurise was once London as well," I said. "But

that changed, just after we discovered orthogonagen. And fantillium, too, I suppose. Everything changed after the discovery of orthogonagen. We suddenly had fuel to do anything we wanted. Aerial cities, rail travel over ocean—"

"—Steel airships. Undefeated airguardsmen," said Lockwood.

"I mean, it frightened everyone. All that power," I said. "It frightened the world. And we held an Assemblage— *the* Assemblage—where the people had Parliament meet, and they created a new government. Something that stood on principles and not power. The virtues of our past—of King Arthur and his knights. And we became the Arthurisian Empire."

Anna listened to all this with interest, fingering the ends of her curls like Hannah would always do during class. Lockwood unpinned the sword clasp from his collar and handed it to her. She turned the steel carefully around in her slender hands.

"That's the Excalibur medal," Lockwood explained. "That means I'm an Arthurisian knight. Every time it pricks my throat, I'm reminded of the Assemblage and what Arthurise stands for."

"A knight," said Anna, a curve of a smile on her face. "So, chivalry really does exist. . . ."

Lockwood returned the half smile.

"I *wish* Nod'ol had something like your Assemblage," said Anna abruptly. She handed Lockwood the sword clasp, and pressed her finger at the end of the Nod'olian dust line, looking miserable. "But—Nod'ol did whatever Nod'ol wanted. And now—look at how far away we are."

We left the manor in poor humor, both learning Nod'ol's unhappy past and anxiety of getting the cure weighing upon us. The late afternoon sun sent warped yellows and pinks through the never-ending Archglass above and cast shadows over the mess of bridges and ruinous buildings as we hurried through them.

We had agreed that dressing like Nod'olians would be our best way to forge onward to the theater without getting caught, and we'd made a fast search of Lord Glamwell's manor. It ended in the attic. Two Riven lay in the corner, beside pieces of furniture and old wicker baskets, dead. They'd appeared to have died long ago. I avoided looking at their numerous hollow eyes and splayed fingers as we dug through a trunk in the corner. The mess of clothes inside were torn and frayed bits of costume. We'd fit in nicely.

I wore a black-and-white mask that fit uncomfortably over my face and squashed my glasses up against my eyes. Hannah's mask was bright purple, and she jingled in an oversized man's coat that drowned her in buckles and sleeves. Lockwood wore a combination of long black coats and a black mask. He could have been distilled into purified Dashing.[21]

Now, minutes later, we rose from the lower levels of the city on Anna's heels, drawing closer to the theater. And the closer we drew, the more labyrinthine the city became. Once we turned into an abandoned alleyway and drew up sharply; three Riven huddled over something with fur, smacking their lips as they plucked the flesh from its bones. A cat. Their many-eyed faces caught ours and instantly they dove for us, howling and snarling. We ran and ricocheted around corners and ducked under pipes until we lost them once again to the mercy of the maze.

And we became lost ourselves, stumbling over walkways that twisted in on themselves, dead-ending through gates and up stairways that led to nowhere. I became more and more impatient. Dusk arrived, marking the fact that I had only one day left. Anna, seeing I was upset, put a hand on my arm. That rather made things worse.

At times, civilization appeared. Airships hung by vertical docks, and the Nod'olians who lived inside them ventured down into the open areas of the maze, milling through broken brick shops and inns of rotten wood, laughing in hoarse voices and sharing fantillium

---

[21] Surprise, surprise.

masks, pressing them over their porcelain faces.

"They don't see illusions without an illusionist, do they?" I said as we carefully edged a group of gutturally laughing Nod'olians.

"Of course not," said Anna. "They just breathe it because—well, it makes them forget about how horrible everything is."

"Don't know why; Nod'ol seems like such a lovely place," said Lockwood.

Masked guardsmen appeared among the crowd, walking through the people in even, measured strides. Everyone gave them a large berth, including us three as we casually walked away from them, turned a corner, and fled into more abandoned paths.

"It won't always be like this," Anna said, rather defensively I thought, as we climbed over a giant fallen statue. The marble head of a former illusionist, years ago.

"No, I don't expect it can be," said Lockwood.

"I mean," said Anna hotly. "It's going to get better. There's a—a—legend that things will get better."

"A legend?" I said.

"Well—more of a . . . foretelling, or . . . a prophecy," said Anna, twisting the curls of her hair, which Hannah always did when she was embarrassed. "*The Writing on the Wall,* it's called."

Lockwood didn't help things by "coughing" suddenly.

"A prophecy? I mean, a real one?" I said as we picked our way over railway tracks. "Who made it? An illusionist?"

"I don't know the exact words," Anna admitted, twisting even harder. "It happened ages ago. Over eighty years ago. The winter solstice festival that year, something really strange happened. During the main illusionarium. In the theater lobby, actually."

Lockwood and I had stopped, riveted.

"What happened?" I said.

"Words," said Anna. "Words happened. They seared themselves into the marble above the doors. The head illusionist—that was King Ignis then—hadn't illusioned them, and neither did any of the other illusionists. The words appeared on the wall by themselves. And when the illusion was over . . . *the words didn't disappear.*"

A shiver ran up my back.

"What did the words say?" I said.

"I don't know the exact words," Anna admitted. "But my father told me mostly what they said. They said the Nod'olian empire was going to be destroyed. And nothing would save it—unless everyone changed their ways and followed a virtuous path. And they said, a Virtuous One would come from another world and show us how to turn Nod'ol back into London."

Hairs rose on my scalp.

"Everyone was frightened of it, at first. My father said

because of *The Writing on the Wall,* everyone almost *did* change. But King Ignis laughed at it all, and he burned all the books and newspapers that printed the words, and he had the words on the wall destroyed, and—well, it all became a big joke."

"I saw that wall!" I said, remembering Queen Honoria and the reporter both staring at the marble that had been chiseled away.

Anna sat on the metal rail of a track.

"That's why the winter solstice festival is called Masked Virtue," she explained. "Because everyone made a joke of it. King Ignis changed his name to King Prudence, and since then, they've named all the illusionists after sort-of virtues, and they still have Masked Virtue every year. It's all a big joke to them. It . . . it sometimes would make my father cry."

Anna's eyes glistened at her hands.

Lockwood adjusted the rifles slung over his shoulders.

I placed a hand on Anna's shoulder.

"It's all right," I said, kindly.

"Done catching our breaths?" Lockwood said abruptly. "Theater isn't far; I see the domes. Come on, Johnny, stop slowing us down."

Lockwood led the way after that, storming over the crumbling walkways. As we drew closer, the brick walls gave way to pocked marble and overgrown hedges. Laughter wafted over the foliage, and several minutes later we emerged from the weeds into an open pavilion filled with Nod'olian miners. Above us their ships bobbed, chained to the docking towers, and they milled and danced gracelessly about the terrace, drinking colored liquid from thin glasses, talking, laughing in rasping laughs, and sharing fantillium masks with each other. They all wore diseased-looking feathers, which hung from their coats and sleeves and masks, making the gathering look like a flock of drunken birds. Everything smelt of burned orthogonagen and sour sugar. Even the harpsichord music was out of tune.

Lockwood took Anna's hand and we pulled back against the hedge walls as crimson guardsmen appeared at the other end of the terrace. They silently dragged with them an overlarge man with a gray pointed beard, buggy eyes blinking through his yellow mask, and feathers jutting from his torn clothes like a ruffled blackbird. I recognized Edward—my miner—immediately.

"His Highness!" said Lockwood.

"Not in this world," I said in a low voice. I hurried along the sides of the terrace, past the musicians and behind the table filled with scraps of food, still out of notice yet close enough to hear what was going on.

At the end of the stream of masked guardsmen, Queen

Honoria strode from the labyrinthine hedges, pistol at her hip. The music halted. Constantine flanked her side, wearing a tiger's mask of orange and black jewels.

Every miner in the pavilion ceased dancing, backed away, and bowed deeply. Queen Honoria ignored all of them, paying attention only to the mewling, whimpering mass of Edward that the masked guardsmen threw at her feet.

"I—I—I'm not hiding him!" he whimpered, covering his face. "I *swear*!"

"Of course you're not hiding him," Queen Honoria spat. "You would have told us far before now if you were. We're just giving you a friendly *warning*."

Crack. The marble tile by Edward's hand shattered. He screamed and scrambled back into the crimson guard, biting his knuckle. The bullet Queen Honoria had fired still steamed in the center of the broken tile.

Queen Honoria holstered her steam pistol and flicked her hand, and the crimson guard was at her side once more, leaving Edward on the marble, a lump of quivering feathers. Anna and Lockwood had joined me in the shadows of the hedge, warily watching the scene. Anna gripped my arm, hard, as Constantine hulked through the dancers after Queen Honoria, his mask of jewels flashing.

"He's not here, all right?" he growled. "We're wasting our time! *You* promised we'd find Anna first!"

Twigs dug into my back. Lockwood made a sound in his throat.

Queen Honoria ignored Constantine, her eyes continuing to search over the dancers, the musicians, and finally—with cold, beady severity—stopping on me. Her eyes narrowed through her mask. I could clearly read what she was thinking: *Someone is not dressed for a ball. . . .*

A scream ripped the air.

A feathered woman among the flock of miners on the terrace pitched with violent jolts, throwing herself against the other dancers, clawing at the eyeholes of their masks. The miners responded by falling back against each other, scrambling out of her way and crying in broken voices, "Riven!"

In a streak of movement, the woman threw herself at Queen Honoria.

Utter terror flashed on Queen Honoria's face. She yanked the pistol from the holster at her hip and fired it.

The woman miner fell mid-lunge and crumpled at Queen Honoria's feet. Trembling, Queen Honoria holstered her gun, wiped sweat away from the edges of her mask, and gulped a breath.

Almost as quickly, she was smiling sweetly. It was a horrible thing, that smile. She seemed to have too many teeth for her mouth.

"It's all right," she said to the miners, who were as ruffled as real birds. "Back to dancing, please. And for heavens' sake, if you're at that stage of Rivening, shoot yourselves so I *don't have to*!"

She snapped about and made to leave with masked guard and Constantine, who stormed back into the maze as though he couldn't wait to get lost. Queen Honoria paused a moment, then swept back to the Rivened woman's side and stripped the fantillium mask from her face. She pressed it against her own face and inhaled deeply. It only took a few seconds of breathing before her eyes relaxed and her hand ceased trembling.

A moment, and Queen Honoria cast the mask aside. It clattered beside the fallen woman.

"Back to the theater," she commanded her guard. "Where it's safe."

They disappeared into the tangle. The figure of the woman on the ground shuddered with final breaths. I made to go to her side and was held back by Lockwood.

"Don't," he growled.

I shook him off and ran to the dying, broken figure anyway. Kneeling by her side, I gently removed her porcelain mask. Swollen eyes sagged to her neck, two noses and five nostrils and a mouth that drooped beyond her chin—and even teeth growing at her throat—marred what might have once been a pretty face.

She expired in my arms, her many eyes glazing over. I allowed a moment before I laid her head down. The miners swirled in a dance around us. Somehow they had already forgotten about her.

I withdrew from the terrace unsteadily, beyond the dancers to the giant metal beams of a vertical dock, enshrouded in shadows and hedges. Lockwood and Anna had retreated here, and I joined them. They paid me no attention as I collapsed against the beam, pulled off my mask, and let the night air cool the sweat on my face.

Lockwood was trimming his thumbnails with Lord Glamwell's hunting dagger, speaking in a lazy drawl: "This other illusionist, Constantine," he was saying. "Know him, do you?"

"Of course not," said Anna, glowering at her feet. "He's practically royalty."

"Only he seemed dead set on finding you."

"Well, I don't know why," said Anna stubbornly, pulling her tangle of hair back and tucking it into the collar of her oversized coat. Her eyes caught me, and they brightened. "Jonathan! Oh—Jonathan. You look sick."

I shook my head. Seeing the woman die had reminded me how Hannah had illusion-died in my arms, and the urgency of finding the theater hit me full in the gut.

"We've got to get to the theater. *Now!*" I said. I made to dive back into the maze.

"Johnny, wait!" Lockwood seethed, grabbing me and pulling back, pushing the three of us into the shadows. Footfalls had broken through the hedges.

It was Edward, who thudded to the docking lift from the Dance of Ravens, crouched and trembling still. He rubbed his hands over and over absentmindedly muttering to himself, and turning the docking wheel to summon the lift. He did not notice the three of us, huddled in the shadows a length away.

I glanced upward. Docked at the top of the vertical dock was what must have been Edward's ship: an old-fashioned machine that was something between a sea ship and a hot-air balloon, with exposed rigging and open deck. Far different from the sleek Arthurisian airships, with their long envelopes and great engines. A thought lit hope through me.

"Idea," I whispered to Anna and Lockwood, refitting my mask. "We'll fly to the theater. We'll get there before Queen Honoria and her masked guard do."

I slipped onto the lift with Edward. Lockwood and Anna hurried in after, squashing us together, just as the gates closed. That pressed Anna against Lockwood's chest, and Lockwood looked as though he didn't mind this in the least. I had a marvelous view of Edward's armpit, his feathers jabbing my ear and face. He smelled of sweat.

"Hello, Edward," I said as the lift hummed up to the dock.

"What? What?" said Edward, snapping out of his own thoughts. He looked at me with disgust, sniffing. "Well, what do you want?"

I pulled my mask off with flair, giving Edward the full view of my face, complete with broken glasses.

Lockwood kicked my shins. Edward the Miner squealed like a girl and bit his knuckles.

"Fancy we ride with you?" I said.

CHAPTER 15

"I am going to be in *so much trouble*!" Edward cried in the highest voice I'd ever heard come from a man. "So so *so* much trouble!"

Minutes before, he had hurried us onto his ship, pale as a ghost, and "battened down the hatches." Which is to say, locked every door we passed and closed every shutter on the windows as his navigator cast off. We found ourselves in a dark little game room in the center of his ship, with large overstuffed chairs, swaths of fabric, and a threadbare billiards table in the middle of the room.

It smelled of old wood and thick cigar smoke. Unlike the Arthurisian ships, which were beasts of sleek steel and machinery, this ship was wood, and the furniture was either nailed down or lashed to the sides with fraying ropes. Dim lanterns swung from the ceiling.

A manservant, dressed in swatches of fabrics cobbled

together in varying blacks and grays and wearing a half mask, brought in tea. Starving, we threw our masks aside and seized upon it. The dry biscuits were gone in an instant.

The manservant did not leave. He stared at me, and when I finally noticed him at the peak moment my cheeks were stuffed with biscuits, he bowed deeply to me. He wore a gold kerchief tied around his neck.

Edward, huddled in a large mass on the main sofa, kept looking around and over his shoulder, rubbing his gloved hands together. The fingers of his gloves were misshapen and thick. I convulsively felt my own splitting fingers, reminded that I was Rivening as well. I suddenly wasn't hungry anymore.

"Fly you to the theater?" Edward echoed my request. "But—but—but—I *can't*! They've searched this ship three times already! They thought I was hiding you! And now that I actually *am* . . . !" He was reduced to whimpers.

"I've never heard anyone whine so much," said Lockwood.

"And not just you! The—the—" He pointed a trembling finger at Anna, who sat on the opposite sofa, politely drinking tea and ignoring him. "The Sacrificial Offering! *Eep!* And I don't know who that fellow is, but I am *certain* he is up to no good!" He fell into the mass of pillows on the sofa, a ball of jutting feathers, and buried his masked face in his hands. "I am going to be in *so much trouble*."

"Can you believe he's a king in Arthurise?" said Lockwood.

"Look, you won't get caught," I said. "Have your navigator steer us to the theater. Send down a line. Lockwood and I climb down, you sail a turnabout, come back, we'll be waiting, and you bring us back up. Nothing to worry about."

"*Everything* to worry about!" he snapped back. "You can't just—just break into the theater! They've got masked guards everywhere in there! They have *pistols*!"

Lockwood and I threw back our cloaks, revealing the steam rifles slung over our shoulders.

"Oh," said Edward.

"Edward," said Anna, setting her teacup down with a *clink*. "You're an air miner, aren't you? Don't air miners have fantillium on their ships?"

We all paused. I let this sink in, light filling me, and turned to Anna, a smile growing on my face. She grinned mischievously back. It made the scar under her eye wrinkle.

"You have fantillium on board?" I said to Edward.

Edward burrowed deeper into his sofa, wringing his hands.

"Edward," I said, ideas growing within me like frost

on a window, "have you ever had a *private illusioning* before?"

"A—a what?"

"An illusionarium. Just for you. On this ship. Without Her Ladyship or any of the other miners?"

Edward stared at me with wide buggy eyes.

"My own illusionarium?" he whispered.

"Edward," I said, kneeling in front of his sofa, "if you help us, I will illusion for you something so *incredible*, so achingly beautiful, it will knock the beard from your face!"

Edward blinked and blinked and blinked.

"You will?" he whispered.

"On your life. Right here. In this very room. The moment we return."

Edward gripped my hands in a sudden movement.

"My boy!" he said hoarsely. "Yes! *Yes!* My boy, let us steer, *steer*, I say! Onward to the theah-tah!"

He released me and bounded from his sofa, lolloping out of the room and singing hoarsely, looking like a flapping, overstuffed bird. The door to the game room slid closed behind him. Lockwood grinned.

"I might like this Edward better after all," he said. "Any chance we could switch him out for the real one?"

I collapsed on the sofa next to Anna, overwhelmed. We were going to get the cure. We had fantillium. We'd be home before the stars came out, and with a day to spare. Mum and Hannah would be well again, I'd be off to the university, and Alice might even want to write me. After I'd properly healed, of course. I glanced at my thumbs— still splayed from each other, purple at the ends—and grabbed a musty pillow, kneading it.

As the lanterns in the game room swung with the ship's ascent, Anna quizzed me again about the observatory doors—iron latches, wood pocked from ice storms—and Edward's servants visited the room, setting down another plate of biscuits or dusting the billiards table or just peering at me from the doorway. When I looked back at them, they fled.

"They seem fascinated with you, Johnny," Lockwood said after another maidservant left the room. "Don't suppose it has to do with your extra fingers, does it?"

I tossed a pillow at him, which he dodged, grinning.

"They think . . . you're the Virtuous One," said Anna quietly.

Lockwood and I both frowned at her. Anna blushed at her teacup.

"The person from *The Writing on the Wall*?" I said.

Anna nodded, eyes still fixed desperately on her cup.

"What? No!" I said. "I mean—I'm nothing special. Anyway, I can't stay here. I have to go back and cure the Venen. Save my own empire, all that."

Anna's blue eyes glistened as she drew a hand through her dark curls, awkwardly trying to smooth them. Her dress was still streaked with mud. By the way she tried to disappear into the sofa's cushions, I could tell she rather wished she hadn't spoken up.

"Well, it isn't Queen Honoria," she said in a tiny voice. "I know that much. She became the queen by convincing the miners that *she* was the Virtuous One. She had the masked guard fight the Riven out of the theater. Still. Everyone knows it's not her."

I remembered our conversation with Queen Honoria in the room full of plants. She'd seemed utterly dead on saving this world. "She certainly *believes* she's the One," I admitted. "She told us nothing meant more to her than restoring Nod'ol. Remember, Lockwood?"

"Not really, no," said Lockwood. "Mostly I just remember her trying to kill us. At any rate, what kind of zealot believes in tripe like prophecies? Fodder for idiots who walk around sucking airship offal—"

"My father believed in it," said Anna.

"—and are actually intelligent, bright sorts who have given it a lot of thought, of course," Lockwood finished. "Of course."

"*Believed*, Anna?" I said, frowning. "He doesn't believe it anymore?"

"I meant, *believes*," said Anna, nearly toppling her

teacup. "He believes in it still. Of course he does. And—Jonathan—who's to say it *isn't* you? You're from another world. *You stood up to Queen Honoria.* How can it not be you?"

The words soaked into the furniture like red punch. Anna's face glowed with fervency. I shifted, uncomfortably. I rather didn't want to spend any more time in Nod'ol than I had to.

"'Course it's not Johnny," Lockwood drawled. He stood casually at the side of the room, leaning against a display case of an old sea ship. "Can't be him, can it? He's toddling back to his aerial city tonight. Virtuous One has to stay in Nod'ol. Maybe . . . well, maybe I'm the one all the hullabaloo is about. Ever thought about that?"

"You, Lockwood?" I scoffed. "Part of a prophecy? Come on. You're not thinking of staying here, are you?"

Lockwood shrugged, nonchalant.

"Dunno," he said lightly to the model ship. "Sort of feel funny about leaving Anna alone here. Took the Knightly Oath. Chivalry, that sort of thing. Can't go back on that, even with my ranking stripped."

He glanced at Anna, who was blushing even redder at her teacup, and I caught that Look again in his one eye. The watching-airships-exploding helpless Look.

I stifled a cough. Lockwood was dead in love!

What, already? It was months before I'd even *noticed* Alice. I still hadn't plucked up the courage to talk to her.

My thoughts overthought. Well, Lockwood was an *absolute* sort of person, wasn't he? He wouldn't fall in love like tripping over a brick. He was the sort to rear back, run, *catapult* over the side of an airship's railing, and fall, fall, *fall* into love before smacking into the Ocean of Delirious Wanderings.[22]

I felt rather peevish about this. Anna was *my* sister, after all! Who did he think he jolly well was?

I scrutinized Anna, still gripping her teacup, and blinked. I couldn't tell her feelings on the subject. Her dark lashes brushed her cheek as she remained looking down.

"I could help you find your father," said Lockwood gently. "If you want."

Anna blinked rapidly.

"I . . . don't know," she finally said.

Lockwood, who had laid his soul bare before her, hastily retreated, anger and embarrassment across his face.

"Right, well," he muttered. " 'Course. Sort it out later. Better go up on deck. Bet we're close to the theater."

---

[22] Which would sever his limbs from his body on impact, causing Death by Unmitigated Joy.

Lockwood was right—by now, among the sea of airships, we were close enough to the theater that its light glowed over us. We watched the maze below turn from overgrown hedge and brick to trimmed foliage and polished marble. The pennants that drooped from the sides of the painted envelope above us barely fluttered in the wind. That's because there was no wind to speak of. Nod'olian air was stagnant and smelled of over-boiled laundry. The only breeze came from the ship's propeller.

Lockwood and I both wore our masks and the layers of coats we'd found in Lord Glamwell's manor. I adjusted the rifle slung over my shoulder. I knew how to shoot—not like Lockwood, of course, but every academy boy at the age of fourteen had to take Empirical Combat 101. But every time I shot a target, the Reformed Puritan inside me kicked me in the proverbial shins. I was a surgeon, not a soldier. My plan was to slip in, grab the cure, slip out; stick to drawing blood and sawing off legs, that's my style.

Anna stood a length away from us at the aft of the ship, staring daggers at the maze below, her teeth gritted and her arms crossed. Lockwood and I had had a quick discussion minutes before, and I'd pulled her aside and told her (in very calm and measured tones) that we really, really thought it was a much better idea if she stayed here and made certain Edward stuck to the plan and anyway, it was much safer if she didn't come along where there might be gunfire.

She took it pretty well.

"Stay *here*?" she cried in a voice that could break glass. "Who do you think you are? You need me!"

"Come on, Anna," I said. "You could barely lift that rail-yard pipe! D'you really think you could even climb down the line?"

"Oh, and *you* can?" she said, her eyes blazing. "Lockwood! You'd better not be behind this!"

Lockwood, putting the rifle he was cleaning back together, had suddenly acquired incredible powers of deafness.

"Keep an eye on Edward," I told her. "Make sure he comes back for us."

"I *know* that theater!" Anna seethed. "You'll both get lost!"

"We get caught, we only get killed, Anna," said Lockwood coldly. He shouldered his rifle. "What do you think will happen to *you*?"

And Anna was reduced to blushing furiously, looking embarrassed and wanting to break Lockwood's neck at the same time.

Now, as the theater roof drew near, Edward's servant handed Lockwood and me each a coiled line attached to the docking anchor. Anna's lips were razor thin and she refused to look at either of us. Lockwood cast a glance at her.

"Think I could ask for a token?" he asked me, nodding to her. It was an airguardsman tradition, asking a girl for a ribbon or lock of hair before they left to battle.

I glanced at Anna.

"Not if you like your eye," I said.

"Ah, well."

And all at once, the theater roof extended far below us, a landscape of green panels, all slopes and gables, chimneys and grime. Lockwood and I threw the lines overboard and they uncoiled to the rooftop.

In a blur of muddy white, Anna grabbed Lockwood's line, threw herself over the railing, sliding down the cord until her arms released and she fell onto the roof's slope, tumbling over and over until she hit a gable.

"Anna!" Lockwood yelled. He leapt over the railing after her, rappelling down the line and releasing halfway, and several seconds later he landed lightly on the roof. I followed suit, graceless, the line burning my gloved hands until I hit the roof and did not die.

Lockwood had run to Anna's side by the time I got to my feet and had chased after him across the gritty metal landscape. Lockwood grabbed Anna and pulled her to her feet, but didn't let go. His face was deathly white. Anna's hands were bleeding.

"Ending was a bit of a jolt," she said, laughing weakly.

"What d'you think you're doing?" Lockwood said angrily. "You think this is a joke?"

"I *know* the theater!" she pled. "I can help! I can't just stay on the ship and—and—and agonize!"

"Better on the ship than in Constantine's arms!" Lockwood snarled back.

Anna's blue eyes glistened.

"I—I can't let you die," she said.

Lockwood mouthed wordlessly.

"Da—*darn* you, Anna," he finally said. "I don't know whether to—to embrace you or throw myself off this building!"

"Don't let's do them at the same time," Anna said with a laugh. In a smooth motion she reached up, and tousled Lockwood's blond hair.

Lockwood looked as though he'd been hit by a brick.

"Right, don't mind me," I said, arriving at their side, winded. "Only I don't think there's much time for, you know . . . being soppish. . . ." I glanced up at Edward's ship. It had already sailed beyond the roof, lines dangling. Edward had given us exactly thirty minutes to fetch the cure.

"What . . . ?" said Lockwood, dazed. "Right. 'Course we don't have time, Johnny. We have to find that cure. Why are you always slowing us down? Anna, you wrap your arms around my neck as tight as you can. Stay right by me and not a hair of your head'll be lost!"

Anna bit her lip, inhaled, and wrapped her arms around his neck and shoulders. Lockwood carried her to the ledge, crouched, and swung from the roof to a ledge along the wall like a shadow. He carried Anna against his chest like it was nothing.

"We're going to splatter on the cement below!" Anna said through gritted teeth.

"The cement will never be prettier!" said Lockwood happily.

I followed after, lowering myself to the ledge, fighting against gravity and vertigo. We were at least seven stories up. I had to grab a carved pillar between two windows to keep from overbalancing. The wall extended out in long rows of windows to either side of me. In the distance stood the Tower of London. High above us, the sea of airships.

And among them, rumbling straight above the theater, a ship's hull trimmed with crimson, red pennants dripping from the envelope like streams of blood. It shadowed us with its vastness. An emotionless red mask of a guardsman peered down at us from over the railing. Fear stole the strength from my muscles.

"That's Queen Honoria's ship!" Anna yelled.

"Spotted!" Lockwood sounded far too cheery. "Windows, Johnny! We're going to bash them in! Hold tight, Anna, and close your eyes—"

With Anna still clinging to him, Lockwood grasped the eaves above the window in front of him. I wrestled my muscles into submission and copied Lockwood, grabbing the ledge above the window next. We pulled ourselves up, kicked back against the window, gathering momentum with each swing. One final shove off from the glass and we bashed through it, feet first.

I released and careened through the broken pane, toppling over shards of glass and crashing, again, into more glass, knocking against wall, water and flowers pouring over my head. Two minutes of standing, banging into more porcelain, falling, crashing, more crashing, a rain of flowers, and I found my feet.

I stood in the middle of a large suite, decorated in all shades of green, and now, all sorts of broken vases and flowers. Divinity's suite!

Lockwood and Anna were nowhere to be found. They must have bashed through a window that led to another room, or the hall.

"Hello?" Divinity's voice chimed from beyond the sitting room wall. "Who's there?"

I dove for the door in long strides. She arrived at her bedroom door, only wearing a frayed bathrobe, just as I slammed the door behind me. This was going all wrong. With any luck we *wouldn't* see every illusionist and masked guard in the city.

My heart pounded so hard my vision pulsed. I ran along the deserted hall, searching desperately for Lockwood and Anna. They were nowhere. We'd planned, if we were separated, to still follow through and find the cure. We'd meet up on the roof in thirty minutes.

Frustrated, I hurried down the hall, checking around the corners before diving into more corridors, running down stairs, until I recognized the familiar main hall that led to the lobby. Rifle banging against my back, I ran through the massive arched doorway and into the mezzanine above the marble floor.

The lobby was deserted.

The light of the chandelier flickered and cast gentle shadows across the walls.

The velvet stairs muffled my footfalls.

And there, in the glass of the round display case between the split stairways, stood the little brown bottle. In a moment I stood before it.

I pulled off my mask, sweat fogging up my glasses, unsure of what to do. I didn't have a key. Well—I'd broken the theater window and about a hundred glass vases, so what was a little more? I threw myself against the case.

It fell to the floor. Glass smashed. Thousands of shards rippled across the marble. The brown bottle rolled off the velvet with a *clinkety clink clink*. I swooped down and the bottle was in my pocket.

My ears thudded. All right, time to meet on the roof. I made for the stairs, and then stopped. A slip of paper among the wreckage pulled me back to the overturned cabinet.

PASSAGE TICKET
Airship #278, Theater Station
Destination: Sussex, dock 4

I stared at the ticket. The words swam.

Anna's way out of the city.

On impulse, I snatched it from the broken pieces and shoved it into my pocket. And—a slip of paper, next to it, caught my eye.

ANNA.

I picked it up and tore it in half, wishing I could do it in front of Constantine's beastly face.

"Piece of filth," I said, glowering. I cast the pieces to the floor.

Bang.

A pair of glass doors behind me banged open. I whipped around, rifle hitting my shoulder, to see masked guards pouring through the door, and an unending stream of red.

Bang. The pair of glass doors to my side. Eyeless masks on crimson figures poured through. Crimson figures dropped from airship lines from all sides outside the theater lobby. . . .

Bang. The door to my other side.

Bang. The door behind the stairs.

Bang.

Bang.

Bang.

"Oh, *great*!" I said, and bounded up the stairs. They poured like blood from an artery after me.

Through the archway. Down the corridor. Up the stairs. It felt slow, like trying to swim the moat all over again. I lost sight of them, but their sticky silence clung to me and dragged me down.

I couldn't breathe. I had to rest. I pivoted around a corner to a dead-end hall and threw myself into the nearest door, slamming it behind me.

I was encased in darkness. My eyes adjusted to the sparse furniture, and my nose adjusted to the smell of thick medicinal tea. I swallowed, catching my breath, examining the large four-poster bed that sat in the shadows at the far end of the room.

Someone slept in it.

I pressed the door against my back. Sweat dripped down my neck.

The person in the bed, a woman, didn't move. When she inhaled, the breath rattled in her throat. She was ill. Always the surgeon, I immediately hastened to her side.

I recognized her before I'd reached the bed. Angry, arching eyebrows, tiny mouth and eyes, all severe as steel, hands that looked like they had bandaged a thousand wounds.

It was Lady Florel.

CHAPTER 16

"Heinrich?"

Lady Florel's cracked, hard voice rose from the bed like a ghost from the grave. Each breath rasped. I marveled at how much she looked like Queen Honoria—but with black veins that covered her neck and cheeks. Her arms, too, had become mottled black. The Venen.

"Well, come closer," she commanded severely. "Let me see you."

I hurried and propped her up on the pillows to help her to breathe, and felt the pulse at her neck. I hardly felt it, it was so weak. She was close to death. And yet, here she was, barking commands at me. She really was made of steel.

"Heinrich Gouden is my father," I said. "I'm his son, Jonathan. Lady Florel, how long have you been here? Have you been in the theater this whole time? Did Queen

Honoria bring you here? She must have—"

"Hush, boy," she barked. "You're making my head pound. Stand up straight."

I stood up straight.

"I—thought Queen Honoria had killed you," I muttered, emotions twisting inside me.

"Ha!" Lady Florel's laughter turned into a cough. I quickly poured her a cup of cold tea from her bedside teapot. "Queen Honoria," she continued, "is a vindictive little recreant who is too cowardly to even see my death. She's died before—that ridiculous illusion-dying, at least—and whatever she saw, she's afraid of it. And as *such* she is afraid to *kill* me—"

She broke into whisper-coughs again. I recalled the look of utter terror on Queen Honoria's face, when the Rivening woman had almost attacked her.

"She's letting you die anyway," I muttered, disgusted.

"She's keeping me alive," Lady Florel wheezed. "Just. I am only administered just enough antitoxin to be kept alive. . . ."

She trailed off, leaning weakly into the mess of pillows with guttural breaths, and said nothing more. My hands were clenched so tightly they shook. Queen Honoria!

I had the cure.

I pulled the bottle from my pocket, and the brown liquid swished inside.

Three doses. If I used one, there'd still be enough for Mum and Hannah. My father could reconstruct the cure from the bottle's label. I hesitated for just a moment, and my father's voice rang in my chest: *My own son cannot even tell right from wrong. . . .*

"Yes I *can*," I said firmly, and unsnapped and uncorked the glass lid.

I mixed a third of the bottle with her cup of cold tea, quickly, expecting the masked guard to burst through the door at any moment.

They did not. With especial care, I brought it to Lady Florel's thin lips.

BANG.

A distant shot rang out. I jolted and nearly spilled the cup.

"JOHNNY!"

"Lockwood!" I said. I hastily helped Lady Florel finish the last of the tea. She fell into unconsciousness as softly as a sigh. I prayed it wasn't too late.

"Johnny boy!" Lockwood yelled, louder this time.

BLAM BLAM BLAM. The gunshots were followed by a massive crash of glass exploding.

"Jooooh-nnnnyyyyy!" Lockwood yelled again. "I know you're hee-eeere! You've summoned the ruddy guard from the gates of somewhere not very niii-iiice! JOHNNY!!"

Lockwood's voice drove my feet into action. In a blaze I flew out of the room to his rescue and crashed full-on into the torn-uniformed, rifle-bearing, unmasked, flashing-eyed Lockwood.

"Idiot!" he yelled, throwing me out of the line of fire. He brought the steam rifle to his shoulder and shots rang out. Masked guards barreled at us, pouring down the hall in a red barrage. Two of them fell, silent as a snowfall. Pistols fell from their hands. Beyond them, more fallen masked guards. In Lockwood's wake, he'd left them strewn down the hall like roses. I felt sick.

We retreated, taking cover behind a massive heap of crystals at the end of the hall. A glance at the ceiling, revealing torn bolts, confirmed it was a fallen chandelier.

"You shot the chandelier down, Lockwood?" I yelled as bullets ricocheted past my head and jangled as they shot the prisms of the chandelier. I ducked down and shook the rifle from my shoulder.

"Of course not!" Lockwood yelled, his rifle firing so rapidly it fogged the air with steam. "I climbed up the wall and pulled it down with my weight, what do you think?"

"Oh!" I said. "Right! The old climb-up-the-wall-and-tear-the-chandelier-away-from-its-bolts maneuver! Where's Anna?"

"She's—"

A crimson figure appeared through the fog, its pistol levered at Lockwood's head.

Like a flash I raised the rifle to my shoulder, aimed, and squeezed the trigger. The pistons hissed, and a shot rang out.

The masked guard dropped his pistol and fell to the rug with eerie silence.

I dropped my rifle with shaking hands and scrambled to pick it up, air choking my throat.

"All right there, surgeon?" said Lockwood, glancing at me. "Take a breather. Second time you've saved my life—thanks."

I nodded, still gulping steam, and managed to pull the pistol back up. If I ever had to face combat again it would be too soon.

"I've got it, Lockwood. Let's get out of here—"

A giggle sounded behind us like scratched glass. I'd recognize that wonderfully chalk-on-slate laugh any day. Divinity. She sat crouched in the doorway behind us, barricaded with us behind the chandelier, trapped at the end of the hall. She was biting her pink lip and laughing as merrily as if she were attending a puppet show. Her hands had been tied together with what looked like a hair ribbon.

"You are going to be in *so much trouble*, Jonathan," she said, looking absolutely delighted.

"You tied up a girl, Lockwood?" I said.

"Yeah, *real* angel. Tried to kill me with this—" Lockwood aimed a tiny green steam pistol, studded with emeralds, at an oncoming masked guard, and shot.

"Queen Honoria's going to catch you," she said smugly. "She's going to tear your thumbnails from your—"

"Shut *up*!" said Lockwood and I in unison.

Divinity broke into chiming laughs all over again. The bathrobe she wore had slipped down her shoulder, revealing the upper part of her corset—my face reddened— and exposing something more at the base of her neck.

A swollen slit of an eye stared back at me.

I grabbed Divinity and pulled her to her feet.

"All right, tell them to stop!" I said, going against every iota of my upbringing and strong-arming her past the chandelier barricade. A sea of masked guardsmen legions deep had appeared at the end of the hall, sending hailstorms of bullets, then halting up short as Divinity showed herself. "Tell them to stop and put their pistols down. *Now*."

Divinity rolled her green eyes and with great exaggeration stepped forward into the line of fire. The masked guardsmen lowered their rifles.

"Stop," she said lazily. She shook her golden hair back. "Stop fighting already. These silly little boys, they're just playing, aren't you, you silly little boys?"

"That's right, we're having a *tea party*," I said.

"With *guns*," said Lockwood as the masked guardsmen that filled the hall froze in perfect formation, like chess pieces in a stalemate. The eye on Divinity's shoulder blinked blearily at me.[23]

"Lockwood!" Anna's voice broke through the silence. "Lockwood—I've found the stairway to the roof—"

A door down the hall yielded and Anna appeared, throwing herself into the mass of masked guards. Before anyone could even react, Lockwood had leapt over the chandelier and grabbed her by the waist.

"All right, girly," Lockwood yelled at Divinity, who stood there, both petulant and amused. "Keep them happy, keep them still while we get out of here, and we won't shoot you in the eye. *You know which one.*"

That wiped the smile off of Divinity's face.

I caught up to Lockwood and Anna, and we were off, through the door at the side of the hall, barreling down corridors, the lamps along the walls a blur, and careening through a doorway into a rickety stairwell.

"All right, *now* you can kill them!" Divinity's voice cheerfully rang out. "Shoot them dead!"

"What a lovely girl!" Lockwood snarled as the three

---

[23] *Niiiiiice.*

of us raced up the stairs, two at a time. "I fancy she's got *loads* of beaus!"

"Yes, someone you bring home to Mother," I said.

Shots hissed and pinged below us. We extended our leaps to three stairs at a time, and moments later we fell through a door at the top of the stairs, up an even ricketier set of stairs, and ending at a dim room full of old props. Anna led us out an old gable door—and the stagnant black air of night. The grit of green tile ground under our feet.

And there, looming over the theater, Edward's creaking airship whirred. Two lines still hung over the side of its deck, brushing the sloping rooftop.

Lockwood pounded me on the shoulder. "The ruddy coward came back! Ha-ha! I hardly believe it!"

I ran to the line and began climbing, hand over hand, pulling, reaching, pulling up again. My muscles wept for their loss of innocence. With Anna's arms wrapped tightly around his neck, Lockwood climbed the line as easy as a knife to pudding.

Below us, the masked guard poured from the roof gables and stopped short, eerie masks peering up at us, and growing smaller as the ship rumbled forward. They lowered their rifles, still staring.

"Quiz yourself on those observatory doors, Johnny!" Lockwood said as we fell over the railing onto the large empty deck of Edward's ship. My muscles screamed and twitched in agony. "Tonight!" Lockwood crowed, "tonight we save the Empire!"

"We did it! We did it!" said Anna weakly, collapsing against the railing. "Huzzah!"

"Just," said Lockwood, rising to his feet. We were alone on the abandoned deck, the balloon above us echoing our voices in a booming, hollow way, our clothes torn and all three of us beaten thoroughly and marvelously happy. "Nearly thought I'd lost you," Lockwood continued. "The way you threw yourself into the pit of masked guardsmen— might be a good habit to break, Anna, throwing yourself at Death without thinking."

"Better me than you," said Anna haughtily.

"*No*, Anna," said Lockwood. "*Not* better you than me. Look, airguardsmen, we're all right with dying. It's our job. Anyway, I've told you, I'm not worth dying over."

"Jonathan, are you all right?" said Anna, who had noticed that I wasn't as jovial as the both of them. I was gripping the bottle of antitoxin in my pocket, pensive.

"Lady Florel is down there, Lockwood," I said. "In the theater."

And to Anna's wide eyes and Lockwood's grim face, I told them everything; finding Lady Florel, how she was only just being kept alive, giving her a dose of the antitoxin—

and even how Queen Honoria was afraid of death.

Anna was as white as the snow on Fata when I'd finished. Lockwood was still stolidly grim.

"We've got to go back and get her," I said.

"One thing at a time, Johnny," he said. "We save Arthurise first."

"I wonder what she saw," Anna whispered. "Queen Honoria. When she fantillium-died."

"Who knows?" said Lockwood. He shifted, almost as though he were about to wrap his arms around Anna and pull her to his chest. He refrained and instead said, "Demons, maybe. Brimstone. You religious, Johnny? I bet you are."

"Well—yes. My family is Reformed Puritan," I said.

"Never seen you wear black."

"Well," I coughed. "It *is* reformed. We don't really believe in a Lower World, though. Mostly the soul serves as intermediaries. Sending light sigs of prayers to heaven, that kind of thing. You?"

"'Course I'm not," Lockwood scoffed, then glanced at Anna and quickly revised. "That is to say—not *a lot*. I'm Maritime Protestant, same as every airguardsman."

"Is that the religion that only goes to church on Christmas?" I said innocently.

"And Easter, please, don't cheat us. If there's a church near the port."

"And uses curse words in their prayers?"

"Shut up," Lockwood said, with another look at Anna. "No," he continued. "Celestial airships. That's what every airman looks forward to. If we captain our souls well in life, we pilot our own airship after death. Sailing among the stars, steering among the solar flares . . ."

We turned our eyes upward to the sky, which was mostly filled with Edward's airship balloon and riggings. But even through the glass beyond, we could see the prickles of stars. That was a ruddy nice thought, I decided, living in the eternities with stars and moons in your wake.

"Anna," I said, turning to her. "Didn't you say you fantillium-died last year? What did you see?"

Anna couldn't seem to talk.

"Well, we can talk about it later," I said hastily, embarrassed I'd brought it up. "Let's illusion the doors. Oh—wait, Anna—" I dug into my pocket, producing the airship ticket. "Got this for you. That's nice, isn't it?"

I presented the paper to her. She stared at it with wide eyes, then looked at me, then looked at it. She slipped it from my hands and read it, and her eyes grew shiny.

"A ticket out of the city," said Lockwood in a hollow voice, reading the ticket over her shoulder. "So. I guess Johnny kept his promise after all."

Tears began to stream down Anna's face. It wasn't noisy crying—the tears came with utter silence. It was a Weep.

"Oh, hulloa, it's not that wonderful," I said, sensing something was getting out of hand. I pulled Anna into a hug, and she silent-cried into my shoulder. "I mean, I sort of took it from Divinity. Hannah—I mean, *Anna*. Stop. Don't cry. All right? I'm doing pretty badly at cheering you up, aren't I? You know, save all this crying for when you see your father, hey?"

"My father," Anna sobbed into my shoulder.

"You'll see him soon," I said.

"My—my father," Anna wept. "Oh, Jonathan. My father is dead."

It was like being stabbed. Lockwood and I blinked at each other over her hair.

"What?" I said.

Anna wiped her eyes with her sleeve. It took her a moment to dry off enough to stitch together an answer for me.

"The masked guard killed him," she said to my shoulder. "They took me away and they burned the *Compass Rose*. He's dead. I couldn't tell you before because you look *so much like him*, but now you're here with an actual ticket and you nearly had holes blown through you for it and I *hate* myself for that—"

She burst into a renewed round of tears. I pulled her

in to my shoulder again, remembering the horrible words I'd last spoken to Hannah. Strangely, I felt I could atone for them now.

"Come with us, Anna," I said.

Lockwood, a pace away, straightened. Anna hiccoughed and laughed.

"Sure," she said. "Just like that."

"Yeah, just like that," I said, growing more fervent. "Come with us. Tonight. Now. Anna, you'll *love* Arthurise! And Fata Morgana—I mean, the place is like an ice palace in the winter! And you'll never have to worry about going hungry or being chased or hurt or anything. Not ever again, Anna. Come with us."

Anna mouthed wordlessly.

"I—can't," she finally stammered. "Don't be stupid. I—I don't have any money or a home or anything—"

"Yes, you do," I said stolidly. "You'll be a part of my family. And my father will be your father, and my sister your sister, and me? Well, I'll be your brother. What's wrong with that?"

The tears streamed anew. Anna wrapped her arms around me, laughing and crying at the same time. I hugged her so tightly it lifted her feet off the ground.

"You'll love my sister," I said. "Ha! Actually, you'll probably fight, but—in a good way. And Mum—she has this rice dish, you'll never want to eat anything else again.

And my father. You'll like him, Anna. You'll like him very much, I think."

"Jonathan is very brotherly," said Lockwood, warily eyeing us.

Anna finally pulled away, flushing to her ears, still hiccoughing but beaming.

"Thank you," she whispered.

I shoved my hands in my pockets, fingers wrapped around the bottle of antitoxin, rocking on the balls of my feet, my ears burning but feeling so utterly *right*.

Anna turned about to Lockwood, who was leaning back against the deck's railing, his face a picture of sprezzatura. Only his eye gave him away. Wary. Like a creature about to get eaten.

"And you, Lockwood," said Anna, smiling. "Are you still going to stay here, in wonderful and enchanting Nod'ol? Or . . ."—Anna blushed a merry pink— ". . . will I still see you?"

Lockwood's eye widened. A smile grew on his face like the sun rising. Before he could open his mouth to speak, however, Anna cut him short with: "Wait. First. Your eye. How did you lose it? Sorry. I've been dying to ask that all day."

Lockwood laughed, then swept Anna up and set her onto the railing of the ship. Anna wound her arm through the rigging and leaned on the ropes, laughing as Lockwood pulled a dagger from his boot and began with: "Darkness! Winter over the Balearic Sea turned everything black, and miles away from my airguardsman ship, under the same storm in Madrid, the duke and duchess of Bourbon-Parma and their eleven children huddled in the shadows of the servants' quarters of their palace, gun blasts from the coup-d'état sounding in the halls, the exiled prime minister seeking vengeance—"

"And you're the closest airguardsman ship!" Anna exulted.

"You're getting ahead of the story," said Lockwood reproachfully. "Where was I? Oh, yes. Eleven frightened children, huddled together, scared for their very innocent lives—"

I pulled away from Lockwood's long-winded Brag about breeching Spanish airships and scaling palace walls, and for the first time, paid attention to the ship deck.

It was abandoned.

Lanterns swung slowly with the ship's bob.

Hairs rose on the back of my neck.

"Not to interrupt or anything," I said, "but shouldn't there be someone on deck? Edward's manservant—or—someone? Possibly? Lockwood? Am I actually noticing something before you?"

Lockwood dragged himself out of the story long enough to cast me an annoyed glare, which quickly snapped to attention when he saw the silent deck. The riggings around us creaked. The sea of airships whirred around us. Lockwood's brow creased.

The three of us dove for the hull door at once.

Our steps pounded and thudded through the spiral staircase as we descended into the belly of the ship. The silence thickened.

"Probably hiding behind one of his sofas, right?" said Lockwood. "Shivering on about getting caught—"

We burst into the game room with the overstuffed chairs and dim lighting—

Thwack—

White burst through my vision. Gloved hands grabbed me and wrenched my arms behind my back. Misshapen fingers dug into my wrists. The masked guard.

They filled the room, flanking every side, standing as a wall of soldiers. They grabbed Anna as she came through the doorway, dragging her to Constantine, who, arrayed in all layers of leather suits, stood by the polished table in the middle of the room. He clenched her to his side. She grew feral against his grip and fought tooth and nail.

It took four masked guardsmen to keep Lockwood from attacking and strangling Constantine with his bare hands. They threw him to the ground and shoved his head against the wood, removing the rifle from his shoulder.

"Anna!" said Lockwood, which earned him a kick in the throat.

"Yes, *Anna*," Constantine growled, "who is not *yours*."

Edward huddled behind one of his sofas, a mountain of anxiety, wringing his hands and biting his knuckles. His mask was askew and sweat dripped down his face.

"I'm sorry," he whimpered, tugging his beard. "I'm so sorry. They just *came*! I *knew* we would be in so much trouble! I knew it!"

The masked guard dragged us to the side of the room, and Queen Honoria's boot stepped in front of me. My eyes followed up her long coats to the mask that covered half her face. She was smiling.

"Ah, and the prodigal son," she said, "has returned. Kicking and screaming, of course, but he *has* returned."

CHAPTER 17

The masked guard held us hostage, and the ship navigated back to the theater, hovering above it long enough to bring Divinity on board. She'd dressed in a wreckage of a dress with a tall collar that covered the face growing from her neck. The emaciated reporter, too, joined us from the theater. He set up a camera tripod at the edge of the room with shaking hands. A gold piece of fabric was pinned to his frayed jacket pocket.

And all the while, the masked guard built a network of piping around the room, behind the sofas, connecting to a small boiler by the door. It hissed and gurgled.

Edward remained behind the sofa, moaning.

The masked guard had removed Anna from the room and returned with her as the boiler began to steam. She wore a new outfit of white—a long, patched gown that licked the floor, a bleached corset, a white jacket. Her hair had been brushed shiny, her face washed and powdered, covering her scar, and she stubbornly held her chin up. Lockwood made a sound from the corner of the room.

I was forced to the table, between Divinity and Constantine, wary of the situation. Queen Honoria was determined to finish the botched ceremonies from this morning, here and now on this ship. Her brown beady eyes shone from her wrinkled face as Anna was brought to the table.

"Your Highness," said Constantine as the pipes *hisshed* around us. "We don't need to sacrifice Anna. Why can't we kill him instead?" Constantine nodded his beastly mask at Lockwood. "He's worthless!"

"Yes, why can't you?" said Lockwood fiercely.

"Constantine," said Queen Honoria, ignoring both of them. "If Jonathan so much as illusions an ember, *shoot him.*"

Constantine leveled the rifle at me. I stared stonily at its barrel, then at his unnaturally bright eyes. They almost seemed to burn.

Hisssssss.

Steam burned my skin. The game room was immersed in a fog. I inhaled. Ice air prickled down my throat and stung my lungs. The room grew unbearably bright, and the smell of rotting wood and musty pillows engulfed us. Guardsmen turned the lamps down as my thoughts grew heavy and swirled in my head. Constantine's rifle seemed far away, and my agonized soul rested.

The masked guard pressed Anna down on the billiards table, her cheek flat against the green felt, her dark curls spilling over her shoulders. Her glistening eyes caught mine and cut through the euphoria of the fantillium's spell.

Illusion. Her lips formed the word. *Jonathan. The doors!*

I glanced at Lockwood. He nodded, imperceptibly. A muscle twitched in his jaw. At the table, Queen Honoria illusioned over Anna. Wearily, jerkily. She slowly drew silver wisps from the air, forming them into pointed steel.

"Are you writing this down?" she asked the reporter. "All of it?"

The reporter nodded, sagging so close to his notebook his nose touched the paper.

Constantine stared at Anna, his lurid orange eyes betraying nothing. But the rifle, still pointed at my head, trembled.

I'm calling your bluff, Constantine, I thought. *Whatever you are, you don't want Anna to die, either.*

I closed my eyes and inhaled. *The observatory doors.*

Twice my height. Dark walnut. Four carved panels on each door, iron latches, hail-pocked, worn. I even pulled to mind the groan they made when opened. I thought of the chemical structure of wood and iron I'd committed to memory. My head grew heavy, weighing me down. I opened my eyes and exhaled.

The thoughts evaporated from me. They wisped from my head like vapors. The illusion sucked itself from my head and air stole from my lungs.

Queen Honoria finished illusioning the dagger, all eyes on her but mine. Behind her, between the model airship and the wall, the air shimmered.

The walnut panels grew opaque, then bold, dark, polished, and then regressed with age and weather. Hail pocked them in shadowy staccatos.

Divinity screeched, noticing it first. Queen Honoria dropped the knife and twisted around.

The latches burned white hot as I manipulated iron construct in my head. The hinges, the white curls at each end of the latch, glowed and then faded to black. I warped the wood of it forward, molding lions' heads and manes of walnut until my vision blotched and sweat poured down my face.

There before us stood the observatory doors.

"Now!" I yelled.

Lockwood fought out of the masked guard's grip like an assassin, twisting necks, kicking joints backward.

I did better than that. I mentally grasped an oxygen particle from the air, then multiplied it thousands and millions of times over, mixed it with one methane particle, and with the speed of someone who actually listened in his chemistry class—

Contracted it all to the size of a pin.

BOOM.

The explosion in the game room hit like a spark in an airship balloon. The force threw Divinity, Constantine, Queen Honoria, and the guardsmen against the wall, sprawling over sofas, top hats flying, and setting Lockwood free.

Black and red embers chased a vortex around us as Lockwood and I leapt onto the billiards table and pulled Anna into our stream of cool air. One lope, and I was grasping the latches of the illusioned doors.

I twisted. They opened with a groan.

We leapt through—

—a rush of air—

—and slammed into Edward's game room wall.

The door had opened into nothing.

We stumbled backward. I shoved the doors closed and opened them again, revealing the plank wood of Edward's wall. I ran through the door once more, and hit wall.

I twisted about, managing a second look at the doors I'd illusioned, and took in what I hadn't seen the first time: the carved panels were the wrong dimensions. The latches looked as though they'd been molded by a child. The lions were toothless, their eyes misshapen.

I hadn't created the observatory doors. I'd created a cheap imitation. The doors glistened, then faded in wisps, to nothing.

Queen Honoria had shut off the boiler. The room darkened. Utter failure encased me. My knees gave way beneath me, and my hands hit the floor. Around us, the masked guardsmen, still strewn across the room, slowly roused and took possession of Lockwood and Anna.

"Oh, Jonathan," said Queen Honoria wearily. Then, to the remaining masked guard pulling themselves to their feet, "Search him."

A multitude of gloved hands seized me and shuffled over my clothes until they found the bottle in my pocket. They flipped me back to my knees, holding me tight, and handed the bottle to Queen Honoria. She received it with cold eyes.

"No," I said, panicked. "No! Your Highness! You said if I illusioned for you—"

Queen Honoria reared back and smashed the bottle to the floor, sending a burst of glittering minuscule shards and brown liquid droplets across the wood. My soul shattered with it.

"Why, Jonathan?" Queen Honoria pled. "*Why* couldn't you have just illusioned for me?"

The liquid seeped into the wooden cracks of the floor.

Lockwood had not yet given up the fight, still

thrashing against the guard. Unconscious guardsmen lay at his feet. It took six more guardsmen to hold him still.

"Lieutenant, *please*," said Queen Honoria wearily, tearing her focus away from me. "You really are destroying your chances."

"Chances for *what*?" Lockwood snarled, mid-punch.

"As captain of my masked guard, of course," said Queen Honoria.

Lockwood kicked a masked guard in the face.

"Excuse *me*?" he said.

Queen Honoria smiled the long-suffering smile of a thousand saints.

"Stop. Stop fighting, please," she said, and the masked guard fighting Lockwood immediately ceased. They remained in a ring around him, and Lockwood's fists remained up, his eye darting to each of them, then stopping on Queen Honoria. She smiled, taut.

"Captain of my masked guard," she said.

"*What?*" said Lockwood.

"Come, Lieutenant. We had our . . . disagreements on the *Chivalry*, but now is the chance to redeem yourself. Our last captain Rivened two months ago. We need someone with military prowess. Someone who is *you*."

"Really?" said Lockwood. "Captain of the guard? *Your* guard? This same ruddy guard who murdered all those yeomen in Arthurise?"

"They had to," Queen Honoria said coldly. "It hardly even makes a difference in your world. Your world will thrive notwithstanding. But Nod'ol—we need you, Lieutenant. You and Jonathan both. You can help me breech the doorway to Arthurise and bring Arthurisians to Nod'ol. This city *can be great again*."

Queen Honoria had started to twitch in her fervent plea. Almost like the woman who had Rivened. I shifted uncomfortably in the grip of my guardsmen.

Lockwood's eye narrowed.

"Pretty sure this city's beyond help," he said.

"Or I could have Constantine shoot you," Queen Honoria said, cold as ice.

Masked guardsmen seized upon Lockwood before he could fight back. Constantine, who had just pulled himself to his feet in a misshapen lump, gripped the rifle that had fallen from his hands, fumbled, and pointed it at Lockwood's head. He breathed heavily.

"No!" said Anna, struggling.

Sweat beaded on Lockwood's face, which remained stonily staring at the barrel of the rifle. A drop coursed from his forehead, traveling down the seam of his eye patch until it dripped from his chin to the floor.

The tip of the sword clasp at his collar pricked his throat.

Lockwood spat at Queen Honoria's feet.

Queen Honoria slowly closed her eyes.

"Shoot him," she said.

Constantine pulled the trigger of his rifle. The pistons hissed:

BANG.

And in that ear-rending *BANG*, everything happened.

Anna writhed from the masked guard with sudden strength. In a blur of white she threw herself forward, grasping the barrel as the rifle discharged.

And slowly, with trembling hands, Anna released the end of the gun.

Constantine dropped the rifle.

"Anna!" he rasped.

A crimson stain grew over Anna's side. She rippled to the floor like a cloudfall.

Before the room could even gasp, Lockwood fought the masked guard like a demon, pulled Anna into his arms and fled, bashing through the guard at the door. My guardsmen released me to fly after him, but I was faster, leaping to my feet and bounding after Lockwood and Anna, dodging the brush of crimson gloves. I careened through the doorway and into the hall.

My leaps up the spiraled stairs were weighted. I could only glimpse Lockwood's foot and a trail of white skirt as he barreled through the door hatch and flew onto the deck. He kept running until he slammed into the railing and fell to his knees, his front stained with Anna's blood.

I arrived at their side, chest heaving. The airship had drifted from the theater to over the tangled, abandoned maze. Nowhere left to run. Lockwood held her in his arms, tight against him.

"You're a surgeon!" Lockwood snarled, grabbing me by the collar and throwing me down beside her. "*Fix* her!"

I'd already pulled off my jacket and rolled it into a bandage, pressing it to the bullet wound in her side. It soaked through. My hands became slick and red with blood, and horror numbed me. A mortal wound. I knew it. Still I pulled off my vest, wadded it, and pressed it hard over the jacket.

"Anna, Anna," said Lockwood, stroking her hair back, his face as white as her skirt. His hands trembled.

"Lockwood," Anna whispered.

"Fix her!" Lockwood yelled again at me.

"Your jacket!" I said, blood-soaked fabric beneath my hand.

Lockwood hurriedly unbuttoned his blue uniform jacket, the sword clasp snapping off and skittering across the deck.

Anna reached up and touched his face before he'd gotten the jacket halfway off, her fingertips brushing his cheek, stopping him cold.

"You're worth dying over," she whispered.

"Anna—"

Anna closed her eyes. Exhaled; and the spark of life faded from her face.

She did not inhale again.

My soul screamed her name.

"Anna!" Lockwood cried, pulling her tightly into his arms.

The masked guard rose around us. Their long coats flapped silently in the propellers' wind; the black holes of their masks bore down upon us. Constantine shoved his way through them, and when he caught sight of Anna, limp in Lockwood's arms, he fell to his knees. He raised his snout to the air and howled an inhuman, feral banshee of a howl. It reverberated in the balloon and echoed to the Archglass.

The masked guard seized upon Lockwood. They dragged him away from Anna's body. He fought with otherworldly strength, sending masked guardsmen hitting the deck, cracking masks. They cornered him against the railing.

Gritting his jaw, and without a backward glance, he flipped himself over the side of the ship in a graceful swoop.

I ran to the railing in time to see him catch—midair— one of the lines that still trailed behind the ship. He slid down it, pounced onto a roof below, and disappeared into the city.

CHAPTER 18

The masked guardsmen allowed me to wrap Anna tightly in my jacket, succumbing to the grief that welled in my throat. Queen Honoria commanded the ship's navigator to steer back to the theater, and all the time Edward remained crumpled in a corner of the deck, wringing his hands and saying, "I'm so sorry, I'm *so* sorry! What a horrible night this has been!"

The airship docked. The masked guard pried me away from Anna's form and silently escorted me down the vertical dock—but not before I noticed the gleam of silver that lay by the anchor line. Lockwood's Excalibur pin. I numbly slipped it into my pocket.

Ten minutes later, I'd been locked in my golden suite. Demons of regret plagued me, twisting webs of darkness over my soul. *Your fault*, they whispered. Every decision I'd made schismed into dozens of others in my head, all of them ending with Anna still alive. If I had bandaged her sooner. If I had stopped her from throwing herself at Constantine's rifle. If I hadn't tried to illusion the stupid doors, and done what Queen Honoria had told me to.

I sat on one of the spindly chairs, wishing Masked Virtue had already begun, just so I could breathe fantillium and just so I couldn't *feel* anymore.

A clean set of clothes lay folded over my sitting-room screen. Gold tureens and lidded platters sat on every available surface in the room, tables and chairs and all of them steaming hot. They smelled of breads and soups and roasted bird.

In one stride I kicked and overturned a table, sending soup across the rug. I kicked the table next to it, and it bashed to the ground, tureens clanging and food splashing. I couldn't stop. I overthrew a chair, sending it crashing, and commenced to destroy the room. I shoved the furniture on its side. I punched holes in the painted screen. I smashed the mirrors to pieces with a chair. I reduced my suite to shambles.

"Are you finished?"

Queen Honoria regarded me from the doorway. She wore new clothes—new for Nod'ol—which covered every inch of her. Her half-masked face looked as though it were coming out of a heap of rags.

I reared back with the chair and bashed it across the

last mirror. The glass shattered. Shards rained over the floor.

"And that's enough," said Queen Honoria. "You're acting like a child, Jonathan."

I threw the chair in the sitting room pool—it splashed and bobbed—and kicked a tureen lid across the room.

"Masked Virtue begins in three hours. You ought to at least use the time for rest," Queen Honoria said.

"Masked Virtue?" I said, incredulous. "What in the world makes you think I'm still going to illusion for you?"

"Because you have nothing else," said Queen Honoria. "Because your mother and sister will be dead by tonight, and Arthurise soon after, and Nod'ol will be all you have left."

I lunged at her. The masked guard countered me midair and dragged me back. Queen Honoria stepped forward and gently tried to put her gloved hand on my head.

"I need you, Jonathan," she said, giving up and pulling her hand away as I struggled. "I'll need you to illusion doors back to Arthurise for me. There will be so many people looking for a new life, here in Nod'ol. We can revive the city again with Arthurisians. That's why I infected your world with the Venen. I had to make them see—"

"You *what*?" I screamed.

And everything screeched and ground together, the gears sorting themselves out into a macabre mechanism. The Venen, a strange and unknown disease, originating in Old London. *Queen Honoria had brought the Venen to Arthurise.*

"You've ruddy killed Arthurise!" I yelled, writhing against the guard.

"I had to!" Queen Honoria pled. "I had to, Jonathan. I had to make them see how much they *needed* Nod'ol! I'm not a murderer! It was all for Nod'ol!"

"My mother and sister—"

"Are soon dead," Queen Honoria finished. "And Nod'ol is your home now."

I broke free of the guard with a burst of strength and charged at Queen Honoria.

Constantine arose from nowhere and stopped me short with a box across my head, disorienting me enough for the masked guard to pull me back into their gloved tentacles.

"Leave me with Jonathan," he growled to Queen Honoria. He wore a mask with a protruding snout, several rows of fangs on both top and bottom. "I'd like to give him some . . . tips. For Masked Virtue."

Queen Honoria waved her hand dismissively and swept from the room without a backward look. Constantine slammed the door. The masked guards' fingers tightened around my wrists and I was brought to my knees.

Constantine knelt in front of me, his long coat-of-many-coats brushing my face. He placed his gloved finger under my chin and lifted my face to meet his. His eyes had been dyed again; one yellow, the other red. The clumps of hair that stuck out from beneath his hood had been dyed lurid white. He pulled off my glasses and threw them into the pool behind us with a little *ploosh*.

Then he brought his arm back, balled his fingers, and slammed me in the cheek with the hardest punch I'd ever gotten in my life. Bone and cartilage crunched. White glittered in my vision. And when it cleared, Constantine's snout was in my face with rancid breath.

"You killed Anna," he seethed.

"Sorry?" I coughed, spitting blood. "*You* killed Anna. Pretty sure. The rifle was in *your* hands—"

He slammed his fist into my head again. The world turned black.

"Why didn't you just do what Queen Honoria told you to do? Anna would still be alive!"

"She'd still be alive if you hadn't shot her," I snapped back as the world regained colors.

Constantine stood, walked away, then made a running start. It ended with him kicking me so hard I lost the air in my chest. The masked guardsmen set me back on my knees, readying for another of Constantine's blows.

"I, at least, had the decency," he said, "to make sure

she'll be laid to rest where the rest of her family is buried. Unlike *you*."

I coughed.

"Constantine," I said, "I *really* don't get you, you know?"

"She was all I *had*," he said. Rivulets of sweat ran down his neck from beneath his mask.

No, I realized. It wasn't sweat.

They were *tears*. From his other eyes.

The rain of blows continued. Constantine beat me across the head, knocking it against the floor, kicked me in the chest and throat, produced a whip and struck it across my back and face. Blood specked the floor.

I struggled, but couldn't fight back. Anger, instead, grew within me like a demon. If I'd ever had a compass, it had broken and disintegrated thoroughly, leaving only razor shards of hate coursing through my bloodstream.

He finished just as the sun rose in the windows, leaving me in a heap on the suite floor.

"I'll kill you, Constantine," I said hoarsely, too broken to move. "I'll kill you. I'm ten times the illusionist you are. I'll make you feel death the way you made Anna feel it, but a thousand times slower, until you are screaming in agony and *begging to die*."

Constantine stared coldly at me from the doorway.

"I'd like to see you try it," he said, and left.

271

Hours later, it seemed, I gathered enough strength to pull myself to my feet, holding my hand to the stinging cuts on my face. I didn't dare pull my glasses from the pool, because I didn't have the strength to swim. I knew I needed to find bandages, at least, because I was leaving a trail of blood, but instead I set to finding Constantine, hate flaring in hot tendrils through my veins. I staggered into the hall, and collapsed.

"Oh, you poor thing." Divinity's voice whispered above me.

I awoke in a soft green aura not long after. I lay on a pale green sofa in Divinity's sitting room. The broken vases and strewn flowers from the night before had been cleaned up and replaced, the broken windows covered with a screen. I pulled myself up against the arm with agony; I ached and throbbed all over.

Divinity arrived, wearing a dress with gauzy bits and a black corset, carrying rags of bandages. She sat on the edge of the sofa, just touching my side, and began to gently nurse my wounds, touching ointment to the stinging cuts on my cheek and cooing.

I hated Divinity almost as much as I hated Constantine. I grabbed her wrist just as she was about to touch my face again.

—and recoiled. The fingers I gripped her with had split at the ends. The illusion on Edward's ship must have progressed my schisming. My thumb was coming apart down to the knuckle now, giving me an extra piece of thumb I could wiggle freely. My fingers had each widened into extra fingertips that melded together at the first knuckle. I hurriedly felt my face.

A thorough examination revealed the bridge of my nose was so wide it was almost two bridges. One of my nostrils was wider than the other. I had an indentation in my temple. I kneaded it, feeling a cavity in the bone. It was tender to my touch. An extra eye. I was growing an extra eye.

I gagged.

"It's always worse around Masked Virtue," Divinity said soothingly, stroking a hand through my hair and pressing her other hand to my chest. "You'll heal. We all do. Well—I'm not sure Constantine does, anymore. Don't illusion again after M.V. for a few weeks, and you'll be fine.

"What?" I said.

"Unless, of course, you've started seeing demons," said Divinity, rather peevishly. "That means your brain is splitting, and you've become a Riven."

I grasped Divinity's slender, delicate, perfect hand.

"You don't have extra fingers," I accused.

A strange smile curved over Divinity's face, as though to say, *You have no idea where I'm schisming. . . .*

Appalled, I pushed her away and got to my feet. My vision sparkled with lack of blood and I fell back to the sofa.

"Hush," Divinity said, pressing me to the pillows as I tried to get to my feet again. "Hush. You're in a bad way. Here, I've brought you something warm to drink. It'll calm you down."

She fetched a mug of steaming tea from a small room at the side of her suite, then gently sat down next to me and held the mug full of black liquid to my lips.

I immediately recognized the familiar, sweet, and rather chemical smell I'd known from Dr. Palmer's medicine cabinet. I stood sharply and shoved Divinity away, sending her knocking against ornamental tables and chairs. The mug hit the floor and sent liquid everywhere.

"Trithyloform, Divinity?" I said, anger logarithming inside me. Divinity scrambled back, flower vases tumbling behind her. She cowered. "You know," I said, "we use that stuff in the infirmary in Fata Morgana, Divinity. Dip a rag in it, press it over the patient's face, and if it doesn't put them right to sleep, it makes them good and sluggish. Trying to drug me, are you, Divinity? In time for Masked Virtue, Divinity?"

She squeaked, faltering to her feet and then backward, tripping over her dress as I bore down on her. Fumbling, she grabbed a fallen vase of flowers and brandished it at my head.

"You stole my airship ticket!" she cried.

"Boo-*hoo*!" I snarled, snatching the vase from her hand

and smashing it to the floor. Shards rained over our feet.

"You made Queen Honoria's illusion a thousand times larger!" she said, cowering against the wall. "How am I supposed to compete with that? I can't! I don't want to die again!"

"You'd better get used to it," I said. "You and Constantine both are going to die at my hand and I *cannot wait*, you little piece of garbage."

I strode unevenly from the suite, leaving Divinity a mewling little mess among the broken vases and strewn flowers.

The rumble of Masked Virtue emanated through my suite. Endless airships docked around the theater, unloading their passengers. The clang of bells and drums, and an organ grinder's tune that prickled and stuck like taffy to the air. Such jolly music for a massacre.

A masked guard arrived, presenting me with a gold coat. It was the only new piece of cloth I'd seen in Nod'ol. They fished my glasses from the pool and also offered me a new gold mask.

This mask covered my whole face. The eyes were furrowed to slits, and the mouth opened to rows of pointed teeth, as though it were yelling. I put it on without hesitation.

Noon, December 22: my family would die in just hours.

I would make certain they weren't the only ones.

The masked guard flanked me as I limped from my suite, escorting me into the vast halls and up stairways to the roof. It was like swimming; Nod'olians filled every inch of the halls, a susurrus of hoarse voices and masks and all of them wearing either orange or green. Venders swam among them, selling sticks with dingy ribbons attached for people to wave around. They had abundances of yellow.

That didn't bother me. I wouldn't be winning for *them*.

We arrived at a far west door on the roof, which was filled with more Nod'olians. High above, the sea of airships had congregated over the theater, with dozens docked at the docking towers that extended across the roof. In the distance, across the landscape of slopes and domes, I saw the pinprick of a beast mask skulking among the crowd: Constantine. Another distance away: Divinity. Each of them was headed to a docking tower that hosted a mass of airships with pennants in their color.

I peered up at the closest tower; a single airship with frayed riggings and patched envelope bobbed at the top. Gold pennants hung from it like dead fish. Edward's airship—my only airship in the game.

It was at a disadvantage, of course. The idea was, we would sail to different parts of the city, fantillium mist would fill the air, and then we would drop into the city and hunt each other down on foot. Constantine and Divinity could disappear anywhere into the city with the help of their multiple airships, but I could not.

A delicate cough sounded behind me.

It was the dangerously thin reporter. He tremulously clutched his notebook, and, I noted, still wore the torn piece of yellow fabric pinned to his lapel. He hesitated, then produced a newspaper page from his vest.

"I wrote about the girl," he said haltingly. "I tried to give her a proper eulogy. Perhaps you would like to see it?"

I fixed a frigid glare on him.

He nodded and folded the paper back into his vest. He opened his mouth to say something, then closed it, then opened it; then finally, words came out.

"What you did," said the reporter. "Standing up to Queen Honoria. It was—noble—and—and good—and—virtuous—and—your name shows up nowhere and you've come at just the right moment in history—it—it all makes sense—"

I stepped into the lift that led up to the docking platform, squeezed between two guardsmen. The reporter dared to follow, stopping short before entering.

"The press," the reporter continued, stammering, "well—me, anyway, that's all that's left of us—we've named you."

He beamed expectantly at me. I stared back at him.

"Hope!" he burst. "Your illusionist name is *Hope*."

"Hope is a girl's name!" I snapped, and slammed the grate shut in his face.

At the top of the lift, Edward greeted us, wearing a tiny gold mask and huddled at the docking plank of his ship, a great hulking mass of Cower.

"So," I said, when we reached him. "You're still allowed to help me in Masked Virtue, are you? After everything that happened?"

"Oh—yes. Well," he said. "The miners all agreed the game wouldn't be much fun if *no one* supported you. But—but, my boy! I have great faith in you! Great faith in you, indeed!"

"It won't be misplaced," I said, striding past him onto his ship's deck. "I'll make certain they both die within minutes."

"Oh. Wonderful," said Edward, paling.

Edward's ship sputtered to life, engines churning, propellers spinning. The airships docked across the roof did the same, casting off their docking chains and all of us rising to the top of the Archglass. Among them flew an ornate ship with a bloodred balloon and crimson pennant hanging from it. Queen Honoria's ship. I could see her on the edge of the deck, a dot of red, with something over her face. A fantillium mask. No—a fresh-air mask, so she wouldn't breathe in the fantillium. Schisming underneath all those clothes, Queen Honoria? How close are you, exactly, to becoming a Riven?

I stood on the deck, watching the waves of airships repositioning themselves against the backdrop of glass and broken city, memories choking me. I tried not to look at the deck floor, where Anna's blood had been scrubbed away from the wood. Edward distracted me by thumping me on the shoulder, jolly as ever, as though he hadn't been such a spineless fool the night before.

"Where shall we sail, boy?" he boomed.

I glowered at the landscape of ships. Oranges and greens. Where would Constantine and Divinity hide? Divinity would be the sort to tuck herself away, hiding until she could sneak up behind you and slit your throat. Constantine, on the other hand, would fight head-on.

One of the airships from the ocean of balloons broke free of the rest and whirred closer to where we flew. It was the largest Nod'olian ship I'd seen, carved tiers lined with window and cannon and sails—though I doubted the sails did much in this stagnant city.

"Sail to that ship," I nodded. "Constantine's on that one."

"The *Argus*? How do you know?"

"It's headed right for us."

"Head-on attack, then," Edward said, laughing

tremulously. "Very, ah, bold! As you say, of course! As you say!"

Edward's navigator steered us forward, and we drew near to the abomination of an airship. From the theater roof, now in the distance, fireworks boomed, glittering and dropping to embers in the watery daylight. The beginning of Masked Virtue. Distant cheering filled the air. A low groaning with harmonics of *hissssssssssssh* echoed through the buildings. And so it began.

All along the city, in the distant beams of the Archglass, great clouds of mist and steam roared. Steam rose from aqueducts along the middle of the city. The mist masked the city below us, and soon the airships disappeared into the white billows as well. Steam masked the *Argus*. And when the fantillium mist hit us, I let it wash over me and coat me with ice. It deadened my soul and sharpened my senses. I felt alive again. Anna was right. Fantillium dulled the pain.

Edward's manservant handed me a line attached to the docking anchor. The same line Lockwood and I had slipped down to the theater with. He smiled encouragingly as I stepped onto the railing, ship creaking under my feet. Below, the abandoned city skyline rose from the mist.

"Constantine first," I muttered, towers slowing beneath as the ship slowed. "I will kill him like he killed Anna, but ten times slower and a thousand times more painfully."

"I—I say," said Edward tenuously from behind me. "That's rather—bloodthirsty—"

"Says the man who eagerly watches Masked Virtue every year," I sneered.

I pushed off, line in my hands, and free-fell, my coat a shimmering sail behind me. I jolted and skated down the rest of the line, gloves burning, and it slid between my palms. I fell into an abandoned street at a crouch.

Broken houses and pubs stared down at me. The line flipped back and whipped away into the mist.

Masks appeared from the white billows. Orange masks. They fleshed and surfaced into figures of torn orange and brown coats and dresses. I twisted sharply; every inch of open street was now filled with Constantine's supporters.

They converged on me, drowning me in orange. They wrenched my hands behind me, grew bold when I didn't illusion, and cheered with raspy voices. I waited for Constantine.

And he came. Moments later, the crowd parted to receive him.

His yellow-and-red eyes took me in, and he shook his beast-masked head.

"You must *really* want to die," he said.

CHAPTER 19

Grit, mud, and centuries-old cobblestone filled my vision as Constantine's supporters shoved my head down, making me bow to him. Everything smelled sharply of rotting sewage.

"'Lo, Constantine," I said, friendly-like, as he knelt next to me. His boot had so many buckles it was obscene.

"*Ten times* the illusionist I am, Jonathan?" he said, tangling his fingers in my hair and wrenching my face up to meet his. "You pathetic little scab!"

I smiled at him beneath my mask.

He released my hair, and without another word, moved his hands in and out quickly. The air between them flashed of metal and wisps. The illusion glowed.

Above us, lightning flashed. The mist around us had begun to draw upward into storm clouds. Without meaning to, I was illusioning a storm. The pent-up anger inside me eked from my eyes and mouth like a fever. Raindrops began to ping on the people around us, surprising them. They must never have felt rain in their lives.

Do you realize how powerful you are? Anna's voice echoed in my head.

My mind whipped into action as a rifle formed between Constantine's hands. He was going to illusion-kill me the way Anna had died.

Numbers. I wasn't good at mechanics like Constantine, but I knew numbers. I knew how to manipulate them. And I knew chemical structures. Steel. Iron. Steam. An idea took hold of me, and I pulled to mind the first chemical I'd memorized from *The Illusionist's Handbook*: iron.

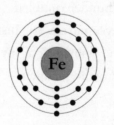

And placed a negative sign in front of it:

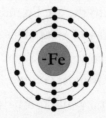

I did this with lightning speed for each molecule and metal bond, forming an *anti-rifle*, with anti-pistons and anti-bullets, and as Constantine finished forming his rifle, a sleek construct of black iron, I had created a *negative rifle*. It emanated from me in flash-wisps of thought. Constantine raised the rifle to his shoulder, aimed at my chest, and shot.

Almost shot. The rifle dissolved to nothing. His hands fell together, and he stumbled forward, as though he had missed a step. The crowd cried aloud, and Constantine stared at his empty hands.

I exhaled slowly, regaining my swimming thoughts.

"Nice try," I said.

Rain pattered across the crumbling cobblestones in watery staccatos. Thunder rumbled.

Constantine's eyes narrowed. Instantly he formed a misshapen pistol and pointed it at my head. He shot it in a flash of illusioned orthogonagen—

BANG.

The bullet went:

Phffzz.

And dissolved into the air. I'd managed to illusion an anti-bullet of iron just in time. The crowd at my hands released me and began to back away.

"Ten time the illusionist you are," I said. I rose to my feet, facing him with my mask of bared fangs.

Constantine backed away. He shot bullet after bullet, illusioning new balls in the chamber. The steam offal encased us in haze. I met each bullet with anti-bullets, dissolving them in transit with the sound of *ffzzt*. Constantine yelled aloud.

I took that moment and illusioned an anti-pistol out of it, casting it at Constantine. His pistol dissolved in his fingers just as he pulled the trigger. The bullet inside fell to the ground.

"How are you *doing this*?" he yelled.

The rain fell in sheets. I harnessed the wind, dropped the temperature, and conjured a gale of razor-sharp ice. It blew Constantine off his feet, sending him flying in a flapping mass of orange-brown before hitting the pavement.

Thunder crackled. The Nod'olians around me drew sharply away.

"Run," I snarled at them. "Or I will kill you next."

They fled into the mist.

Fair-weather supporters.

Now I was alone with Constantine. He shakily tried to pull himself to his feet. I threw him back with a gust of frozen rain and, drawing from my experience with Lockwood, froze his hands and feet to the ground, solidifying his clothing stiff with ice so he could not move.

I casually walked to him, smiling, as he struggled in

a desperate attempt to illusion warmth. I anti-illusioned every wisp from his head.

"Ice, that old thing," I said conversationally. "I'm good at temperatures, you know. Because temperatures are numbers. And as it turns out—I am *very* good at numbers."

I illusioned a pistol. It was an ugly thing, with a misshapen barrel and tiny steam pistons that whined and leaked. It lay in my hands like a wet brick. It would have to do.

"You're him," Constantine rasped as I drew near. He almost sounded frightened. "You're—you're the person—that—that writing—wall, whatever it was, legend talked about—"

I laughed, incredulous.

"If I were the Virtuous One, Constantine," I said, "I wouldn't want to kill you *so badly*. You disgusting animal, you half-human filth, you snarling little piece of muck, before I fantillium-kill you, shall we see the hideous remnant of human that lives underneath that mask? I can hardly wait."

With the illusioned pistol still in my hand, I brought my fingers up beneath his mask, tearing it away from its leather buckle. It skittered across the street. Constantine held his chin up, eyes burning with hatred.

He wasn't human.

He had three faces. Like mine, his nose split at the bridge. It continued on to form another nose next to the first, with five nostrils. His mouths—all three of them—gaped open on the other side of his face, revealing sinews at his jaw, with extra tongues. They foamed at the edges.

And his eyes. They were everywhere. Eyes and slits of eyes melted down his cheeks, misshapen and crusted. A thin sliver of gold-brown ringed the dilated pupil. The same gold-brown as my eyes.

His curly white hair, brown at the roots. The same color as mine.

What was left of his face. The same face as mine.

He was me.

Constantine was me.

I yelled and stumbled back.

Lightning flashed. Thunder crashed so loudly the pistol fell from my hands and clattered against stone. Deep gray of a virulent storm encased us, wind whipping and hiding the airships above in thick black clouds. I needed to rein it in. But I couldn't illusion. My thoughts couldn't form a thing.

"Silly boys!" came a jingly voice from behind us. "I've *found* you!"

Divinity.

She rose from the alley across from us, laughing her

horrible laugh that made the hairs on my neck stand on end. The pouring rain drenched her, her stringy yellow hair dripping over her sodden green coat, her dress clinging to her figure. An entourage of green-masked miners flanked her as she emerged into the open street. I glanced upward—a green ship was anchored to the nearest vertical dock. She'd followed Edward's airship.

"You know," she said, beaming at me, "you accidentally taught me something, Jonathan. When you had taken over Queen Honoria's illusion. I realized *I* can harness illusions, too! I've been in control of this storm for nearly the whole time!"

Sparks ignited at her fingertips. The black pools of her dilated eyes echoed the flash, and the rain came in sheets, clouds fizzing above us in a whorl of black.

"Divinity!"

"You stole my airship ticket!" she screeched.

Lightning struck.

Every individual bit of me—esophagus, lungs, stomach, heart, spleen, all my splitting fingers and toes—suddenly *splintered* into a thousand shards, all at once, in blinding pain. White blew my senses out.

My eardrums exploded.

My nerves splayed.

My vertebrae ruptured.

My heart burst.

My vision filled red and I surrendered, each minuscule piece of me crying for mercy from the excruciating pain.

And—

It disappeared.

Cool washed over me, soothing my burns, and faded the pain away completely.

I gathered my consciousness in pieces. It wasn't quite an awakening, but rather, pulling myself together, becoming aware in shades and shards, like a dissected picture piecing together, settling into a world of white. It tasted of ice and snow. The pain I'd just felt was distant, like a faded memory, replaced in my soul with Quiet. Not happiness, not sadness. Just, quiet.

The white receded into polar blue shadows. Shapes formed around me. Telescopes mounted on stands. Benches. I was on Fata Morgana! Dock three! The southern platform! That ruddy old thing with telescopes that played a tune and a lift that only worked sometimes! I walked down the platform, brushing the railing and benches with my fingertips. My splayed fingers and extra thumbs were gone.

I'm dead, I thought. I said it aloud: "I'm dead." And then I amended: "But—not *actually* dead. Fantillium-dead." I examined my clothes and saw my gold coat and mask had gone, replaced by what I'd always worn on Fata: shirt, vest, trousers, cap.

The mist receded further. Docked at the end of the platform was a Nod'olian ship, with creaking riggings and a pennant, held up by a balloon envelope that had been patched numerous times. Faded words across the hull read: the *Compass Rose*. And from the airship, a figure ran toward me, her footfalls clanging on the platform.

Anna.

I knew it was Anna and not Hannah, even though her scar had disappeared. I simply knew.

She wore a purple ribbon in her dark hair, tied neatly in a bow, a long skirt, and a thick Nod'olian coat that flapped around her ankles.

"Jonathan!" she said as she drew near.

I scooped her up into a tight embrace, lifting her feet off the ground. All the pain and hurt and horror of her death released itself from me, the anger leaving me in tears, and I was glad she couldn't see my face. I released her finally, after the bone-crushing hug, and dried my face quickly.

"It's the cold, you know," I said. "Stings the eyes. It does that here."

"Oh just," she said, grinning.

She looked curiously around her, taking in the expanse of black ocean and bright colored ribbons of the northerly sky. Far away, lightning flashed in a distant storm.

"Is this your home?" she said. "It's beautiful."

"Yeah," I agreed. Cold air whipped my face. The city behind us faded in white layers of mist. "At least—it's *like* my home. Is this real, Anna?"

"No," said Anna. "Not at all. I'm an illusion. This dock is an illusion. It's all part of an illusion, inside your head." She reached up and knocked gently on the crown of my head.

"Hmmm. Ah," I said, smiling, confused. "Quite an illusion. Is that what I would actually see? If I were truly dead?"

"I don't know," Anna admitted. "It isn't what I saw, either time. But this is your home, so—perhaps."

Lightning flashed, closer this time. The storm was drawing near.

"Jonathan, I don't have much time," said Anna, biting her lip at the growing clouds. "Any moment now, they'll pump fresh air into the Archglass, and you'll wake up. You can't let them take you away. You've got to find Lockwood and Lady Florel. You still have a chance to save everything. Your family, too."

I stared blankly at the black ocean below us.

"Yeah," I muttered. "That all ended so well before. . . ."

Anna kicked me as hard as she could in the knees.

I collapsed to a bench, pain shooting up my legs.[24]

"Anna!" I seethed, massaging my kneecaps. *"Honestly!"*

"Sorry. Actually, no, I'm not. I wish I could kick you in the head," she said, all innocence. "The Nod'ol—their religion—it's lodging itself inside you. You've been breathing fantillium so much, you're turning into one of them. You were trying to kill people!"

Guilt filled me. I limped back up to my feet, wordless. I'd been turning into Constantine.

"I—wasn't myself," I muttered.

Anna pursed her lips. From her skirt pocket, she produced two gold coins. She showed them to me, and to my surprise, one had the profile of my face on it. The other coin: the hideous gold mask I'd been wearing—the one with the pointed teeth.

"Do you remember talking about airships and compasses?" she said. "How veering just a little can send everything miles off course?"

"Of course."

Anna took the first coin and inserted it into the coin slot on the first telescope. Most of the time, the mechanics on these old telescopes did not work, due to the ice and frigid temperatures. They worked now, playing a jaunty

---

[24] Which really wasn't fair, being dead and all.

tune—*Deeedle deeedle deeee-dee-deeeeeeeeeCLONK*—as the blinders dropped.

Anna offered me the first look. I peered south into the freezing eyepiece.

The Scandinavian coastline did not appear, but a city did. Arthurise! Or—perhaps, Nod'ol without the Archglass? I recognized the Tower of London, the bridges, the buildings. But there was more: golden spires, buildings I'd never seen, and semaphore towers that lit the sky with all colors; sleek, massive airships that traveled far too quickly for their size.

CLONK. The blinders closed and blocked the view.

Anna dropped the other coin—the one with the fanged mask—into the telescope.

A jaunty tune played.

The blinders dropped again, this time revealing the same city, but in ruins. There wasn't an Archglass; there were no airships. No people, only crumpled buildings. I pushed away from the telescope before the blinders clonked shut.

"Was that Arthurise?" I said. "Or was it Nod'ol?"

"It's both," said Anna. "Both cities. Both empires will fall. Tonight. Unless you remember which way you point. It all hinges upon you."

"Oh, is that all?" I said. "Nothing to worry about, then."

Anna took my hands in hers and gripped them so hard and stared at me with such fervency that I amended: "Anna, I honestly don't know if I *can*. I'm not even sure what I can do. I've already bungled everything up. If I'd done what Queen Honoria had wanted, at least you'd still be alive—"

The stupid, stinging cold air. I turned my head.

"No, Jonathan," said Anna, her blue eyes shiny. "What you did for me was the most noble, wonderful thing you could have done. And it's what you *should* have done. If you had allowed yourself to bend to Queen Honoria, do you know what would have happened?"

We both knew. I would have played Masked Virtue, I would have illusion-killed people, and Queen Honoria would never have taken me back, and Arthurise would die of the Venen. The compass inside me would have broken more and more until I'd become a not-human. Like Constantine.

"You must *always* point north," said Anna. "No matter what the cost."

She touched the middle of my chest with her fingers.

The strangest sensation of warmth and peace gathered at her touch and solidified within me. It grew from my heart to my fingers and head, and my mind cleared completely. Suddenly, desperately, I *knew* I needed to come back to life.

"Find Lockwood," she said, her eyes glistening when she spoke his name. "He needs you, too. He's veering. And Constantine—"

"Constantine!" I said. "Anna, you said your brother had died!"

"I thought he had!" she said. "We didn't know. The masked guard destroyed everything; we thought he had been killed with Mum, not taken away to be an illusionist. And now he's so off course, he's . . . he's not even recognizable anymore."

She wiped her face.

"Cold air," I said.

"Right," she said. She smiled, and added, "Jonathan. When you see Constantine. Tell him he has a second chance. He can still change his course. Tell him—tell him I know he's still Jonathan."

Thunder shook the platform. Lightning flashed. More thunder.

Anna embraced me so quickly I barely had a chance to hug her back before she'd slipped away and was running back to the *Compass Rose*.

"Until we meet again, my good brother," she said.

"Anna, wait!" I called after her. She stopped and turned, her coat twisting around her, hail popping at her feet. I stammered, hundreds of questions rising from my chest. Where would I find Lockwood? Forget

Lockwood, where would I find the cure? And how would I get back to Arthurise? I garbled what came to my lips, surprising myself: "What did Queen Honoria see? When she died?"

Anna smiled.

"What you just saw, actually," she said. "All around her. Queen Honoria was trapped in the abandoned world. The one the Writing on the Wall had foretold."

And leaving me with that odd answer, Anna ran back to the Nod'olian ship. The hull door and loading plank were open and extended, and in the bright rectangle of the doorway stood my father. My—Nod'olian father. He lacked the glasses and apron, but everything else about him was the mirror image of my own father. He smiled and raised his hand, hailing me.

I raised my hand and bowed.

The falling ice around me intensified, growing thick and pulling a curtain of hail around me, until the *Compass Rose* disappeared and Fata Morgana faded, and I only saw shadows of the telescopes and benches.

White flashed through me. Lightning poured itself through my soul.

I gasped anew, and rose from the dead.

CHAPTER 20

It was what the pain of being born probably felt like—each piece of your body clinging to your soul with sticky agony. I gagged and gagged and then balled up in a thousand needles of sharp pain.

The rain had disappeared. The alleyway and the Archglass above was no longer thick with storm clouds or the mist of fantillium. The citywide hissing of pipes pumping out fantillium had ebbed. I was breathing untainted air again.

I took everything in with one glance. Constantine and Divinity stood a length away, next to Queen Honoria, clothes dry once more, all of them flanked by the crimson of the masked guard and a few spare miners. I sensed they were preparing for the second round of Masked Virtue.

Behind the masked guard stood Edward, looking crestfallen. Behind *him*, docked at the top of a vertical dock, loomed Queen Honoria's scarlet airship. I'd be taken back to the theater.

I lay on the grit of the stone, gathering my wits. Then, calmly, I pulled myself to my feet, pulled off my mask, and shoved it in one of the large pockets of my coat, and then offered myself to the masked guard. They hesitated before gripping my hands and shoulders and escorting me to the dock's lift.

"Well done, Divinity," I said as I passed her, burying my pride in a deep grave and placing a vase of flowers on it. "I wouldn't have thought of harnessing the lightning."

"No, you wouldn't have," she said smugly.

This didn't inspire one iota of anger within me.

"I'm sorry about the airship ticket," I said, and I meant it. "What's in Sussex?"

"Her mum," said Constantine lazily from behind us.

Divinity colored pink.

"I haven't seen her since I was six." She brushed the words away with a careless wave of her hand. "I hardly even care."[25]

Constantine and Divinity disappeared with their miners into the winding alleyways, making their way back to their ships. I stepped onto the lift with Queen Honoria and the masked guard, and we rose to the dock platform.

[25] Liar.

Queen Honoria. She still wore the *hsshing* fresh-air mask over her face, which meant that almost every bit of her was covered. She shifted nervously, adjusting little things: tugging her gloves further up her wrists, pulling her collar up higher, adjusting her mask, hiding whatever she was schisming into.

I remained in the corner of the lift, thinking.

Trapped in the foretold Nod'ol . . .

The abandoned city skyline, utterly bereft of life, passed through my mind. Trapped forever, in a place like that. Alone. No wonder she was so dead set on fixing Nod'ol. It wasn't because she cared about the city or anyone in it. It was because she was afraid she'd die and spend eternity there if she didn't do something about it.

But even I knew a person couldn't fix something by breaking everything else. Queen Honoria was making Nod'ol even worse. I almost felt sorry for her.

We boarded the ship without a word, the propellers blurred to life, and I peered over the railing at the snarl of the city below as we rose higher. Already the Archglass rumbled and mist was pumping through the maze of pathways and alleys below us, beginning the second round. It reminded me of the cloud canals on Fata.

"You'll speak to the reporter when we reach the theater. After you awake, of course," Queen Honoria was saying, the masked guard a length away. "Do make your fight to the death exciting; the miners *live* to read those things."

My head was calculating gravity vs. height vs. impact fall of a 174-pound human.

"Did you hear me, Jonathan?"

"Yes, quite. After I awake." My brain did a double take. "Awake?"

I couldn't see Queen Honoria's smile, other than her eyes squinting through the holes in her mask. One of the guardsmen next to her wetted a cloth with a medical bottle full of clear liquid, and I backed away against the railing. Trithyloform. Probably even from the same bottle Divinity had tried to use on me earlier.

"I am sorry," Queen Honoria said as the guard drew near. "But really, after your abysmal behavior at the opening ceremonies and then on Edward's ship, we can hardly have you illusioning out of turn anymore. When you speak to the reporter, I do believe you should apologize for that."

I glanced below, the brown and decaying gray of towers disappearing into layer after layer of mist, and the buildings of Old London just a brush away from the hull as we sailed past.

"No, no, I don't think I will," I said heartily as the masked guardsman with the cloth grabbed my wrist.

"What?" said Queen Honoria.

"Good-bye!" I said, and pulling yet another page from Lockwood's book, yanked out of the guardsman's grip, twisting away just as he brought the cloth to my mouth. I leapt onto the railing—

—and threw myself over, plunging gracefully into the mist.

I'd died once before. . . .

I slammed onto the roof of a tower that jutted up out of the white, grabbing the iron weathervane before sliding down its dome to a brick ledge. I regained balance, dazed and impressed with myself. Not even a broken bone! Shame Lockwood hadn't seen that!

Growing mist encased me, filling my lungs with frigid air and brightening everything to an unbearable white. I inhaled, determined to keep the infuriatingly calm chemical from dashing my resolve. In the distance above, Queen Honoria's voice yelled.

Scarlet forms of the masked guardsmen leapt onto the roof after me, descending out of the white like demon angels. With dexterity to impress even Lockwood, I half slid, half climbed down the tower, gripping the crumbling ledges beneath broken windows. Craggy brick scraped my hands. The masked guard climbed down after me like crimson spiders.

I recognized the decaying yellow brick as I slid to the ground, falling into knee-high weeds of a hilly courtyard. The Tower of London. I always managed to end up here.

The masked guard seized me, dropping from the sky. I pulled together a hot wind and threw them off, knocking them against the brick of the White Tower and throwing them across the courtyard, top hats tumbling. They leapt to their feet and dove for me again with indefatigable stamina. And then, just as suddenly, they stopped.

Frozen, as still as red-painted statues.

A new sound, among the silence, rose up from the old stone walls.

It sounded like someone sucking foam.

A lot of someones.

The masked guard fled. They scurried back up the White Tower, they made for the wall, they climbed through the windows of the towers around us. I frowned at their receding backs and turned around, face-to-face with a mass of creatures.

Riven.

They poured out of the abandoned doorways, down the walls of the stone towers, over the hills of weeds, and from the mouth of the White Tower. They leapt from broken windows, a gray mass of torn clothes, too many arms and noses and elbows and *teeth*—far, *far* too many teeth—dragging one another down and crawling over one another to get at me quicker. Their many-fingered hands clawed at my throat and chest, throwing me to the ground as they pounded me into the earth.

Numbers! my mind yelled uselessly as they buried me. *Illusion numbers! Any numbers! You're good with numbers! Illusion, Jonathan! Aaaaah!*

A memory immediately flashed through me.

A classroom, in the Fata Morgana Academy. The glaring lights above us, the long rows of tables, and the rumbling of the city generator nearby. Sitting at the front table of my physics class, Professor Stromberg speaking of the force of gravity and writing in bony chalk on the wall:

$$F = G \frac{m_1 \, m_2}{r^2}$$

And then another memory of him standing in the same place, drawing the imaginary element:

$$i$$

—and explaining how the square root of negative 1, if applied to certain equations and graphs, has the property of turning it, in fact, *ninety degrees*. I sat there, doodling on my slate and thinking, I am never, never, never, never going to use this in real life. . . .

Real life overtook me in the form of Riven. Feverishly

I formed the sheer i within my head—it slid around my thoughts like a glimmering wisp—harnessed it, molded it, and pressed it to the G in the formula, imagining all the numbers taking upon themselves the burden of the impossible and melding with gravity.

$$F = i\left(G\frac{m_1\ m_2}{r^2}\right)$$

My brain turned first. My organs next, and then every individual blood cell and heartbeat inside me turned ninety degrees. I shook as the immensity of the illusion took over. Every piece of me struggled to hold it together. I couldn't breathe.

And then, I released it. The world balanced precariously.

Mist rolled past me. I grabbed the support beam of the White Tower's stairs at my back, bracing myself. Riven held back, hissing and recoiling as the world turned . . .

Sideways.

The weeds bent downward.

Water flooded from beyond the wall, rushing through the abandoned Tower of London windows and pouring down the hills of weeds in the courtyard. The current drenched me. The water took the Riven with it, and they slid across the steep incline of ground and then fell into one another, hitting the stone wall below, jutting out beneath us. One remained, dangling from my foot, his grip breaking and sending him down the length of the courtyard as well. He smashed onto a window of one of the tower walls. They all hissed, a mass of torn clothes and limbs as they tried to maneuver their way with this new center of gravity.

Moat water coursed its way down the courtyard in streams of black. I pushed myself onto the sideways wood beam and climbed the crisscrossing beams to what was once the wall of the White Tower—now a brick floor with windows across it. I ran along it to the far end, near the dome and weathervane.

Here I took in the entire expanse of the city I'd illusioned on its side. Towers and houses and buildings jutted out beneath me from the perpendicular landscape. The dome of the distant theater lay far below. Above me, the shadows of the decaying city rained debris and dust through the Tower courtyard. In front of me, now in a vertical sky, the sea of airships had remained upright in the ninety-degree turning, innocently bobbing, unconcerned with this new center of gravity.

O-*kay*, I thought. I'm not entirely sure how to turn this back upright.

Well. It would catch Lockwood's attention, *that* was certain.

I ran back down the tower, jumping over windows, to

the grass that extended up in a wall before me, mapping out my course. I wasn't actually running up and down the side of a tower. The fantillium was only making me *think* I was. In actuality, I was most likely walking next to the foundation of the White Tower, knee deep in weeds. I had to be careful. I could step somewhere in this illusion that seemed perfectly safe—the edge of a bridge, or the side of a gate—and my real self would tumble down stairs or fall into the moat and drown.

I pressed forward. I had less than two hours, if I had any time at all. Anna's words of hope echoed in my head. I still had a chance. Lockwood had to be near here, in this old part of Nod'ol. It was the closest thing to Arthurise. I carefully climbed down across the courtyard, grabbing weeds to slow my sliding descent. The Riven had disappeared, though I could hear them in the distance. Another ruckus sounded further away. Airships. Constantine and Divinity, I guessed, re-navigating themselves. Hope you love it, I thought, and pushed off from the weeds, landing on the stone wall below.

I carefully made my way to the stone entrance of the Tower, crawling, sliding down the courtyard bridge, air rushing through my coat and hair, faster and faster, until my feet hit a jutting gate. Out of the tower fortress, I commenced running and climbing my way through the city. Across walls of buildings. Sides of stairways. Stumbling through alleyway sides and leaping from storefront to abandoned storefront. If I were a fierce-as-blades, over-keen, rifle-bearing one-eyed soldier, where would I hide?

Time slows when panic's in the blood. I felt as though I ran forever. I pulled up sharply, light-headed and breathless, amid a mass of old pipes and crumbling walls, to see a little boy standing all alone, huddled over the door of a hovel. He was a grimy little thing, wearing a patched vest and breeches. His face was pinched from hunger, his hair matted. He looked up at me and my gold coat with wide eyes. Far too wide for his face.

"Hello," I said, looking around for parents. There were none. It was strange to see a child here in Nod'ol—this one, in fact, was the first I'd met. Didn't exactly seem like a prime place to raise a child, Nod'ol. Or even fall in love. I buried my splitting hands in my coat pockets. A sliver of gold glinted from one of them.

The boy's eyes lit when he saw my hand touching the golden mask. Slowly, he reached into his vest and produced a makeshift stick with a grimy yellow ribbon tied to the end. He waved it.

"I say!" I said, affection filling me. I lifted him up into a giant hug.

He stumbled against the wall of his house when I released him, blinking, but not running away. He seemed too frightened to speak.

"Boy," I said. "I bet you keep an ear to the ground, eh? Have you seen a soldier about my age around here? He wears an eye patch? No mask?"

The boy blinked at me with wide brown eyes.

"He's wearing a blue uniform," I said. "Rows of buttons? A belt? Stripes on the sleeves?"

The boy blinked at me.

"He's a devil with a gun," I said.

The boy broke into a giant grin. He took off running like mad, jumping with reckless abandon over pipes and across walls. Up the sides of stairs, even through a pipe. My muddy coat slopped against me, chasing after him.

"Well done!" I said happily. "Well done, go on!"

He stopped moments later at an airship that hung just a few feet over us. It was so low flying it nearly scraped stone. A frayed rope kept it docked to a small set of stairs. Like the other airships, it had continued to bob upright in the gravity change. A sign above the half-broken door of the hull read THE THREE-EYED KING. A pub.

A gunshot sounded from beyond the door. If a gunshot could sound crisp and cold, this one did in spades. Lockwood!

"Thanks!" I said to the boy, who stared at me with wide, wistful eyes. Without hesitation, I pulled the golden mask from my pocket and offered it to him.

"Bet you can trade that for food or something," I said.

He nipped it from my fingers, leapt from the stairs of the dock, and disappeared into the dark mists of the city, waving his grimy ribbon stick all the way.

I entered the pub, hopping through the door from the protruding stairs into a large room that filled the entire hull of the ship. The walls were bowed. Glowing in dim lantern light stood a wreckage of tables and chairs. Classical Nod'olian style. Which meant: everything was falling to pieces. Broken orthogonagen lanterns, torn curtains, rotting wood floors and walls, shards of glass everywhere.

Men wearily sat in some of the chairs, talking, lower-class Nod'olians with years of Riven scars across their faces, and some with extra noses. Their clothes were faded gray, fabric of colors that had washed out years ago, and it made them blend in with the walls. They didn't, I noted, wear orange or green. In fact, they didn't even seem to care about Masked Virtue or the world beyond, but for two men in the corner.

"Ooo, this *nooothin'*," one was saying, nodding to a grimy nearby window. "Why, when I woos a boy, they'd have proper illusions, great rivers of blooood, plagues, locusts, that's the ticket. O'course, that was when there were more people in the city—"

"Aye, but I'll remember this one too. . . ."

No one in the pub noticed me enter. They all were too

preoccupied with the person in the middle of the dank room, who had a row of glasses lined up in front of him. It looked like they held water, but from what I could smell, didn't. A water-logged prune[26] rested in the bottom of each glass. The person they stared fixedly at had a mess of blond hair, an unbuttoned uniform jacket that flapped around his white linen shirt, and a Nod'olian steam pistol at his side. Lockwood.

He took a glass, drank the liquid in one gulp, then threw it into the air. In a blur he drew the pistol from his belt and shot the glass without even looking at it. It exploded into a firework of shards and rained over the men.

Cheers erupted throughout the pub. The men around him gathered money and placed more bets among one another.

"He hasn't missed one!" said one man, noticing me advance. "Care to make a wager? We reckon he'll drink hisself to death before he misses."

"Another! Ha-ha!" a man yelled.

Lockwood took a drink, but before he could lift it to his lips, I'd reached the table, placed my hand over the cup, and pressed it back down. Lockwood tugged at it, then his cold blue eye met mine. He blinked in bleary recognition.

---

[26] Fata Morgana's shipped foods had given me a vast knowledge of all things dried.

"Hi," I said.

Lockwood tugged on the glass. His hand slipped and he stumbled back.

"You done here?" I said as he regained his balance.

"Get out!" he said, shoving me away and grabbing for another glass. He drank half of it, the other half splashing onto his uniform, spat the prune out, threw the glass up into the air, drew his pistol, and shot it again. It rained glass and prune alcohol.

Everyone cheered and passed money around.

"Lockwood," I said, maneuvering around the table to meet his eye again. "I need your help. There's not much time. I have *one last chance* to find the cure and get us home."

"*Home?*" said Lockwood. "Ha! Why don't *you* go home, Johnny? You have one."

"I ruddy well won't if you don't help!" I snapped. "Isn't that part of an oath you took? To fight and defend Arthurise? I thought you were an Arthurisian knight!"

"And *I* thought you were only one person," Lockwood fired back, smiling nastily and grabbing another drink. "Because unless I'm *very* drunk, you're splitting into several."

At Lockwood's words, I quickly examined my hands, and my stomach sank. Breathing in all this fantillium had split them even further. My thumbs each had split down to the knuckle and stuck out in misshappen digits. My schisming fingertips had widened and split, fusing together at the second knuckle. My hands had deformed into fleshy spiders.

I hurriedly felt my face, probing the bridge of my nose under my broken glasses. It had grown wider. I had three nostrils now. I felt higher and to the side and discovered a rim of hair growing along my temple—an eyebrow. The indent below it had become deeper and tender to the touch.

Horrified, I made to desperately hide myself. I dug into my coat pocket for the mask, and when I grabbed nothing, remembered I'd given it away to the boy. Instead, my fingers closed around a tiny metal sword.

The Excalibur medal. That was right—I'd kept it from the deck of Edward's ship, and had slipped it into the coat when I'd changed, earlier today. And here it was. The tip of it pricked my finger.

I slowly wrapped my hand around it. Resolve solidified in my chest.

With lightning speed I grabbed Lockwood by the front of his uniform and slammed him down across the tabletop, knocking glasses to the floor. The men of the pub cried out in indignation. Lockwood blinked at me. I was surprised myself. Lockwood was so heavy he must have been made entirely of compressed muscle. I shoved him down when he tried to get back up.

"Now you listen to me, you rudderless rankless twit," I said. "I've turned this city sideways looking for you! D'you expect me to just let you slosh yourself to death? Especially after all that talk about airships and navigation and compasses? What, suddenly it's all right to not steer if there's a storm? You make me sick!"

In a blur, Lockwood grabbed my wrist with such strength he could have snapped it. My numerous fingers opened, and the sword clasp fell out and clattered onto the table.

Lockwood stared at it.

I yanked my hand from his grip.

"Find me when your rudder isn't broken," I said.

I stormed from the pub, leaping from the door back to the stairs. One last glance at Lockwood—he still stared expressionlessly at the sword clasp on the table—and I was on my way. I didn't have time to wait around for him.

I peered forward into the misty sideways sky. Above and below, beyond the cliffside buildings, airships hung. I'd have to fly to the theater. Once again I was running across brick walls and storefronts to the nearest vertical lift, where a small airship with green pennants was docked. Too small for weaponry or importance. This airship was mean for quick flight. Perfect.

I couldn't just climb out on the now-horizontal

dock to reach it—I'd have to take the lift, so when the illusion ended, I'd actually be in the airship, not clawing at the dock, *thinking* I was in an airship. In spite of being illusioned sideways, the lift still worked. I paced impatiently on its wall as it groaned and moved forward.

I mentally broke the steps down in my mind as I carefully climbed out of the lift onto the side of the docking platform, praying my actual self was leaping onto the ship's deck as well. I fell kneecaps first, hitting on all fours. I hadn't kept balance on my feet. By the feel of it—and my painfully tight shoes—my fingers weren't the only things schisming.

"Don't move."

The rasping voice came from behind me. It was the voice of someone who *decidedly* had a weapon. I didn't move.

"Stand up, illusionist."

I stood, hands up, catching a glance behind me. A lone airman in a green mask stood by the docking gear. He held a pistol level to my head. I reluctantly turned and looked ahead at the balloon envelope, riggings, and mist.

"Right," said the airman in guttural tones, and then he screamed. "Captain! Captaaaaaaa—"

THWUMPF.

The sound was followed by more sounds: the *thump*

of a body hitting the floor, the *clunk* of a mask hitting the wood face-first, and the skitter of a pistol across the deck.

"Shut up, shut *up*," came a familiar voice. "You little Nod'olian worm!"

I twisted about. The airman lay in a heap on the deck, knocked unconscious. Above him stood Lockwood, wincing, one hand holding a pistol, the other pressed against his head as though he had a massive headache.

"Lockwood!" I said.

"Hullo, Johnny," said Lockwood, and he smiled. Pinned haphazardly to his open uniform jacket was the Excalibur medal.

CHAPTER 21

I couldn't describe how I felt, seeing Lockwood on course again. I almost wanted to hug him.[27]

Instead, we raced to the small navigation room at the forecastle, Lockwood growling at me the entire way.

"*You* made this illusion?" he seethed. "This complete sideways nightmare? Do you know what a ghastly piece of mind-twist it was to try walking up a vertical dock and have gravity jerk you both ways? *Do you?* When we get back to Arthurise, remind me to break your neck!"

"I'm glad you understand the *gravity* of the situation, ha-ha," I said, breathless. "I was afraid things were taking a wrong *turn.* . . ."

"I don't get your jokes!" Lockwood snapped.

"Look," I said. "We still have a chance to save

---

[27] Or smack him across the head. I couldn't decide.

Arthurise. My mum and sister, even. We've only got a few minutes—we've got to get to the theater and find Lady Florel. Can you fly one of these things?"

"Of *course* I can fly one of *these things*! Even these *stupid*, outdated pieces of rubbish I could fly ten times as drunk as I am now with one arm, my eye put out, and both my legs chopped off, what do you think, you sober two-eyed twit?"

"Three-eyed," I corrected, running up the forecastle stairs after him.

"That's even worse!"

We arrived at the navigation room, silent as a snowfall. Lockwood opened the door slowly with a soft *click*. It was an enclosed room with glass along the sides, giving us a full view of the mist and airships above and below.

A balding man in a scuffed green uniform and scuffed green mask sat in the captain's seat, hands at the engine and rudder wheels. And behind him stood Divinity, drawing her fingers nervously through her golden hair. They argued at the scene of sideways rooftops and tangled hedges before them.

"I'll fly wherever you want," said the captain with strained patience. "But it would be nice if you could turn the city right so I'm certain we're not actually crashing into anything."

"I *can't* illusion it away," Divinity snarled. "No

one can! It's not a *normal* illusion! It's—it's that idiot Jonath*Eeee!*"

Divinity leapt backward as Lockwood cocked his steam pistol and pressed the barrel against the back of the captain's head. The captain stiffened.

The windows around us bowed of their own accord, creating nebulous blotches of light, before building and gathering into a long whip of glass. It snapped past our faces and knocked the pistol from Lockwood's hand before breaking from the window and crashing to the ground in shards.

Glass! Divinity! In haste she illusion-pulled the glass from the window again. A large arm formed with fingers the size of fuel cells. Lockwood and I dodged it as it, too, broke over us and smashed to the ground.

The captain threw himself from the chair and attacked Lockwood, pulling a revolver from his holster. Divinity illusioned the glass forward from the window again—and without a second thought, I nullified it from her fingers with an anti-glass illusion. I'd learned something from *The Illusionist's Handbook* after all.

Divinity tried to enliven the glass again, shaping it into tentacles. I nullified them all, *again*, and the glass bowed back to its window port. Divinity stared at her fingers with wide eyes.

"What did you just do?" she cried.

"Divinity," I said, dodging a stream of glass once more and nullifying it. "Sorry. I know it's a bad time to say it, but—really, I'm sorry."

Divinity gave up illusioning and dove at me with clawed hands. I ducked out of the way. She tripped over the captain's chair and stumbled into the wall.

"I'm sorry I took your airship ticket, and I'm sorry I said those things. About hurting you."

Divinity struck me with sparks flying from her fingers. She screeched and made an effort to gouge my eyes out.

"Admittedly," I said, shoving her hands away from my face, "I'm a whole lot *less* sorry when you're trying to kill me!"

Lockwood pulled a dagger from his boot and lunged at the captain.

"Lockwood!" I yelled, drawing him short. I inhaled, pulling together the chemical formula I'd known on Fata. I pushed it from my head and fingers to Divinity and the captain in a glistening, swirling flow of thought.

They folded up and hit the floor with a *thum-thumpf* and lay there gracefully sprawled in a dreamless sleep.

Lockwood stared at me with a wide eye.

"What did you just do?" he said.

"Trithyloform," I said sheepishly. "Surgeons use it."

"Ha! Maybe *I* should become a surgeon!" he said. He threw himself into the captain's chair and shoved the gear sticks forward. The engine deep inside the ship ground and whined and rumbled, and we dropped down into the expanse of airships. I turned Divinity over, carefully, and gently set her by the wall, where she wouldn't get stepped on.

"I really *am* sorry, Jane," I said, remembering her real name. "If I could, I'd stay and help make a world where you could visit Sussex, anytime you wanted."

She exhaled gently.

Spires and the rooftops of towers whizzed past us as Lockwood lowered the ship along the length of the city, narrowly avoiding other airships. The theater appeared from the mist below us. Lockwood maneuvered the ship with surprising dexterity, his face grim, until we were flush with the theater side. The side that faced up was the same side we'd broken through the night before. The windows were still broken, even.

I explained to Lockwood the difficulty of getting from the ship into the windows—the gravity in the real world had the final say, and if we didn't make certain we were careful at all angles, in real life we'd end up falling to our deaths on the marble below and not realizing it until the sudden black.

"What a dear little sunshine you *are*," he said, navigating the ship so close that the hull scraped the marble veneer, shaving away little curls of wood. He jammed the wheel with the captain's belt and we raced down the stairs and over the deck. Of all the airships above us, only one descended itself after us to the theater. The giant red of Queen Honoria's airship.

"O-kay, I *say* we have maybe fifteen *minutes*, at *most,*" Lockwood yelled, and he jumped into the broken window, grabbing the ledge and swinging himself through. I followed after with much less grace.

Green curtains swished past me as I slid down the length of the room and smashed into the wall, sending vases and more flowers crashing around me, breaking the arrangements and furniture all over again. I ran along the wall, jumping over mirrors and leaping over the edge of the doorway into the hall.

I gasped sharply. Here, beyond the broken windows of the suite, the air lacked the icy chemical flavor of fantillium. My stomach upended. The world flipped. My head spun. In the unsettling moment when gravity pulled me every direction and none, I saw monsters.

Demons made of glass and spiders, crawling over me in a thousand delicate *clickety click clicks*, their feet puncturing my skin as they split and split again into a plague of hundreds more. I yelled aloud and tried to shake them off.

Lockwood burst from Divinity's suite, kicking off a green swath of curtain.

"On your feet, up up up!" he barked, yanking me to my feet. I stumbled and jerked my head so hard it knocked against the wainscot.

"Jonathan!" he said, shaking me. "You're—you're not a Riven yet, are you? They—shake their heads like that, yeah?"

"No! No, I'm not," I said as the visions faded. "Let's go."

I led the way through the corridors, tripping over whatever was schisming in my shoes. Thankfully the world was right ways up now. We turned a corner—and there was the fallen chandelier, still a mess of glittering prisms at the end of the hall. I ran for Lady Florel's room—

And masked guardsmen filled the hall from the doorway at the end. They poured into the corridor, filling every inch. They swarmed over Lockwood and me, pinned us by the dozens before we could fight, wrenched our hands behind our backs and pinned us down. Queen Honoria's voice broke through the walls of crimson: "Let me through. This *instant*."

She strode through, dressed in a nightgown and thick boots. Her hair was pulled back into a severe bun. At her waist, over the nightgown, she wore a holster with a Nod'olian pistol, and at her face, *no* mask, but an angry frown.

There was no eye, not even a divot, between her eyes.

She strode through the guard, and each of her steps echoed severity and function.

A thin man straggled after her, looking utterly dumbfounded, lost, shocked, and hopeful all rolled into one with a dab of cream on the top. It was the reporter, though he'd lost his little notebook and pen. He drew a quavering hand through his mussed hair.

"Her Ladyship has gone . . . gone *good*!" he cried.

"Release them! *This instant!*" she snapped at the guard, and they released us so quickly we hit the rug.

"Lady Florel," I said hoarsely.

"Jonathan Gouden," she said, and she smiled. I doubted she smiled at anyone, because it looked like she had to practice to do it. But she smiled at me, a real, sincere smile. She knelt down, took my hand, and pressed a brown bottle full of liquid into my palm.

The antitoxin.

"On my feet in less than a day," said Lady Florel, striding down the hall after the masked guard, who led the way up to the roof. We hurried after. "Amazing, really, how quickly the cure resolved things. Obviously the first thing I did was surmise the situation. Find the cure, of course, and then find you. *Button up your uniform, soldier! You're a disgrace!*"

Lockwood buttoned up his jacket like a man on fire.

"These guard fellows have been a great help," Lady Florel said crisply, striding on. "They do whatever I ask. I could have certainly used them years ago at the battlefield hospital."

"They, ah, they think you're the other . . . queen," said the reporter timidly, scurrying along after us. "They're some of the children from outside the city. The . . . *other* . . . queen, you see, she took them away from their families when they were young and raised them to be guards—"

"She *what*?" Lady Florel whipped around, bearing down on the reporter, who cowered. I grinned. *This* was the Lady Florel Knight of Arthurisian legend! Every movement, action, and word from her resonated with intimidation, power, and . . . *virtue*. "This city is a mess!" she continued angrily, whipping back around. "Stealing children! Corrupt governments! Insensible, indecent clothes! Corsets worn *over* your clothes? *Really?* And Nod'ol! What an utterly ridiculous name! It *will* change!"

We turned a corner and hurried up the stairs after the masked guard. I'd explained to her that we needed to go out again into the fantillium, in order to illusion a door, and the roof was nearest. We reached the theater attic, full of old broken statues and smelling of moldy rugs, the domed roof with peeling plaster, and I stopped short before going through the door. The bottle of antitoxin felt heavy in my pocket.

"What is wrong?" said Lady Florel, frowning at my hesitation.

"I don't know if I can illusion the doors," I said honestly. You didn't lie to someone like Lady Florel. "I—I tried before. I failed. Miserably, Lady Florel. I didn't know them well enough."

Lady Florel holstered her pistol and took me by the shoulders with firm hands, staring down at me with her arched, angry eyebrows and dark eyes.

"Look at me, boy," she said, not unkindly. "There must be a doorway you know well. Think!"

I thought. I thought of every door I'd grown up with, all them vague, shifting masses of colors. My family's row house . . . the panels swam in my memory. The infirmary doors—I couldn't even remember what they were made of. I'd never paid attention to doors before.

I shook my head, distraught.

"Think! I know it is in you!"

I scraped my memory, gritting my teeth. The statues bore down on me, and the attic room's dark walls felt like prison.

Prison.

"Prison!" I said, inspiration hitting me like an airship hull. "The cell door! On the *Valor*!"

And the gridiron of the bolted metal plates formed so vividly in my vision it could have been standing just there in front of me. I remembered everything; the crisscrossing grate, the smell of rusting iron, everything I'd taken in during the journey to Arthurise. It was embedded in my mind.

Lady Florel gripped my shoulder and nodded to the gable door. Our obedient masked guard threw it open, granting us access to the roof. Fantillium mist poured in.

"Good luck, Jonathan Gouden." Lady Florel saluted me and returned to our faithful reporter, who had been watching us from the shadows of the old props.

"You're not coming?" I said.

"I am not," she said. She smiled at my expression, but her eyes had a bright kind of sadness.

The reporter behind us gulped air.

"Yes, Mr. Wickes," said Lady Florel severely. "I am staying."

"You can't stay here," I said. "Not in a place like—"

"Quiet, boy," she said, looking at me intently, and I fell to silence. "Yes. Yes, I can. There have been times in my life, Jonathan, when I have seen as clearly as day a course unfold before me, as though I were sailing on a long journey, and I know precisely where I must navigate. This is one of those times. Do you understand that, Jonathan Gouden?"

I touched my chest.

"Yes," I said. "I do."

"Then do tell the king for me, won't you?" she said, smiling. "I'm staying behind to turn this city back into London."

"Johnny!" Lockwood yelled, plunging through the doorway.

I bowed, glimpsing Lady Florel for the last time before I gulped a breath of untainted air and held it, dove through the doorway and into the mist. The reporter had pulled off his mask and was wiping his eyes.

"Why are you crying?" Lady Florel's voice carried severely through the doorway. "That is silly. Please refrain, Mr. Wickes!"

"There is a—a f-f-foretelling a—a prophecy," the reporter was stammering.

"Prophecies! Superstitious loads of tripe, excuses to sit back and do nothing while you let the world around you fall to dust. Don't *speak* to me of any such ridiculous—"

Lockwood slammed the gabled door closed, and we stood in the center of a landscape full of green rooftop slopes, gables, and mist. We inhaled the fantillium air at the same time. The world, once again, flipped underneath our feet. Lockwood and I slid and hit the jutting gable door now beneath us, knocking our heads against it.

"I'll kill you for this illusion!" he snapped as we scrambled to find our footing on the gable.

I closed my eyes and pulled together my memory

of the cell door on the *Valor*. The square window with scratches, rims with bolts, the latticework of the iron at the handle, the clanging it made when the ship rumbled . . . I inhaled deeply and exhaled the thoughts from my head and numerous fingers onto the door at our feet.

It took my blood and bones with it. It sucked everything from me and left my skin a shell. The cell door formed over the gable door at our feet. Every rusted plate, hinge, and bolt drew itself from me in glowing strings of mist. The cell door of the *Valor* lay before us, glowing white hot and then fading to bronze with such *completeness* that I knew I had illusioned it to the very scratch.

Above us, the air rumbled. The silhouette of Queen Honoria's airship loomed. I saw a glimpse of her peering below at us over the deck, removing her fresh-air mask.

"We *fly!*" Lockwood yelled, diving and grabbing the cell door latch, tugging it upward in a shriek of iron.[28] We leapt into the dark, gaping rectangle as red forms slid down lines cast over the side of the airship.

Black enveloped me. All my organs and veins twisted and *blipped* as the threshold blurred past me.

BAM.

We smacked against the metal wall, and with our first gulp of air, the dim metal hall around us flipped ninety

---

[28] I had the sense to illusion it *unlocked*.

degrees, and we toppled again onto the floor. We'd landed in the brig hall of the *Valor*. I had done it.

"Ha-ha!" Lockwood exulted, throwing cell door shut behind us. Nod'ol had vanished, leaving only the cell of bronze walls and a tiny port window. "You did it, Johnny, you great fool! Ha!"

His laugh was distant.

I writhed. Glass and mechanical creatures with numerous legs crawled up and down my head and chest, into my ears and mouth, hissing, hissing inside my head.

Jon . . . a . . . than, they clicked.

Lockwood's hand broke through the darkness and boxed me.

"Come on!" he yelled, lifting me to my feet. The reticulated creatures crawling through my orifices skittered away. My muscles felt surgically removed. Lockwood half carried me away from the brig. "On your feet! Stop daydreaming, Johnny boy!"

The cell door bent outward behind us, and then *burst*. It exploded forward and hit the opposite wall with a thunderous clang.

The masked guard poured forth as blood from a mortal wound. They smashed into the wall and over one another in a tangle of red fabric, hats, gloves, and masks, and pulled themselves to their feet like liquid, streaming down the hall and up the stairs after us.

Lockwood and I bounded. We clanged up the stairs, three at a time. The brig master, an elderly airguardsman with white hair, stood at the top of the stairs and leapt backward as we barreled past.

"Get out of here!" I yelled at him.

He furrowed his brow at us. I glanced back. The rivers of guards swept him up, casting him to the side and flowing on. Lockwood and I kept running, up more stairs, to the main floor and out onto the observation deck. Cold air hit us like a hammer.

Fata Morgana lay before us like a white castle, ringed with vertical docks, northern airguard ships, the *Westminster*, spires, and docks touching the black polar sky and canal offal falling down the sides in slow drifts.

We ran around the arc of the deck to the back of the ship as the masked guard poured through the entrance and out onto the dock. I caught a glimpse of Queen Honoria, graying hair frizzing wildly, her mask askew and red lips pursed, entirely pressed in the crush of the masked guard descending down the long dock and into the city.

We rushed past the row of airship dinghies, their balloons tied to the underbelly of the envelope above us. Lockwood hurriedly unharnessed the pulleys and ropes and dropped one to the deck between us. It *clonged* to the ground, and the metal deck thundered under our feet.

Lockwood shoved me in, and I hit back-first into the hull of the boat.

"*No* one," he snarled, leaping in after, "accuses *me* of not being able to steer an airship! Figur-a-tively or otherwise! Hang on, Joooohnnyyyyy!"

He flung the orthogonagen wheel open and shoved the accelerator stick forward. I tumbled back into cases of food and ropes, just as the masked guard poured from around the side of the *Valor* after us. Their gloved fingertips just brushed the edge of our dinghy, and we fell, down—down—down—

The blood-red masks staring down at us over the railing grew smaller and smaller. My excitement turned to panic as they unharnessed the dinghies themselves, boarded, and sailed over the side of the ship, descending after us.

"Lockwood!" I yelled.

"I know!" he snapped, wincing. He turned the ascension wheel in a blur, firing the engines, throwing the ship sharply upward. "Good luck to them finding the altitude lever on these stupid boats!" He shoved the stick forward, and I knocked back again, banging around the ship's supplies as we zipped forward.

The ships that had been plunging downward like dead flies immediately fired up at the same time, shot upward, and zoomed after us.

"Looks like they found it," I said.

Lockwood gritted his teeth and we raced forward in a polished blur. Fata Morgana's spires and observatory dome grew larger.

"Where's the infirmary?" he said.

I pointed out the building, in the center of the city. The ship propelled forward. Freezing air whipped around us. The ships behind us grew larger.

"No one outsails *me*," Lockwood snarled. He shoved another lever forward and we shot up again, narrowly avoiding a masked guardsman's dinghy, which crashed into a vertical dock, then spiraled into the silver city below. My throat fell into my stomach, we rose so fast. Within seconds the dock had become a silver ribbon and the weathervanes on the city's towers spun in our wake. A few seconds more, and the entirety of the city lay before us.

Lockwood pulled steady at this new altitude. My ears rang.

"I didn't know ships could do this," I rasped.

"Yes, neither did I," said Lockwood.

The dinghies below us rose as spirits from the grave.

"Hold on," said Lockwood, and he cut the engine.

We plummeted freely. Our clothes lifted from our shoulders, my stomach lifted into my throat, our entire selves lifted away from the floor of the ship. We blurred past the masked guard, catching a glimpse of their masks and hulls.

Lockwood fired the engines. We smacked onto the dinghy floor, and before we crashed into a cloud canal, Lockwood jolted the ship forward. We skimmed the surface of the river of mist, dipping and bobbing. He gave the engine more fuel and we shot forward in a wake of white. The canal-front townhouses and white brick buildings smeared past on both sides.

Lockwood turned the boat around corners, tightly dipped it beneath walkways, just brushing the top of the balloon. The engine whined. Lockwood grabbed my arm.

"Jump!" he said.

"What?"

He shoved me over and leapt after me. I plunged into the misty black depths of the canal, suspended in orthogonagen-smelling fog, slopping against a curved brick wall and sliding down in a trail of slime. We slid to a stop on the mucky canal floor.

I coughed up mist. I used to play in these canal bottoms when I was boy, but you couldn't breathe this generator offal for long. Your lungs would fill with water.

The *bang* of our dinghy crashing into the canal side sounded in the distance. Lockwood's form appeared next to me, caked with muck.

"Yeah," I said. "All those things I said, about you not

being able to steer a ship, you know, I think I take them back."

Lockwood laughed, and then winced and held his head. I took the lead now, slopping through the bottom of the canals. Chemical light behind metal grates cast strange shadows around us, illuminating sky mussels clinging to the walls. Beneath them, numbers and letters marked the location. S-C-498. Stratus Circle, where the infirmary stood.

Metal rings had been built into the wall. Lockwood and I climbed them. I stumbled and slipped in my now too-small shoes, reminding me of my Rivening. I didn't dare look at my hands. Breaking through the mist surface and inhaling dry air, I pulled myself onto the smooth pavement, shivering. I helped Lockwood up.

The infirmary loomed before us. Frosted light shone from the windows.

My over-tight shoes squished and squashed as we careened through the entrance hall, shoving doors open and running to the main wing. It was evening now. I prayed I wasn't too late. The infirmary felt silent. Far too silent.

I should have recognized that.

Slamming through the main wing's doors shoulder-first, I pulled up sharp.

The entire infirmary, normally a stark white, was

filled with crimson. Masked guardsmen flanked the walls, filled the spaces between the beds of dying women, and swarmed upon Lockwood and me. Blue-uniformed men lay at their feet, either unconscious or dead. King Edward lay in a mountainous heap in the corner, knocked out next to the unconscious form of Dr. Palmer.

At the end of the wing, standing among the chess pieces of masked guardsmen, my father stood, chin up, his jaw set. A pistol was held to his ear. On the other side of the pistol was Queen Honoria, her chin raised haughtily.

"Jonathan!" she said, and she smiled, sweet as sugar. "Well! Isn't *this* familiar!"

CHAPTER 22

The masked guard forced me to my knees. Constantine came up from behind Lockwood and with a swoop of his clawed glove, knocked his head so hard that Lockwood—already drunk—glazed over. He folded up into a blue brass-buttoned heap.

My father stared at me. He looked terrible. Unshaven, unkempt. Like he hadn't slept in a week. He probably hadn't. His horrified expression made me reach up and feel my face. My splitting fingers felt two bridges of a nose, extra nostrils, and the indent at my temple had a bulb of an eye beneath the skin. I winced.

Mum and Hannah lay in their beds. Hannah shivered and trembled. Mum didn't move at all.

"Jonathan, I think it's wonderful you illusioned a door so *well*," said Queen Honoria in a patient voice. "This will be helpful in the future, of course. But right now, *Jonathan*, you need to stop this silliness and come back to the theater."

I slowly reached into my pocket, keeping my eyes fixed on my father and the pistol pointed at his head. My fingers closed around the small brown bottle inside.

"Jonathan," said Queen Honoria, smiling.

"Please," I rasped. "Please. Just let me cure my mother and sister. Leave my father alone. Let me cure them, and I'll go back with you, through the doorway. Please."

"Let him," said a hoarse voice behind me. Constantine. Queen Honoria wavered.

"Let him," said Constantine again, his eyes fixed on my father. "Give him five minutes, Your Highness. Then he'll come back with us. He'll get more orthogonagen with his illusions and help fix Nod'ol. Won't you . . . Jon . . . a . . . than?" He said my name with difficulty, like a rusty clock trying to run.

He tore his eyes from my father and fixed them, one yellow, one red, on me. My same eyes.

"Yes," I said, dying inside. "I will. For five minutes, I will."

Queen Honoria regarded me, her eyes glittering. Then, without lowering her pistol from my father's head, took a pocket watch out from a pocket in her layers of dress and clicked it open.

"Five minutes," she said.

The masked guard released me.

Shakily, I found my feet and a pot of tea by a bedside, poured a cup, and mixed it with a dose of the antitoxin. Everyone's eyes were fixed upon me.

I administered the cure to my mother first; she lay breathing in quick, shallow gasps. Even her eyelids and lips had turned black.

"Hello, Mum," I whispered, touching the cup to her lips. She drank it in little sips, then with a trembling hand reached up and brushed my cheek.

"My Johnny," she whispered.

I kissed her fingers.

I poured another for Hannah and pressed it to her black lips. She gagged and tried to push it away.

"Stop being stubborn, for once," I said.

She cringed but allowed me to help her drink, then curled up into her pillow when she'd finished, shivering. I pulled the blanket up to her neck with a shaking hand.

The bottle had one last dosage of antitoxin within. I walked to my father, still frozen with the pistol at his head, and pressed the antitoxin into his hand.

He blinked at the bottle, then at me. A mixture of expressions crossed his face: surprise, confusion, then hope and a glimmer of *pride* as his fingers closed tightly over the bottle.

"Jonathan."

The five minutes had flown. Constantine wore a fantillium mask over his face. Queen Honoria pulled the pistol away from my father's head and fitted her own mask on, illusioning with broad gestures something I could not see. The masked guardsmen all around us produced fantillium masks, strapping them over the mouths and noses of their crimson faces. They handed a mask to me. I buckled it around my head. It pumped and hissed; I closed my eyes, inhaling. And the fantillium filled me once again, fizzing my blood and brightening the lights.

The door Queen Honoria had illusioned stood at the end of the infirmary wing, the same old Tower of London door with rusted hinges.

I faced it, resolved. And that very moment, the invisible compass inside my chest went *click*, an audible noise to soul. I felt Anna's touch on my chest, stronger than the numbing fantillium, and knew exactly what I must do.

I stepped in line next to Constantine. He ignored me. The masked guard streamed around us and through the door, which opened into the overgrown courtyard. Queen Honoria, Constantine, and I passed through the arched doorway at the same time. The moment we crossed over the threshold, the moment when our veins and cells and organs went *blip*, I closed my eyes.

And illusioned.

It wasn't like any illusion I'd created before. It flowed from me like a song, an orchestra of interweaving threads and melodies, painting themselves into a picture around us. The infirmary disappeared, the Tower of London before us disappeared, the masked guard disappeared, and only Constantine, Queen Honoria, and I stood in the Nothing between two worlds.

Walls faded in around us, and we stood in the center round tower. It was a mix of the Tower of London, Nod'ol, Fata Morgana, the observatory, the infirmary wing. The ceiling was made of glass, and weak winter light shone down over us. The floor was tile, the walls stone.

A lone door stood in front of us. It was the same Tower of London door we'd just walked through, moments before.

"What—" Constantine began.

The quickening formula grew in my mind and evaporated from me. The sun above us began to whip around, brightening, darkening, brightening, darkening, faster and faster until it became a flicker and our shadows danced around us. The tile molded and cracked. Weeds blossomed and died at our feet. Trees grew up along the sides of the strange room, filling with leaves in a blur and then dying, falling to seed, seeds growing into trees, dying again. The glass above blackened with grime.

The Tower of London door in front of us blurred out of focus like a bad microscope, until it split into two identical doors, side-by-side. As time flickered over us, the identical doors began to change. One started rotting, hinges rusting even further, wood blackening. The door at the right grew polished, carved, with steel hinges and latch.

"What is going on?" said Queen Honoria severely, her voice muffled underneath her fantillium mask. "Are you illusioning this, Jonathan?"

"Madam," I said calmly. The room had a Quiet that I'd only experienced once before. "You are witnessing . . . a schism."

The glass ceiling cracked and shattered. Shards rained over us and disappeared into dust. The trees grew over our heads and broke the tile with their roots.

I halted the formula. The sun jarred to a stop. We stood knee-high in weeds, the room almost a forest, crumbling stone ruins shadowing us. Moss and vines covered everything. I walked to the doors and yanked the vines aside, exposing their frames. The door on the left had almost completely rotted away, hanging from one hinge. The door on the right stood, polished, solid wood.

"Your Highness," I said, startling the three of us.

"Queen Honoria. Do you recognize these doors? They lead to Nod'ol—one thousand years from today."

Queen Honoria's dilated eyes flashed at me, then at the doors. She took a wary step back.

"You," I said, "are the schism between them. This door"—I nodded to the polished door on the right—"is the result of allowing Lady Florel to take leadership of Nod'ol."

I strode forward, grasped the steel latch, and pushed it open.

Such a world I couldn't even dream.

Constantine, Queen Honoria, and I drew back. The Tower of London stood over us, preserved to a shine, the grass clipped as smooth as velvet, and words appeared in the air of the courtyard, dissolving, pulling together new words in some magical trick of light, or a new form of energy. "Tours from 10 to 6," they formed. History, images of London maps. We stared.

Beyond the Tower of London, golden buildings peaked to the sky. Over each spire, gold pennants rippled. There was no Archglass. Airships flew through the air without balloons, somehow held aloft without wings or sails, mechanical bullets of steam sweeping through the cityscape. And something more—I inhaled sharply. Giant creatures soared between the towers, flapping leathery wings, bridled by people mounted on their backs. Creatures, perhaps, that had once roamed the earth and had somehow been revived.

"*Dragons?*" Constantine rasped.

Queen Honoria snapped forward, grasped the latch, and shoved the door closed. Darkness fell.

"This is madness, Jonathan," she snarled, hands shaking. "Turn time back! *This instant!*"

I did not move.

Queen Honoria whipped an illusion—a bolt of fire. Before she could lash it at me, I had dissolved it from her hands. She tried again to attack with fire; and again it disappeared with my anti-illusion.

"Constantine!" Queen Honoria screeched. "Help me!"

Constantine remained still as a statue.

"No," he whispered.

"Queen Honoria," I said, nullifying her illusion again. "I'm giving you one last chance! You can make Nod'ol the city you just saw! Go back with Constantine and *turn yourself in.* Give the monarchy to Lady Florel. Earn absolution for the crimes you've committed. It's not too late!"

"*I will not,*" she growled, feral. She thrashed as her illusions wisped away.

"Do you want to see what happens to Nod'ol if you *don't?*" I said. "If you go back and still are queen?"

I threw open the door on the left. The wood crashed

from its hinges to the floor, revealing a vast expanse of Nothing. Not even weeds grew. The old stone walls had been reduced to rubble. No city tower stood beyond; there wasn't even a river among the ruins. A far distant post jutted up from the ground, marking an Archglass that had once been. A smoke hazed over the entire landscape.

Queen Honoria stared at it, frozen.

"You recognize this place," I said. "Don't you."

Queen Honoria went mad.

She screeched and threw herself at me, gray hair flying wildly. I fell back, hitting the wall, and immediately she was clawing at me, slashing at my face and neck, catching me unaware with bolts of illusions that seared my skin. I cried aloud, more from fear than from pain, as her clothes tore at the seams and I saw what she had been hiding, perhaps for years: Eyes.

They were everywhere—on her shoulders, wrists, dropping down her arms, melting down her neck. In that horrifying moment, she grasped the pistol at her waist and pressed it to my head.

A new force took over, grasping Queen Honoria and tearing her away from my side. The pistol clattered. With newfound courage, Constantine dragged Queen Honoria to the doorway of the abandoned city.

"You utter *coward*!" he said, tearing off her masks.

I scrambled about in time to see a third eye between her eyes, her dress soaked with tears and gray hair tangling to her elbows as Constantine forced her into the abandoned city, throwing her to her knees.

"Illusion time back, Jonathan!" he screamed, leaping back through the doorway. *"Now!"*

Numbers took over before I could even think of them, searing my vision and coming alive in the illusion. The Quickening Formula:

$$\Omega = x\left(\frac{(2\pi r)\left(\mu\sqrt{\left(\frac{2}{\lambda}-\frac{1}{\theta}\right)}\right)}{\varphi}\right)$$

And $x = -6.3114 \times 10^{10}$, turning the years backward into seconds. Time whirred retrograde. I gasped as the illusion left hollows in my mind. Queen Honoria disappeared as the sun jolted into a strobe and the wood replaced itself. Plants grew backward in the flickering light. The ceiling re-pieced together, shards rising up like billowing steam. The tile mended. The doors unfocused and melded back together, forming once again the unkempt door of the Nod'olian Tower of London. And behind me stood the door that led to the Fata Morgana infirmary.

Time slowed to a stop. The room had returned to its original form. I remained on the tile, heaving, broken and sore all over. Constantine hulked by the door. He ran a hand through his matted hair as I forced my crying muscles to pull me to my feet.

We stared at each other for a moment.

"You're me," he said without a trace of emotion. His eyes looked me up and down. "What I could have been, anyway."

"What you can be still," I said.

"Ha!" Constantine laughed, then broke into a cough. "Look at me, Jonathan. *Look at me*. I'm not you anymore. I'm a monster."

I looked at him. He hulked underneath a thick orange coat, almost disappearing inside it. Every inch of skin was covered, his misshapen form hiding whatever he was splitting into underneath.

And yet, I caught glimpses of myself. The brown at the roots of his hair. The shape of his eyes and the way he rubbed his clawed hands together, over and over, not unlike how I kneaded my cap when I was nervous.

"When I died," I said thoughtfully. "Did I tell you? I saw Anna."

Constantine froze, still crouched. His eyes widened under his mask, hanging on to my every word.

"She said that there still was a Jonathan in you. She said she knew there was."

Constantine was sweating down his neck and collar. No—not sweat. Sweat didn't stream like that.

"She really believed that?" he said. "Underneath all my . . . noses and eyes and dye? She still did? Well—ha! That would make one of us, then."

"Two," I said. "And since I'm *you*, that would make three."

Constantine rasped. I realized it was a laugh.

"It's not too late, Constantine," I said. "I know it's not. Go back to Nod'ol and turn yourself in. Lady Florel is going to need your help. Divinity, you know."

"Oh, I know," said Constantine, rasping. It might have even been a laugh.

On impulse, I embraced Constantine—beast mask and all. I wanted to fix everything—take him back to Fata with me, to stay with my—our—family. He filled my arms in a misshapen hulk of a figure.

"I'll go," he said, breaking away abruptly. And then, with more firmness: "I have to go back."

"Wait," I said, and feverishly searched for something to write on and write with. I settled on a torn piece of my coat, scratching in numbers with one of the numerous cuts on my numerous fingers:

$$x = -6.3114 \times 10^{10}$$

"That's the key," I explained, handing him the scrap of cloth. "The key to Queen Honoria's prison. A thousand years in a few seconds. Lady Florel can decide what to do with it."

Constantine's eyes furrowed underneath his mask, but he pocketed the cloth and nodded. He thumped me on the back, nearly throwing off my glasses. My Nod'olian self had considerably more muscle than I did.

"Thank you, Jonathan Gouden," he said, grasping the rusting latch of the Nod'olian White Tower. When his voice was quiet like that, he almost sounded like my father.

"Thank you, Jonathan Goodwin," I said, and took my own door's latch.

We pushed the doors and crossed over the thresholds at the same time. Every inch of me rearranged itself as I stepped into the clean white of the infirmary and shut the door behind me. Many of the blue uniformed men had revived and stared at me in utter horror. I yanked off my mask, breathing clean air again.

The hallucinations came. Demons crawled on hundreds of legs inside my lungs and stomach and head, mechanical centipedes, schisming into hundreds more, filling my body . . . I fell to my knees, thrashing, clawing at my head.

Jonathan.

Fantillium would feed them. My hands tore and grasped at nothing.

Jonathan.

Arms grabbed me instead, keeping me from writhing on the floor, and pulled me into a tight embrace. The creatures inside me hissed and punctured my veins. I fought, but the hands remained holding me tightly.

And slowly, the demons waned.

Sweating and exhausted, I found myself in the arms of my father.

"My boy," he said, and he was laughing and crying at once.

CHAPTER 23

Dock 3, Fata Morgana (Class. A Aerial City)
January 1, 1883

The sun was a washed coin. It swung above the horizon for an hour a day now—a solar feast!—before plunging below again and sweeping the sky in purples and blues.

Much had happened since I'd stumbled back through the illusioned doorway nearly a week ago. The empire had slowly begun to limp back to life. The Venen had taken its toll. According to the light sigs, Arthurise was clothed in black. There wasn't a person who hadn't lost a mother or a sister, and everyone mourned the queen. But still, many had been saved. Within a few hours in his laboratory, my father had reconstructed the cure and immediately signaled the antitoxin's formula to Arthurise, halting its spread.

The king, who had revived after the attack of the masked guard, listened in my father's laboratory as I told the entire story—from Queen Honoria illusioning the door on the *Chivalry* and the way to falling back through the infirmary doors. I didn't leave anything out—not even Edward the Pathetic Miner.

I couldn't tell if the king believed me or not. He only remained slumped in one of my father's chairs, looking too heartbroken to even breathe. He'd nodded when I'd finished, taken the transcripts from the airguardsman who had been recording my words, and left for his ship. He'd be returning to Arthurise. I suspected this wouldn't be the end of my explanation; but for now, it would do. My father believed me, and that was enough.

In the meantime, Mum and Hannah, like Lady Florel, healed miraculously well. They remained in the infirmary for three more days, getting their strength back, and I took care to visit them at night, talking quietly and helping Hannah with her academy homework. At night, everyone in the infirmary was asleep. And Alice, who was healing without a freckle amiss, gratefully didn't see my splitting face.

The last illusion had hastened me into something like Constantine. My second face looked like it was sliding down my throat, my split nose askew and the eye at my temple splitting open. Another eye had begun to indent on my neck. I had extra fingers splayed from the others, completely movable. Hannah teased that I ought to learn to play the piano, but at the look on my face, clamped her mouth shut. My extra toes made it hurt to walk, and I limped. I made certain to wear a large scarf at all hours of the day.

I'd been having hallucinations, too. They fevered and haunted me ceaselessly, twitching and crawling over me whenever I closed my eyes. I could only drive them from my soul like sweat—pounding them from my mind by running through Fata, over the pathways and by canal fronts, letting the cold sting my face and convincing myself that I didn't need fantillium to make the creatures go away.

But I *was* healing. Anna had been right about that. After the first three days, the hallucinations weren't as vivid; their pricks not as sharp. The Rivening was beginning to heal, too. The eye at my temple had closed and scabbed over, the bridge of my second nose had gone soft, like cartilage, and my extra nostrils had begun to close up. My fingers were taking their jolly time. Dr. Palmer, my father, and I examined the extra pieces of me with great interest, sorting out how the bone and muscle had split.

We decided I ought to accompany my father to Arthurise, and as we helped quell the Venen there, we could consult the top surgeons of the empire. My father had promised, in fact, that I could have a hand at the scalpel and make some incisions![29]

And so it was, just nine days after returning from Nod'ol, my father and I packed our things and prepared for a season-long stay in Arthurise. Longer for me, because after I'd recovered, I'd be remaining in Arthurise to attend the university and become a surgeon myself.

Mum and Hannah, well enough now to brave the cold air, gave us a send-off on dock three, surrounded by benches and jaunty-tune telescopes. Leaving my family in this familiar setting reminded me of Anna, and I couldn't say much. At the top of the vertical dock, the *Chivalry* loomed, engines fired up and ready to brave the polar storms to transport the empire's head medical scientist— and his apprentice—to Arthurise. Northern airguardsmen walked to and fro, up and down the lift, loading the hull. We stood as a family, still among the harried last-minute work. A cold wind caught our backs, flapping our coats.

"I'm going to miss you," said Mum, the breeze blowing dark wisps of hair in her eyes. The mottled black of her skin had disappeared, and she was as soft-spoken

---

[29] I was *really* looking forward to this.*

*I'd taken to marking my hands with pen and ink, drawing out the muscles and veins beneath the skin and labeling them with such intricacy that it almost looked like I had contracted the Venen myself. It was a marvelous diversion.

ACKNOWLEDGMENTS

EDITORS:
Martha Mihalick
Julie Romeis Sanders
Sarah Cloots

AGENTS:
Edward Necarsulmer IV
Christa Heschke

SPECIAL THANKS TO:
Lisa Hale
Joe Fowler
Renee Wilson
Tim Hinton
Jason Kim
Kevin Keele
Travis Deming
Brent Melling
Alan Rex
Chris Melling
Grace Rex
Taylor Todd
&, of course, the Fam—Mom, Dad, Missy,
Peter, Sar, and all the rest of you, you crazy ol' sonuvaguns.